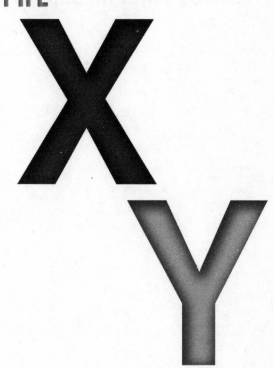

THE

X
Y

ALSO BY VIRGINIA BERGIN

The H$_2$O Series

H$_2$O

The Storm

THE
X
Y

VIRGINIA BERGIN

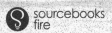
sourcebooks
fire

Published by Sourcebooks Fire, an imprint of Sourcebooks, Inc.
P.O. Box 4410, Naperville, Illinois 60567-4410
(630) 961-3900
Fax: (630) 961-2168
sourcebooks.com

Originally published as *Who Runs the World?* in 2017 in the United Kingdom by
Macmillan Children's Books, an imprint of Pan Macmillan.

Library of Congress Cataloging-in-Publication Data

Names: Bergin, Virginia, author.
Title: XY / Virginia Bergin.
Description: Naperville, Illinois : Sourcebooks Fire, [2018] | Summary: Sixty
  years after a virus wiped out nearly all men on earth, fourteen-year-old
  River finds a sick boy, Mason, and helps restore his health while learning
  dark truths behind the lies she has been told.
Identifiers: LCCN 2017020844 | (hardcover : alk. paper)
Subjects: | CYAC: Science fiction. | Virus diseases--Fiction. | Sex
  role--Fiction.
Classification: LCC PZ7.B452214 Who 2018 | DDC [Fic]--dc23 LC record avail-
able at https://lccn.loc.gov/2017020844

Printed and bound in the United States of America.
MA 10 9 8 7 6 5 4 3 2 1

Have you ever had a book dedicated to you?
No? Neither have I.
Let's fix that.
This book is dedicated to:

_____

THE GLOBAL AGREEMENTS

1.   The Earth comes first.

2.   Every child is our child.

3.   We reject all forms of violence.

4.   We will all help one another.

5.   Knowledge must be shared.

6.   We Agree that we need to Agree.

7.   Everyone has the right to be listened to.

To these Agreements, we are committed.

Signed on behalf of the people of the former nations of:

Afghanistan	Bhutan	Comoros	Fiji
Albania	Bolivia	Congo	Finland
Algeria	Bosnia and	Costa Rica	France
Andorra	Herzegovina	Côte d'Ivoire	Gabon
Angola	Botswana	Croatia	Gambia
Antigua and	Brazil	Cuba	Georgia
Barbuda	Brunei	Cyprus	Germany
Argentina	Bulgaria	Czech Republic	Ghana
Armenia	Burkina Faso	Denmark	Greece
Australia	Burundi	Djibouti	Grenada
Austria	Cabo Verde	Dominica	Guatemala
Azerbaijan	Cambodia	Dominican	Guinea
Bahamas	Cameroon	Republic	Guinea-Bissau
Bahrain	Canada	Ecuador	Guyana
Bangladesh	Central African	Egypt	Haiti
Barbados	Republic	El Salvador	Honduras
Belarus	Chad	Equatorial Guinea	Hungary
Belgium	Chile	Eritrea	Iceland
Belize	China	Estonia	India
Benin	Colombia	Ethiopia	Indonesia

Iran	Marshall Islands	Portugal	Sweden
Iraq	Mauritania	Qatar	Switzerland
Ireland	Mauritius	Romania	Syria
Israel	Mexico	Russia	Taiwan
Italy	Micronesia	Rwanda	Tajikistan
Jamaica	Moldova	Saint Kitts and	Tanzania
Japan	Monaco	Nevis	Thailand
Jerusalem	Mongolia	Saint Lucia	Tibet
Jordan	Montenegro	Saint Vincent and	Timor-Leste
Kazakhstan	Morocco	the Grenadines	Togo
Kenya	Mozambique	Samoa	Tonga
Kiribati	Myanmar	San Marino	Trinidad and
Korea	Namibia	São Tomé and	Tobago
Kosovo	Nauru	Príncipe	Tunisia
Kuwait	Nepal	Saudi Arabia	Turkey
Kyrgyzstan	Netherlands	Senegal	Turkmenistan
Laos	New Zealand	Serbia	Tuvalu
Latvia	Nicaragua	Seychelles	Uganda
Lebanon	Niger	Scotland	Ukraine
Lesotho	Nigeria	Sierra Leone	United Arab
Liberia	Norway	Singapore	Emirates
Libya	Oman	Slovakia	United Kingdom
Liechtenstein	Pakistan	Slovenia	United States of
Lithuania	Palau	Solomon Islands	America
Luxembourg	Palestine	Somalia	Uruguay
Macedonia	Panama	South Africa	Uzbekistan
Madagascar	Papua New	South Sudan	Vanuatu
Malawi	Guinea	Spain	Venezuela
Malaysia	Paraguay	Sri Lanka	Vietnam
Maldives	Peru	Sudan	Yemen
Mali	Philippines	Suriname	Zambia
Malta	Poland	Swaziland	Zimbabwe

She is riding through the woods on what was once a road. The dotted white line that used to separate the comings from the goings is crumbling. The asphalt is slowly being destroyed by tree roots, and small plants—so strong—sprout up all over, wherever they can. In another few years, there won't be any road left at all.

Too bad, so sad, bye-bye—that's what her granmumma Kate (who refuses to be called *Granmumma*) says about all the things that once were and are no more. *Too bad, so sad, bye-bye.*

The horse, a gentle giant of a Shire horse the granmummas call "My Little Pony" (Milpy, for short), pulls a cartload of cider apples: small, hard, bitter things that will be fermented into some fun. The girl has a backpack stuffed with harvest produce on her back; it is easier to carry it than to have to clamber off and then back on the huge horse just for a drink of water.

Her name is River, and she is daydreaming about the exploration of outer space.

It is an autumn evening.

Dark is coming soon.

She is miles from home.

She feels no fear.

Why would she? There are no predators. No such thing as ghosts.

Fear belongs to another time. It lives on only in the memories of others.

She feels no fear at all.

Not even when she sees it: the body lying in the middle of the road.

♀ ♂

She feels surprised. The surprise finds its way into her hands, and she pulls back on the reins the second she spots it, the body in the road. Then there's alarm. A jolt of it. She knows right away it isn't anyone from the village. She's known them, all of them, her whole life, and this person is not one of them. But the jolt of alarm isn't about that instant of seeing; it's about whether the person is hurt.

She slips off the horse and runs to the body.

And stops.

It *is* breathing, this body. A stranger in strange clothes. Under a filthy *white* T-shirt, an enormous, black tick shape on it, a flat chest without even the tiniest of breasts rises and falls. One arm has a horrible gash on it, an open, oozing wound on which flies are feasting. Long, skinny-but-muscley legs in skintight, shiny, red leggings end in cloven hooves: weird, rubbery, black shoes with pockets for big toes. She looks back up to the place her gaze skimmed. There is lumpiness in the crotch. And she looks at the face of the stranger: smudged with dirt, beaded with sweat, and hairy—a substantial crop of wispy facial hair, *more than any person she has ever seen.* And she looks at the throat…where there is also lumpiness.

It snaps into her head: *Adam's apple.* That's what Kate calls that lump in your throat. Because… The why of it she can't exactly remember. *Too bad, so sad, bye-bye.*

In the few astonished seconds she spends staring at that body, River imagines the most extraordinary thing: that this is an XY, a person born genetically male.

But that cannot be. It simply cannot be.

Seconds of astonishment. Seconds of extraordinary. Then River, who nearly always tries to do the right thing, and not just because that's what her mumma would expect, does the right thing: FIRST AID.

#1: She checks for hazards. Nothing dangerous lying about—not even a sun-basking adder—and the power lines that followed this road hang broken and long dead, so no threat of electrocution. There is only a bad stink in the air—from diarrhea and vomit spattered nearby.

#2: She checks for consciousness.

"WAKE UP!" she yells, clapping her hands. "WAKE UP!"

A single puffy eyelid rises. A bloodshot eyeball rolls. A pupil pinpricks against the pretty red and gold of dappled autumn light, focuses and—

A BEGINNING

CHAPTER 1
CONSCIOUSNESS

The person leaps up, there's a hand across my mouth before I can even scream, the other arm wrapped tight around me, and my brain is exploding—instantly—with shock and horror and fear and anger and *confusion* **CONFUSION CONFUSION** because who would just ATTACK another person and—

"*Who's with you? Huh?!*"

The voice! Growling and sick and deep and broken and stinking.

MAN
MEN
MURDER
GUNS

WAR
KILL

Every strange and scary thing I've ever half heard said about XYs comes bursting into my head, but it *cannot* be. It **cannot** be.

"*Don't make me hurt you, junior!*" vile breath threatens.

The grip tightens. The grip HURTS.

WHY would this person be doing this?!

WHY WOULD ANY PERSON DO THIS?!

So maybe this person is crazy, so maybe this person has taken drugs, so maybe whatever sickness this person has got is causing this madness—

"*STOP IT!*" My cry muffled wordless by a stinking, sweaty palm.

"*Shuddup!*"

I get shaken. I get squeezed. It HURTS. So who cares who this is and why? So NO WAY. So I kick. Kick, kick, kick. Boot against shin. Boot against shin. I get another shake and squeeze, then dragged back so fast my boots can't get to shins, but I stamp down hard on a cloven hoof, and the stinking breath lets out a growl that ends in a moan of pain.

"*DON'T MAKE ME HURT YOU.*"

Who would say a thing like that?!

I plant another kick back hard. SHIN!

There is a roar of pain. And words that roar louder:

"*Stop-or-I-swear-to-God-I'll-kill-you.*"

I go limp. It's not that no one swears "to God"—some of

the granmummas still do. It's that no one, *no one… Who would threaten to KILL a person?*

"You on your own?"

The grip releases just a little—and I feel it: I feel how *weak* this person really is. One glance down at the bicep on the arm of the hand that's pinned across my face tells me this body is used to hard work—but sickness trembles in those gripping arms.

"Are ya? Well, are ya?!"

I nod my head. My ribs hurt. My face hurts. My mouth is dry with fear and shock—but my eyes and nose? They're running. With **anger**. I feel **angry**.

The strange, sick, nasty, wild person hesitates…then releases me.

I wipe the trail of tears and snot from my face.

"I do a mile in six point eight. I press sixty."

I have no idea what this means. I have no idea how to respond.

"So don't you bother trying to run, and you should definitely not bother trying to fight me. You *will* lose."

The *creature* wipes my snot off the back of its hand, looking up and down the forest road. Then it looks at me. "Wait a second—have you got a transmitter in?! Your tag—"

It lurches forward, grabbing my upper arms and squeezing them.

"What, did they stick it in your leg? They did that to me once—"

"*Get off me!*" I pull away as it grabs at my thighs.

"Shut up! God, you little screecher! No wonder you're not

9

tagged. You ain't even on T-jabs, are you? How old are you, kid? Hey! You're okay now! Okay?"

The insane question settles it. This person is an *unknown* kind of person. A person who hurts and scares and then asks how you are. A person I must get away from. I nod at it, sniffing hard.

"Then quit with the blubbering, kid."

No one, not even Granmumma Kate, would tell another person to stop crying. Anyone who doesn't know that is definitely an unknown kind of person. Maybe not even a person at all.

"Name's Mason," the creature says, holding out a hand.

Courtesy dictates a hand held out is a hand to be shaken, that the cheek of the person holding out that hand is to be kissed. I take the hand and, swallowing revulsion with my own snot, lean in to kiss.

"What the *hell* are you doing?!" *it* says, shoving me away.

It. That's what this is. No human being I have ever met would behave like this.

"Where did you 'scape from anyway? You weren't hell bound, was you? Come on! What unit you from? What d'you call yourself? I'm not gonna tell anyone, am I? Who'd I tell?! *Why'd* I tell?! How long you been out for? You don't look that sick. Did you get proper sick yet? Where'd you get that horse from? I mean, that is an actual *horse*, right?"

I nod. I have to get away from it. I have to think. I have to stay calm—*and keep it calm*, that's what I decide—because something in its ranting, in its questions asked with no wait for an

10

answer, reminds me of my own granmumma, whose temper can feed like a fire on any sort of disagreement.

"An actual horse… I thought they'd be smaller…" it says, almost to itself, contemplating in amazement. "How'd you even steal that?!"

I just smile politely. The smile feels wonky on my face.

"God's sake…" It grins at me. "How are you alive, li'l thief? Hah. How'd you manage it? You're a walkin' freakin' miracle, ain't you? You got anything to eat and drink in that bag, have you? You got water?" It holds out its filthy paw, its hand making *gimme!* baby grabs in the air. "Come on now, little brother. Don't hold out on me."

Little brother. *Brother…* I slide the backpack from my shoulders and it snatches it.

"Siddown, bro," it tells me.

Bro? I crumple to the ground where I stand. It plonks itself down too—close. Grabbing-distance close.

"See now, we gotta share and share alike, ain't we?" it says, ripping open the backpack. "Us 'scaped ones, that's what we gotta do. We're brothers in the face of death now, brothers in the face of death… Oh, do NOT tell me you've been eating this stuff," it says, holding up a bunch of freshly dug carrots. "KID! This is goddamn filthy jungle poison, that's what. You eat this stuff, you're dead in two seconds, not ten. Get me?!"

It shakes the carrots in my face, then flings them aside. Soil still on them, but Milpy doesn't care, comes plodding up to munch, cart trundling behind, and the creature jumps back to its hoof feet. It looks around, then staggers to grab a branch—a poor choice, so rotten looking it'll probably crumble immediately, but still…Milpy, munching. No one hits her, not even Lenny. She just gets shouted at. She doesn't often listen. I have no idea what Milpy would do if someone struck her—only that she would NOT like it.

"No!" I can't help myself. "She won't hurt you!"

The creature eyes the huge power of Milpy, chomping.

"She's just hungry!"

"That so?" it says, watching Milpy crunch.

Painful seconds tick.

"That's a *she* horse?" it asks.

I nod and watch the creature watch Milpy—Milpy watching it right back, her nostrils flared, scenting, her ears unable to decide between laying back in irritation (because—really!—what is this nonsense on the way home?!) and pricked, twitching, listening (strange *it*, strange smell, general strangeness). Still: fresh carrots?! Too good!

"What's that you got in that wagon anyway?" it asks, pointing at the cart.

"Apples?"

It picks up an apple. It examines the apple. It bites it. It spits it out.

"Brother, these ain't apples!" it says, shaking its head at me, wiping its mouth. A convincingly human look of disgust and pity on its face.

With watchful eyes on Milpy, it sits back down. Places

that branch down on the road, and I can see, for sure, that it is rotten—orange-and-white fungus all over it, wood lice tumbling out, escaping from its broken ends. I've been hit by kisses harder than that.

It rummages again, trying the next compartment in the backpack. Pulls out a cloth-wrapped package, unwraps it.

"And what is this?" it asks.

How could anyone not know these things?! It's sniffing the loaf of bread. My cousins' gorgeous sourdough. Fresh baked.

"Bread."

"Don't look like bread."

It sniffs some more, bites down slowly, tears away a mouthful. It chews, eyes on me.

"'S disgustin'," it mumbles, but it keeps on chewing, biting off more, like it's ravenous, while the other greedy hand searches, finds my water bottle, and…suddenly it tosses the loaf at me, and I catch it.

Regret that immediately: shows so clearly I am watching, alert.

It eyes me.

"Why doncha take a little bite of that yourself?"

Terror alone would stop me. I have also been stuffed full of cake at my cousins' house, but I have got to get out of here, so I pull a chunk of bread off—away from the creature's bread-mauling area—and take a bite.

It, Milpy, and I chew.

Me and Milpy are watching it.

It is watching us.

It unscrews my water bottle, sniffs…

"Water," I whisper.

It glugs—and glugs.

"Don't taste right neither," it mutters—and my heart skips a beat as it pulls my knife out of the backpack. My good knife, my favorite supersharp blade that was given to me by Kate. Belonged to my great granpappa.

It releases the blade—seems to know just how—and holds it up. The blade of the knife shines true in the late, dying sun.

I feel my whole body tense up so hard any fearful shaking stops.

"Was you thinking to stab someone, little brother? That what you was thinkin' of?"

That's a thing men did, isn't it? That's what I've heard. Kate says women did too, but Mumma says there are *statistics*. Men stabbed people, shot people, killed anyone. Prisons rammed full of them and still they did not stop.

"'Spect you'd like to stab me right now, eh?"

It makes a tutting sound and waggles the knife at me.

"It ain't the way, li'l brother. It ain't the way. I mean…I guess sometimes it maybe has to be the way, right? We've all seen that. But—"

Something in the backpack catches its eye. It pulls it out, the jar of honey, holds it up with a puzzled look.

"Honey."

"Think so?! I've heard of that!"

It drops the knife—blade open—on the other side of its body

and manages to get the jar open. Scoops out a fingerful and sniffs it. Looks suspiciously at me.

"You first," it says, offering the fingerful.

Its hands… They are so filthy.

It grunts. "Brother, we are both gonna die anyways," it says, honey running down its finger. "Welcome to the jungle."

With my mouth, I take the honey from its finger.

The touching of it, the creature, makes me shudder.

"That good, huh?" it says and delves another filthy finger into the jar, shoves it into its mouth, and sucks it.

Its eyeballs roll back. "Sweet!" it says. "That *is* good, ain't it? So, kid, you gonna talk to me?"

I can see huge beads of sweat popping out on its forehead. I am sweating too. My sweat is fear; its sweat is sickness—pouring out of it. It keeps eating though, grabbing the bread back, dipping chunks into the honey jar, swigging at the water—and all the while mumbling talk and questions at me. I don't answer. I see streaks of blood in the bready mix of chewed-up food in its mouth, and it winces when it swallows, rubbing at its throat. And its stomach? I hear loud gurgling and churning, smell the stink of vile farts.

"So how come you ain't sick? I been loose FIVE WHOLE DAYS—got sick DAY ONE. Had to drink goddamn filthy water got green stuff growing in it. Green stuff! Veg-et-able material *growing* in the freaking water! Brother, come on, might as well name your unit—and don't go telling me you're Alpha material, because I know a Beta boy when I see one…but how come you

15

ain't on the T-jabs? You oughtta be by now! Kid, you got X-S body fat. X-S! Round the ass—and your pecs! Serious!" it says, jabbing my left breast.

I flinch and shrink and twitch to run.

"Whoa! Don't get all like that! Them flabby pecs is probably what's keepin' you alive! You're probably digestin' yourself!" it laughs, ripping off bread and dunking it into the honey.

It raises its eyes from the jar, studying me as it chews.

"Hey, it doesn't matter at all now, does it?"

I study it right back. I...say nothing. My mind has landed in a bad place. My mind has landed in a place where the thought that *cannot be* **is**.

"D'you even know where you are, Beta boy? 'Cause I sure as hell don't! Hellhole, brother! In-fin-it-y of it! Know what that means? Endless, my brother. This goddamn jungle goes on forever."

It doesn't. It goes to the village. I'm no great runner, but I think, if I can remain calm, I can outrun this sick thing.

"Yup, we is lost...lost and damned and done for. So this is just great, ain't it? This is juuuuuuuust ber-illiant. Two runnin' dead men sharing a last supper and only one of us got anything to say."

"I just want to go home," I whisper. I am telling it to myself. I am willing it to happen.

"Yeah, I'll bet you do. Ah, **HELL**—it ain't me you're scared of at all, is it? It's the wimmin, ain't it? Oh God! You seen them? Have you seen wimmin?!"

16

I nod the tiniest of nods. I feel physically sick—but not as sick as the creature. It's rubbing its belly, sweat popping, hairy face grimmer than grim.

"You seen wimmin...around here?"

I nod an even tinier nod.

"Je-sus." It wipes a shaking hand across its filthy hair, eyes darting. "They'll kill you quicker than the jungle, if they don't— Kid! Oh God, oh brother mine...did they...mess with you? No shame here, brother. If them wimmin touched you, it ain't your fault. We all know that. We all been told what wimmin'll do to any 'scaped male they find—and if they done it to you, IT AIN'T YOUR FAULT. No shame on you, no blame on you. IT AIN'T YOUR FAULT. You listen to Mason now."

I shut my eyes, just to make it STOP for one moment, but the sound of the thing retching makes me open them again—it's doubled over, gripping its belly, head sweat falling like raindrops.

"Get out of here," it says, voice twisted with pain.

I edge myself up, onto my knees, then one foot to the ground, knuckles to the concrete, willing power into my legs. It looks up at me, fighting whatever agonies I can hear battling in its guts.

"D'you hear me? Don't let the wimmin get you!"

It doubles up again with a horrific groan. My legs tense with sprint intention.

It vomits—bread and honey and water and...blood? I should run. I should run—but, even in a nightmare, who leaves a sick person?

"Go," it says, wiping its mouth. "Brother: die free."

CHAPTER 2
MAN

I glance back, midsprint, see it hauling down its shiny, red leggings. See a *penis*, dangling. Scrotum. Strange, floppy things, all of them.

I have never seen an XY in my life. *No one* has seen an XY in sixty years.

I realize, running, that I have hardly even believed they existed.

I mean, sperm has to come from somewhere, so obviously they *do* exist…but not in my world. Not in anyone's world. It didn't matter who a person was or how they lived or who they loved; the virus—"the sickness"—targeted anyone with a Y chromosome. Those who survived, they were put into the Sanctuaries to keep them safe—and they can never leave. The virus is still here. The virus would kill them.

It *cannot* be an XY.

A person might choose to change their body, to make their body male…but no one in my world would randomly attack and hurt another person or call someone "brother" or "man." The genitals, they're just the final confirmation.

This thing that cannot be *is*.

MAN! MAN! MAN! MAN!

The thump of my boots pounds the word into the road as I run and run—and it is only when the road is about to bend, to curve up and around the hill, that I shoot one last fast look back.

And see.

It is lying in the road—not moving.

I stop.

In the UK, it has been Agreed: if *any* creature—a human or any other animal—suffers and cannot be helped, it should be freed—quickly, kindly, and as painlessly as possible—from its misery.

There are no Agreements I know of that apply, specifically, to XYs. Why would there be?

But what I do know is that they can't live outside the Sanctuaries.

It is going to die. It *knows* it is going to die.

I have wrung birds' necks. I have bashed countless fishes' heads. I've taken my turn to slit the throat of a prestunned lamb. I chose to. It was hard, and it was very upsetting—but

19

in our village, anyone older than a littler one who wants to eat meat needs to understand what "meat" is before their teen years are over.

I wish my sharp, sharp knife weren't lying on that road.

It still isn't moving.

Milpy, who has poked her nose into the backpack, investigating, pulls her nose out of it. Stands there, crunching, watching me… *My Little **Conscience***.

It might already be dead… That's the thought I hold on to, clutch on to for my own dear life—as I walk—jog—walk—jog—hesitate—walk back down the hill.

It isn't dead.

It's lying on its back. Its breathing is shallow and fast. The text of the UK version of the Agreement about helping death in humans is very specific, and all of us who are trained and of an age to act upon it know what we must do: no matter how hopeless the situation, no matter how great the suffering, no matter even if death was anticipated and clear instructions left…if at all possible, it should be the decision of the person who suffers as to whether they should be assisted.

Which, in this case, would require checking for consciousness. Again.

I do not want to do it. I'm telling myself that I'm not even sure whether the Agreement applies to an XY…but if it doesn't, wouldn't I have to treat it like any other kind of creature? It is going to die: the kindest, quickest thing I could do would be to slit its throat. Or smother it? Would that be easier? Would that be more bearable than jets of blood? It is doomed…and I feel doomed too. I do not want to risk it waking again…but I do not want to kill it. I do not want this. I do not want any of this.

But this is what I have.

I look down at my knife, lying on the road, blade still out.

I pick up my knife. Angle it, whizzing brain considering as the blade picks up the soft gold of sunlight fading through woods. I take good care of my knife. Granmumma Kate won't tolerate dull edges on any kind of blade, so I was raised to keep tools sharp and clean and ready to do their job. Kate says it's a disservice—to the maker most especially—to do otherwise.

I look at my knife. I look at its throat. Muscles, bones, veins, arteries.

Its eyes barely flicker as I shout, "WAKE UP! WAKE UP!"

But maybe it's a softer shout than before.

And I clap my hands, I do.

But maybe it's a softer clap than before.

I do not want to reach down and shake it. I do not want to touch it.

I clap and shout loudly. I make myself!

It does not stir.

All I can hear is breath: its and my own and Milpy's—she has run out of items to eat and has come up to me to nudge me because she is wanting to get on.

Breath…and a crowd of rooks settling in for the night with a *Hey, hello, how are you, we all here?* rowdy chorus.

Caw, caw, caw.

The warmth of this October day is dying. The chill of night is minutes away.

I have the panting, strained throat of a dying creature bared before me.

I wipe the blade on my shorts.

There is no way I can do it. I just can't.

I fold the knife closed.

I feel that I have failed.

I will have to accept my failure and the consequences of it.

Someone else will have to release the creature from its misery.

I haul it up onto the cart, twist it over—pulling its arms, my feet slipping on apples—so it is tummy down and won't choke on its own vomit. Then I take a run and try to leap up onto Milpy—and find I haven't got the strength. Not good. But easily fixed. I'll lead her on and find a place where there's a roadside bank high enough to scramble onto her back with less effort.

The creature turns, groaning—and I vault over the edge of the cart, clambering over apples, to grab it and shove it back onto its stomach even as it vomits.

Milpy has stopped, ears pricking back—to the side—in front—every which way. She is spooked.

I see how this is and what I'm going to have to do: I'm going to have to walk all the way home, because I cannot leave the dying creature, but I cannot leave Milpy either. There is a *thing* right behind her. A thing that doesn't smell right. A thing that doesn't sound right. A thing that is not right. And with darkness coming on, an ancient horse fear is already taking hold.

There is no point trying to tell a horse she lives in a land without wolves.

I am going to have to walk by Milpy's side—so she knows I'm there—but also keep an eye on the creature…although I could let it choke on its own vomit. Grim job done.

I…can't.

I go up to Milpy's head, expecting to have to jump up and grab the bridle to force her to pay attention to me she's so spooked—but she lowers her head, and I take hold of her muzzle and breathe words of encouragement into her soft, hairy nostrils. She is skeptical; I can tell that. Her ears are panicking even as I speak—and when an owl hoots, her head shoots up so fast she could have knocked me out. No pep talk is going to work here. With a *click-click* of encouragement, I urge her on. Drop back to her side, one reassuring hand on her as she Agrees the deal and hits a pace that's on the brisk side of steady for her and on the exhausting side of a jog for me. I drop back a little farther, so I can see and hear the creature.

It vomits again.

Spooked horse, vomiting creature. Vomiting creature, spooked horse. Vomiting creature. Vomit and diarrhea and delirium.

Ranting, muttered and shouted insanity. And, when a plane flies over, it yells at the sky: "Go to hell!"

In the middle of the nightmare of that night, it rains.

It would have been easier and better to have mercifully killed it.

♀ ♂

Teeth chattering, soaked to the skin. Exhausted.

That's my body. My brain? It stopped working hours ago.

A creature, a horse, darkness, and rain. Vomit. Diarrhea. Delirium.

Hours of it.

But I am home.

I drag open the never-much-used big gate. Milpy refuses to enter.

Kate comes out of the house. Kate worries when I come home late. (*Old habits die hard.*) No one else in the village worries like Kate worries. Maybe the rest of the granmummas would, but they mostly all live together these days and don't know anything about daughters and granddaughters who come home late. And…what is there to worry about?

"Where the hell do you think you've been?" she asks, battered umbrella over her head and no coat on. Kate's breathing is atrocious. It's going to kill her if she's not careful, Mumma says. That and that she should never have smoked. Kate says *Pah!* and blames it on once-was air pollution. She says it's her heart that'll kill her, same as everyone else. (*When it stops, you stop.*) (*Too bad, so sad, bye-bye.*)

"Nowhere" is what I'd usually say, with a huge grin, and Kate would smile and roll her eyes, because that's what she used to say to her mumma, back in the days when a girl late home was apparently a truly scary thing.

Nowhere. That's what I'd usually say, and then I'd tell Kate all about whatever me and Plat had been up to.

Tonight, I have no more words.

"What's happened?" Kate snaps, instantly detecting the not-rightness.

The rain is coming down so hard.

"Is Mumma home?" I ask, shivering.

I know she won't be, but I wish she were.

"Get in!" says Kate.

That's usually a private joke from the once-was too—"*Get in!*"—but tonight it doesn't feel funny at all.

"Kate…"

I don't have the words to explain. All I can manage to do is stand back and point at the cart.

It fell quiet ages ago. It stopped moving.

Kate eyeballs me. It is a sign of how quickly she has understood the not-rightness of the situation that she doesn't even say, *This had better be good.* She walks straight past me to see for herself.

She sees. Even in the darkness, she sees.

She clutches her throat. "Dear God…"

Before she can even start gasping, I run for the house, turning over everything on the kitchen table, searching, then running and flinging open Kate's bedroom door, instantly deciding a hunt through her mess is a BAD IDEA, and running to grab an emergency inhaler—the last—from the drawer in Mumma's study. And running back outside and handing Kate the inhaler—and she shakes it and shoots...and breathes.

"I think it's an XY! I found it in the woods!"

"SHIFT!" Kate shouts at Milpy and thwacks her rump.

Kate is not so strong these days. She is seventy-five. But—

For a split second, Milpy considers this unexpected event; she has been shouted at all night, she has had her head pulled around, she has—as far as she is concerned—escaped the wolves, she has had a wrong-smelling, wrong-sounding thing right behind her, and now: SOMEONE JUST HIT HER!

She rears. The cart bolts bust open as the weight of the apples heaves backward, and the creature and a ton of apples tumble out.

Milpy, having made her point, goes back to still and stubborn and wet and *furious*. She lifts her tail, farts tremendously, and deposits a seriously runny pile of angry, tired, anxious poo.

"Christ!" says Kate, stuffing the inhaler in her pocket and chucking the umbrella aside. "Get his arms!"

I hesitate.

"GO ON!" she shouts at me. "GRAB HIM!"

I clamber over apples slippery with rain and best-not-think-about-what and grab it by the armpits. Stooped, shaking, rained on, freezing... Knowing Kate, who has its knees, has so little strength, I take the weight of its body, and I *make* my arms, legs, and feet work.

"Where—in—the—**hell**—did—you—come—from?" Kate puffs at its body as we carry it in out of the rain.

A strange time to notice a strange thing yet again: the way that the creature and Kate speak. It's so similar, the questions that need no answers, the swearing, and the rudeness.

♀ ♂

In Kate's room—a dining room once-was—we heave and dump it onto the bed.

"Cover him!" she says, searching frantically for the phone she's supposed to keep with her at all times in case of an asthma attack. It's buried under a ton of stuff on her dressing table. It *is* plugged in, but the socket is switched off. The phone is dead.

"Useless!" says Kate, flicking the socket on. She grew up with more tech than any of us but can't be bothered with any of it now that there's nothing "interesting" online. "Go get Akesa on your thing!"

"It's at school!"

My *thing*—a notebook that isn't mine at all—is being assessed and upgraded.

"Then get the other phone!" Kate shouts at my back. I'm already running for it: the only working device left in the house.

Mumma's old mobile is in the emergency items drawer in

her study—and charged (of course it's charged!)—but I'm just not used to phones, so my fumbling, panicky fingers are still trying to figure out how to get PicChat up as I blunder back into Kate's room, where she is taking its pulse at the neck.

"Gimme that," she says, snatching the phone and expertly flicking to PicChat. Her fingers and thumbs have never forgotten.

I dare to speak up: "But…wouldn't it be quicker and kinder if we killed it ourselves?"

For a second, she looks at me in utter horror.

"I'm just saying…I mean…it's going to die, isn't it?"

"It isn't an *it*."

"An XY. A man."

"It's a *boy*," says Kate, and jabs—viciously—at Dial.

CHAPTER 3
BOY

Boy.

That's not a word I often hear.

I hear it even less than I hear the word *man*, which is what I thought it was.

Boy.

I thought they'd be smaller.

And less hairy.

Boy.

I can't find a place in my head where that fits.

We sometimes get told stuff about men in community studies, and every year, we have "men's week." It used to be a whole month, but it was Agreed—even by the granmummas—that it took up too much important study time. And I am all in favor of the mummas' suggestion that there should just be an "International Men's Day," because it's not like it's all that important or anything. I mean, obviously it is important; there would be no aeronautical engineering for me to study if once-was men hadn't been around. So I kind of get it, I do. And I love all that old stuff: the Bernoulli brothers and the Wright brothers—although not as much as I like reading about Valentina Tereshkova and Wally Funk. Once-was people: women and men. In a once-was world that seemed to bother about that—women and men—A LOT. I understand—of course I do!—that reproduction has to happen...but other than that, it's baffling to me why being a woman or a man was such a big deal—when I even think about it. Mostly, I don't.

So about *boys*...what do I know? For me, they exist only as words on the pages of books, words I have spent my whole life... ignoring, I suppose. I can remember Plat pointing out to me that some of the characters in *Twilight* (we were rehearsing it as a play to put on for the granmummas because they loved it so when they were our age) were supposed to be XYs (as well as vampires and werewolves?!) and me going back to the book and trying to understand that these weren't just people (Or vampires! Or werewolves!), but they were supposed to be...male as well as female.

I hadn't seen *he/him/his*. I didn't get it. And honestly? Even when Plat showed me how it was there in black and white on the page...I couldn't seem to rethink that or any other once-was story. It didn't seem important at all: who was male, who was female. The people in the stories behaved in all kinds of ways that seemed strange to me, so what difference did *biology* make?!

It felt as though it would be a wasted effort to even begin to fathom it.

♀ ♂

The phone in Kate's hand rings. The second Akesa's face pops up, I catch a glimpse of just the slightest "unprofessional" frown flicker across it: our doctor *knows* Kate.

"Hello, Kate," says Akesa. "How can I—"

Kate jabs her onto speakerphone. "You need to get here," she shouts at Akesa's face and points the phone at the body so Akesa can see.

"Pulse is one-six-five," says Kate, tracking the phone over its body.

One hundred and sixty-five beats per minute. That's so high its heart must be about to explode.

"Vomiting, diarrhea. Don't know temperature yet—but HOT. Don't know cause, so don't ask. Been like this for…" Kate glances at me. "How long?!"

"I don't know!"

"Roughly!"

"At least three hours." It's got to have taken me at least that long to get home—but there was vomit on the road too, so it was sick before I found it. "Longer."

Me, Kate, and Akesa—via the phone—stare at it. Between

short, sharp bouts of violent shaking (in which its eyes, freakily, roll open and clamp shut), it lies motionless except for that flat, flat chest that's rising-falling-rising-falling—rapid, tiny movements like a terrified, small creature—while torrents of sweat pour.

"I'm on my way," says Akesa. Sound of her grabbing stuff. Sound stops. "Wait—let me see that arm."

Kate shoves the phone at its arm. It's horrible, the jagged mess of a cut on it.

"And the body...show me the body again."

"For crying out loud," mutters Kate, pulling the phone back, panning.

For one long and strange moment, all you can hear is breathing: Kate's (rasping), mine (gulping, trying not to cry from sheer exhaustion), Akesa's (alert: battering down the line like a storm)...and another: its. Soft, rapid, tiny. A dying mouse.

"It's a *MAN*?!" Akesa's disembodied voice says. Shock bouncing.

"A *boy*," says Kate, turning the phone so Akesa faces her.

"A *BOY*?!"

"*YES!*"

Breathing. There's just breathing. All the kinds of breathing.

"I...I've seen one before," Akesa says. "The arm... It's... There was a testosterone implant he'd tried to cut out. Looks like this one has succeeded—"

"You need to get here!"

"I don't know what to do!"

"**HELLO!**" Kate screams. "They-pretty-much-work-the-same-as-us, *DOCTOR!*"

32

I fling myself at Kate, grab the inhaler from her pocket, shake it, and shove it into her mouth—and she breathes deep on the shot of medicine, but her eyes are wild. She shoves my hand away, and we both stare at Akesa.

"There's a protocol," Akesa says, her normally calm doctor's voice so shaky. She clicks about on her notebook. "I have to consult. Before I can attend, I have to—"

Kate grabs my hand and takes another shot from the inhaler.

"A *protocol*?!" she wheezes. Fury. "How can there be a **protocol**?! *What the hell are you talking about?!* He's sick and you've got to come here now!"

"I HAVE TO CONSULT. I'll call you back—"

Kate's furious fingers cut Akesa off before she can hang up.

"A *protocol*?!" she says—not to me, but at me. Then her eyes narrow. She speed swipes at the phone, and Mumma's worried face appears, thinking there's something wrong.

And there is. There is something very wrong.

"Big shot, we've got a situation here," says Kate.

I cringe. "Big shot" is what Kate has taken to calling Mumma since she got elected to represent the region at the National Council. Mumma hates it. Kate knows it. Kate turns the phone so Mumma can see the body.

My Mumma gasps. "Have you called Akesa?" she says immediately. I can hear her dialing PicChat on her notebook without waiting for an answer, and I know what she must be thinking: Why would we be calling her when we should just be calling our doctor? "Do you know what's wrong?" she's asking as I hear the result of her dial; Akesa's line is engaged. Mumma cutting the call, dialing again, now demanding again of us, *"Do you know what's wrong with her?"*

"**It's a boy**," says Kate.

Like me, Mumma has never seen a bio-born male. Like me, she'd struggle with the word *boy*. And she wouldn't think in a million years that this creature is one.

"It's an XY!" I chip in.

Mumma is silent as Akesa's line comes back as busy again.

Kate flips the phone around so she can stare Mumma down: "Your daughter found this *boy* in the woods—you ARE hearing me right—and he's sick as hell. Now we've got a *doctor* talking *protocols*, so how about *you* talking to the *doctor*?"

"Oh my God…" Mumma whispers. My mumma never says that.

"Call Akesa!" yells Kate, and she hangs up.

For a moment, it's like Kate doesn't even know I'm there in the room—and the way I'm feeling, I'm not even sure I am in the room. I feel… It's like I'm floating tens, hundreds, thousands of miles away from myself. Crying, apparently—

"Quit blubbing," Kate says.

That's what *it* said.

Crying is normal. Crying is complex. Crying conveys. No one ever tells anyone to…*quit blubbing.*

Kate grabs her pajama top, sits down heavily on the edge of the bed, and mops its face—even as I mop at my own, wiping away tears I can't make much sense of at the moment.

"I can't go through this again," she's muttering to herself, a rare, lone teardrop escaping. I don't know what that tear means either. The granmummas cried so much they now cry so rarely. Their tears have turned acid with emotion. Too much, too many, feelings…in too few drops.

"I can't do this again. I can't," she whispers, stroking its sweat-sodden hair.

When the phone rings seconds later, she's on it like lightning. Listens, dead faced, to Mumma's words—speakerphone-loud words I don't want to hear:

♀ ♂

There is a protocol. That's what Mumma says. The protocol says there is no permission to treat the *boy*, only to administer pain relief. And not to euthanize, even if it is requested.

Kate bangs the phone against her head in disbelief.

Mumma continues calmly delivering instructions: Kate should send me away to Lenny's—to Lenny's, not the granmummas, because it'll cause less fuss. I mustn't see this. It wouldn't be fair or right for me to see this. It would cause unnecessary trauma to me. (Kate manages to nod at this.) The boy's body will be collected in the morning.

There is a silence from Kate. She smooths the boy's hair. Another acid tear falls.

"He won't live. You know that," Mumma says.

Kate does not reply.

"And perhaps it's best not to say anything to anyone else. It will only cause…*distress*."

Best not to say anything? But everyone always discusses everything. Open discussion: that's how everyone and everything works. *Distress*?

Distress is life. Distress is distress. It might be painful. It might be difficult. But it can be shared. It can be talked about. It can be worked out—always. Can't it?

I look at Kate. Yes, this *is* already causing distress.

"Katherine-Thea, are you listening to me?" Mumma asks. "Is River still there with you? Kate, are you listening?"

"Nope," says Kate, and hangs up on her.

She breathes, lungs wheezing. She chews at her lip. She dials. Gets Akesa. Stares her down.

"What you're seeing right now is a massive reaction to bacteria his body has never encountered before," Akesa says. "He comes from a sealed environment. Sanctuary food is irradiated. Water is purified. This…*boy* has never been outside. Our world is deadly to him."

An apple. Bread. Water. Honey. A finger in my mouth. The same finger in his mouth. *BACTERIA*. Have I killed a **boy**?

"So we need to give him antibiotics," says Kate.

Antibiotics?! In the once-was, they were handed out like cake on a birthday. Even I know the consequences of that: resistant superbugs. These days, they are hardly ever prescribed. And in a hopeless case like this…

"Even if he responded, all we would do would be to

prolong his suffering. He'll already be infected with the virus by now. It will be attacking his immune system. There is only one way this ends. I'm so, so sorry, Kate. I know how hard this must be for you." She swallows. "Permission to treat is refused. Pain relief only. They'll learn more from the body if he…fights to the last. He could help other XYs. He could help all of us."

Finally, Kate speaks: "But we can't help him…"

"There is no permission to euthanize."

"That's disgusting."

"It's the protocol," says Akesa grimly. This must be almost impossible for her; no doctor would allow such a cruel thing. "I am so sorry. I'll come as soon as I can. I will make sure *he* suffers as little as possible."

"*We can't even help him to die?*"

It comes out mangled by anger and pain, but Kate speaks in uptalk—a sure sign of her utter desperation. It is a hundred years old, but it still carries weight. People all over the world still speak it; it wasn't a language in itself, but it was a way of speaking—an aural question mark at the end of a sentence, indicating that although the speaker is fairly sure of what she is saying, the listener is free to disagree. Women pioneered it, back in the once-was—and Kate hates it. She says if you've got something to say, you should just say it…but occasionally, uptalk just bursts out of her. Usually in moments of rage—when, actually, she really couldn't care less what someone else thinks. From Kate's lips, uptalk is a devastating, angry weapon.

"Correct," says Akesa. "But maybe you hung up before I could say that."

"Damn right," says Kate, and ends the call.

The XY is having a shaking fit so massive its whole body convulses. And when it stops, a strange whimpering sound escapes from its lips and its eyes roll open again—just for a second.

I understand what Akesa just said. We *can* help it to die.

"I'll get the pack," I tell Kate.

♀ ♂

It's hard not to slip on the hundreds and hundreds of spilt apples as I run out in the lane—where there's no sign of Milpy, but the apple trail tells me she's lumbered off home, as cross as a horse can be.

I've never had to do this before. The pack we need—the death pack—is kept at the house of the granmummas. There is a heart-start, and there is a pack containing the medical tools to maintain life, and there is a death pack: to end life peacefully and painlessly.

My heart is pounding as I open the front door to the granmummas' huge house, not so much from the exertion of running, but from dread. I don't know how to handle this—coming to get death—and I don't know how to handle the granmummas.

There is crazy noise, as usual, coming from inside as I barge through the hall that's rammed with coats and boots and Casey's walker and Yaz's wheelchair, and fling open the door to the granmummas' vast kitchen, a toasty paradise of sofas, tables, chairs, and comfort. And pumping music.

It is not like anyone else's kitchen—not just because of its size, but because of how the granmummas like to use it. Card games are being played. Even in the din, books are being read. Manicures and pedicures and makeovers are being administered. Hair is being dyed. Smoke hangs heavy in the air. The rest of the harvest might be a bit of a joke, but the granmummas somehow manage to grow a superb crop of cannabis—not all of which gets traded. They also excel at the production of alcohol from pretty much every fruit, herb, and plant there is; Willow's horseradish and potato vodka is currently being considered for export trade, though local consumption is high. There are mugs and fancy cups everywhere, few of which will contain tea.

It is *their* Sanctuary—a small, hard-won handful of happiness—that I am about to destroy.

They all instantly know something is wrong. The music is killed.

"We need the pack," I tell them.

Courtesy telling. I'm first- and last-aid trained, so I could just take it, but I guess the look on my face tells them something else too: it's the death pack I've come for.

"Oh no—no, no, no! Is it Kate?!" cries Willow as Yukiko flings open the cupboard and shoves the death pack into my arms, grabbing the heart-start and the life pack, and flinging the general first-aid pack at Rosie, who grabs it and hugs it to her chest. At the same time, the rest of the granmummas—all those who are fit and able, and some who really aren't—are on their feet immediately, rushing to grab coats, to come and assist. Yaz grabbing at everything in her path—walls, cupboards, tables, people—to get to her wheelchair in the hall.

"Who is it?!" Yukiko shouts at me.

"It's a boy."

The word explodes. A wave of shock breaks across the room. I've seen footage of the weapons people used to have. The word *boy* is an atomic bomb.

CHAPTER 4
PROTOCOL

The granmummas descend on our house en masse and in a frenzy of grief and anguish.

When I look around the room in which the boy lies dying, I see so clearly what I have always somehow known about the granmummas but never witnessed. Fury is not a strong enough word for it. There is an unimaginable sorrow that seeps and bleeds and bubbles beneath their toughness, beneath their wild love of fun. Beneath that? There is phenomenal anger. An ancient, complex rage that is beyond my comprehension—yet I feel it.

It is Casey who is most distraught. Casey is pretty much a national legend. In the early days of the in vitro fertilization program, when virus outbreaks in the Sanctuaries threatened to kill the few remaining XYs, there was fear for the very survival of the human race. Casey volunteered for IVF again and again—and again. Three live-born sons. She had *three* baby boys. No daughter. All three baby boys delivered by cesarean section in a super-sterile IVF clinic right outside the Sanctuary and, once tested to be virus free, immediately handed over into the care of the Sanctuary, as every baby boy must be.

Their mothers are never allowed to hold them. Not even for one second. In the early days, a photograph of the baby was taken and continued virtual contact was allowed—reports of the baby's development, more photographs, then, as the child grew, direct virtual contact. Exchanges of emails, exchanges of photographs and videos. When the consequences of that became apparent—boys would escape and die—contact between mothers and sons was shut down. It is still an option to have a photograph of the newborn, but granmummas tend to counsel against it. They advise that it is better for the mother not to dwell on it. It is better, they say, to forget. They say this, the generation who cannot and will not forget.

I can hardly look into Casey's eyes, so great is the pain in them.

They have sedated the boy and administered immediate pain relief. Sweat is still oozing off him; the still-rapid rise and fall of his chest shows his lungs are struggling. Shows his dying-mouse heart is still beating fast enough to burst.

They have to release him. They know it.

The granmummas wordlessly comfort each other with shared, sorrowful looks and hands reaching to touch hands—but, oh, that anger burns.

"He might live!" Heloise breathes, willing it all to be a lie: the now and the past.

Dora, her sister, puts her arm around Heloise.

"He won't," she says.

"He might!"

"He won't," says Yukiko.

"You know it," says Dora, holding Heloise close.

She does. They do. All of them know.

"It might have changed. The virus might have…gone away," whispers Casey, then shudders with tears. Granmummas reach out hands to pat and soothe her.

Rosie softly whispers, "Your boys will be grown men now. Your boys are safe."

"And this one is a goner," says Kate.

And this one is a goner. From anyone younger than a granmumma, this would sound despicably insensitive, but Kate lived through the sickness. She was fifteen years old when she gently lifted her youngest brother, baby Jaylen, from the arms of her sleeping mother—the mother who did not want to let him go, thought she could somehow keep him safe from the dying all around. The baby was wrapped in a scarf and held tight—by Kate—on the back of her boyfriend's motorbike all the way to the airport. One of the last flights to leave. Crowds and chaos. Kate holding up Jaylen shouting, *He's not sick! He's not sick! Please take him! Take him! Please!*

And a stranger, taking him…

And Jaylen gone.

And Kate only realizing when he had gone, watching that plane take off to who knows where, that she still held the bag of his favorite toys, his bottles and nappies, and his little clothes… and the letter that said who he was and when he was born and where he came from. The letter that told who his family was. The letter that told who loved him and to whom he should be returned.

Only he never did return. None of the babies or the boys or the men who survived ever came back.

♀ ♂

"We need to do the right thing," says Yaz. "You all know it. You all know how it was: no boy or man who caught the virus ever survived for more than twenty-four hours."

I know (Global Agreement No. 7) *Everyone has the right to be listened to*, but I've always found it fairly (very) terrifying to speak in public. I'm OK at home—with Kate in the house you either toughen up or shut up—but in front of other people, I get tongue-tied. But if there's one thing I hate, it's factual errors. My life is math. My future will be NO ERRORS. Errors in engineering kill. If there is one thing that can actually make me talk when I'd rather not, it's an error. Errors must be corrected.

"Five days," I say.

For a moment, it's as though they have not heard me over the din of their own thoughts—but they have.

"What?" says Yukiko.

"Five days," I say, and I shrug from nerves. "That's what it said, that it had been running for five days."

"You...*spoke* to him?" says Kate.

"Yes."

"Why...didn't you say?"

"There wasn't time." Fact.

Silence. Horrified silence.

It feels like a 150—like a Community Meeting. No, it feels like a 150 *Court*—an event, rare, when the one hundred and fifty voting members of our community meet to decide restorative justice. It's set, very strictly, at 150, because it is thought that is the maximum number of human relationships one person is able to handle in any kind of meaningful way. That's how any kind of organization works, how industry works—how the whole of democracy works: from community to national level. It's a gigantic, upside-down pyramid of communication, from the village to the area to the region to the nation to the ever-changing chair of the Global Council. And I avoid contact with it as much as I can.

I'm only having to deal with a tiny—minuscule!—percentage of the world. I'm only having to deal with the granmummas who could make it here, yet I feel as though I am on trial.

All I have done is to be too scared to assist death. I can't be the first. I won't, I'm sure, be the last.

"There wasn't time..." Yaz says, encouraging me to speak.

"There wasn't! And it...what it said...didn't seem relevant. I mean...I didn't really understand what it was saying anyway."

Kate groans.

"I didn't! I was scared!"

A roomful of muttering. Kate takes a hit on her inhaler, heading for a serious overdose. I go to take it from her and she bats me away. *Bats*. It sounds gentle. Kate smacks me in the face with the back of her seventy-five-year-old hand. The force is not deliberate, and she's too distraught to even notice it. "We need antibiotics and everything else you've got. Anything! Everything! All of it! Go get the meds!" Kate shouts at the room.

I'm clutching my face thinking *OW!* and *Meds? Medication?!* The granmummas have medication when no one, to my knowledge, ever has anything more than the basics?

"Outside," Kate barks at me.

Outside. It's one of our jokes that I really don't quite get because I can't quite imagine it. It's only the sense of it I get. It is, apparently, what a man would say to another man when he wanted to fight him. Kate just says it to me for fun when I complain about something I know I shouldn't complain about, such as there being too many inedible, crunchy bits in the cockroach stew she's made.

♀ ♂

"He spoke to you…" Kate is saying to me as granmummas rush past us.

"Yes."

"What did he say?"

46

"I didn't understand most of it."

I can see Kate is in full Kate mode, teetering on the brink of flipping out—a brink from which she pulls herself back.

"What I want you to do," she says, her hands resting with only slight clawing pressure on my shoulders, "is to write down what he said. Every word that you can remember."

"But I didn't—"

"Every word, whether you understood it or not. Understand?"

"Yes."

Not for the first time in my life, I wish my mumma was here. I love Kate's love; she's gruff but understands some things my mumma doesn't. Things to do with how you feel about people. But my mumma…she's my mumma.

I sit down at the kitchen table and I write every word I can remember of what happened.

I'm writing it out as the granmummas return almost immediately, depositing drugs on the kitchen table. No one else gets called upon, because these people, they've seen it all. Dealt with every situation you could think of. They attend the birth of every girl (and always get absolutely wasted when a child is born healthy), they are *on it* when anyone falls sick or is injured (if it's serious—they are scathingly dismissive of minor hurts), but it is death, in particular, that is their specialty.

Thanks to the dying of the XYs, they have seen pretty much every kind of death there is. Even medics like Akesa will consult with granmummas in the event of an illness that is unusual or potentially fatal, and nothing gets more unusual than this: a dying boy they refuse to let die.

A huge sorting out of the drugs happens. Our kitchen table is heaped with boxes and bottles of all kinds of pills and potions. A secret stockpile. It's confirmation of the granmummas' spectacular naughtiness and of their will to survive. Not their own survival, no, but children's and grandchildren's. Relatively few of the granmummas had children of their own. *Every child is our child* is their favorite among the Global Agreements. Without it, there would be no future, and it's that—a future, the very survival of the human race—that they have spent their lives fighting for.

Where normally the granmummas bicker about every single thing—and seem to enjoy it—tonight they are quieter and more efficient than any mumma. Even my own.

They fill the house with their activity.

Drugs are chosen, ground up in the mortar and pestle, mixed with water. A spoon is sterilized to feed the solution into the boy's mouth. An IV from the life pack is set up. Hanging from our coat stand it feeds water laced with salt, sugar, and a touch of death-pack liquid morphine into the XY's vein. Its body is stripped of its weird clothes. It is washed, dried, and tucked up in clean sheets and blankets. Two of the granmummas scuttle off to the community washing machines with the soiled linen, then come scuttling back with fresh reserve bedding from their own supply.

My account of the XY's ramblings written, I now feel useless and helpless. I can only watch, peering around the door to

Kate's room, wincing, stomach churning, as Dora sews up the wound on the arm. Dora, with the best, amazingly neat, needlework skills, elected without dispute to perform the task. Me, not wanting to look but unable to stop myself. I watch her needle puncture flesh. Midstitch, mid-thread-drawing-skin-together, the sound of Akesa's helicopter.

"So listen up," Kate tells them all. "There's a *protocol*. There's a no-treatment protocol for boys."

I see that needle hand momentarily pause, hold itself steady, then continue. Casey softly places a calming hand on Dora's back.

"Since when?" Yukiko says.

"Since I don't know when, but that's what Akesa said."

"We'll call Zoe-River," says Rosie.

Yes, yes, yes! I think at the mention of my mumma's name.

"Big shot said the same," says Kate.

"Well, no one's going to agree with that, are they?" says Casey.

There is a terrible, fraught silence, while outside I can hear the helicopter carrying Akesa landing on the designated spot outside the granmummas' house, a once-was *heated* outdoor swimming pool that has been filled in with rubble.

I do agree. I can completely understand the idea of the protocol (because it WILL die anyway), but I find I cannot speak up.

"I'll head them off," says Yukiko, leaving, and everyone knows what she means: Akesa is one thing, but "them"—the whole of the rest of the village—is another. Yukiko is not going to stop Akesa, but to stop our community. And I don't think it's just because the fuss would escalate if the mummas came—and the teens (even the littler ones). It's because everyone else in the village would understand the protocol like I do. Because the protocol makes sense. The XY is going to die, because that's what happens to an XY who leaves a Sanctuary. The XY should not be treated, so that doctors can learn from its death. What difference could five days make? It's doomed.

Everything about this night, this long night, is happening too fast. And too slow. And too weirdly. All at the same time.

I'm pushed farther into the hall by a surge of granmummas. Outside, in the lane, I can hear Yukiko shouting to concerned neighbors, "It's fine! Everything's fine! It was Kate! Kate's fine! Please tell everyone! It's fine! Kate's fine!" as Rosie lets Akesa and the pilot, Mariam, into the house.

"You keep your mouth shut, kid. This is not for you to have an opinion about," Kate hisses at me. It's not unusual for her to speak harshly to me—so many of the granmummas are almost as blunt—but normally it's to encourage me to speak up, not shut up.

Mariam, who knows me and knows how much I LOVE aircrafts, shakes hands and kisses a special *Hello, how's it going?* on my cheek even as Akesa faces Kate.

"Hello, *Doctor*," says Kate—wheezes Kate, because the stress and the sudden flood of damp, wet cold from the open front door and the general goings-on of it all really are playing heavy on her chest. I detect a battle tone in her voice.

Yukiko comes in and shuts the door behind her. "Everyone is glad Kate is well and sends their best wishes," she announces, i.e., neighborhood invasion averted; mission accomplished.

"Where is he?" Akesa asks.

"Dying," Kate says, staring her down.

"Let me see him," says Akesa.

"Why? He's dying. That's all you need to know, isn't it? *Protocol*," says Kate.

"Let me see him."

It's Casey who calls it. No one stops her or even tries to. She opens the door to Kate's room, and it's as though she and the other granmummas inside that room knew that was going to happen. There they all are: posed in defiance. Standing or sitting around the bed. There it is: arm stitched so neatly, IV in hand of other arm, sweat—endless sweat—pouring. Those closed eyes? Not even twitching anymore. That flat, flat chest no longer rising and falling quite so hard or so quickly. Breath… steady. Faster than it should be still but steady.

"You've given him treatment," says Akesa.

"Yes," says Kate. "And he's responding."

The room crackles with it, with the sorrow and the rage. All I can think is, *They've seen this before*. Each and every one of them saw this happen dozens, hundreds, thousands of times in the year the males were almost wiped out. You'd think all that would be left—all that *could* be left—would be sorrow. But the anger, the anger of the WHY and the anger of the NO, has never ever been forgotten.

Our whole world was built on this, on the angry suffering of the granmummas—most were just teens, like me, when the world that they knew died with the males. No more war. That

51

was the first thing. That was sorted before the Agreements even happened. That was sorted in the very year the males died. And it wasn't even because there were no more males to fire guns or explode bombs. Anyone can pick up a gun and fire it. Anyone can explode a bomb. No training or skill required. Only hate, anger, or fear. All wars ended overnight because it didn't seem to matter much who had killed whom in the past or over what. Everyone's sons, fathers, brothers were dead. War ended because women had no interest in war whatsoever.

Nearly half the population of Earth had died. Human beings faced extinction. All disagreements, all old wounds seemed… *It was all just totally freaking irrelevant*, Kate says.

Religions crumbled. Governments? Dead mainly, because for some strange reason there was a disproportionately high number of XYs in politics—the same with armies. In the UK, the once-was army, air force, and navy collapsed and merged. They are now one: H&R. Help and Rescue.

Akesa…she's mumma age, born in the time when the males had long gone. Born, like my own mumma, in the generation that came after, the generation that started over. So few of them to begin with, but then, as IVF techniques became safer and girls could be selected, more and more. Not enough to stop the population nosediving, but enough, eventually, with the grit and determination to rebuild in a *new* way. A new world, with new Global Agreements, and all of this done, all of this built, on the aching backs and hearts of the granmummas. The mummas grew up with incredible support. They rose because the granmummas, so deeply wounded by sorrow and anger, decided they wanted the world to be different.

All this once-was…it's just stuff I hear. It is not my world. My world is now. The past, my understanding of it, is hazy.

The reality of the sick, sick, sick creature lies before me—and before Akesa.

"Let me examine him," she says.

The granmummas don't answer, but in unison, they shift just a little to allow Akesa to get closer to the bed.

"What have you given him?" she asks, taking its pulse.

"How do we know we can trust you?" says Kate.

Akesa looks down at that sick thing. "I'm a doctor," she says.

"What about the *protocol*?"

"Tell me what you've given him, and we'll work out how to proceed from there."

"We know how we want to proceed," says Heloise.

"We want you to continue treating him," says Kate.

Akesa looks up sharply at Kate. "I can't believe you've done this. You have placed me in an impossible position. He's responded to whatever on earth you've given him, but you know there is no hope. You people of all people *know* this! They do not survive!"

"This one has," says Dora.

"So far—"

"Five days," says Kate. "He's been alive outside a Sanctuary for five days."

"That's not possible."

53

"Ask my great-granddaughter. She found him," says Kate.

I am hanging around by the door, so ready to run away from this ghastly spectacle. Kate seldom, if ever, would refer to me as her "great-granddaughter." And I sense that she is being formal on purpose: the granmummas' views are often clouded by the once-was, but I'm of the now—and the daughter of a representative.

"I...I did," I stutter. It's not just the stress of all eyes on me that makes me stutter; it's that Kate told me to keep my mouth shut and now she wants me to speak.

"She wrote it all down," Kate says. "Everything the boy told her. You can read it if you want."

"She spoke to him?!"

"Five days" is Kate's answer. "So now what, *Doctor*?"

Akesa looks down at the boy. "I will treat him."

The granmummas, who have never before had cause to doubt Akesa, heave a collective sigh of relief.

"Did he tell you his name, River?" Akesa asks.

Such a simple question, but one no one else has thought to ask. In the granmummas' minds, I suppose, this boy is called a thousand names, a thousand ghost names of all the boys that were lost.

"Mason."

CHAPTER 5
UNICORN

I feel lost and exhausted.

I am useless. The granmummas are so expertly busy there doesn't seem to be a thing for me to do, so I drift in a daze between one offer of help and another, all politely but firmly refused.

It's Kate who calls it when she bumps into me yet again in the hall.

"What *are* you doing?"

"Nothing!"

"Precisely. For crying out loud, River, just go to bed!"

"Can I call Mumma?"

"No. Certainly not. No way."

"Can I go see Plat?"

It's Platinum I long for almost more than Mumma. Her arms

and her sweet, sensible, calm-thinking self are just minutes away; she wouldn't even mind that it was four in the morning—not once I told her what's going on.

"You can't tell anyone else about this. For now, you just can't tell." Out of nowhere, she hugs me. I am so shocked—Kate is not a big hugger—I hug back. I feel her skeleton; these days she is more bones than flesh. "Go to bed, eh?"

I go upstairs and flop down fully clothed on top of my bed.

And find I cannot sleep.

Boy. Him. His. Son. He. Male.

It is astonishing to me to think this *boy* is someone, some-where's *son*. *His* mumma won't know he's here. She won't know anything about him. *He* won't know anything about her. A *boy* baby, taken straight into a Sanctuary after a cesarean. A *male* baby grown up. A *son*. A *boy*.

Those words are so seldom used. I just think of everyone as *people*, and even everyday terms like *mumma* and *granmumma* or even *girl* or *woman* have never really seemed to mean that much. It's just to do with maturity, isn't it? I mean, *mumma* doesn't even mean a person with a child. It just means an adult, doesn't it? A person who is working rather than studying or training. People just are who they are. People are…however they want to be.

Boy. Him. His. Son. He. Male.

What *do* they mean?

In my troubled mind, a small, unsure thought starts to form around those strange words. Although I have always been aware of the existence of XYs, and I have always thought in terms of *people*, perhaps, really, I have always thought of the world as essentially *female*.

The heat in my room—the heat in the house—becomes unbearable. The granmummas have piled the stove with wood. They are cooking. I can hear the clank and clatter of it. My brain, also cooking, refuses to sleep. My need to see Plat is almost unbearable—she'd help me cool my thoughts—but I can't see Plat, can I? The granmummas don't want the village to know about this. But why? Doesn't everyone always talk about everything? Doesn't everyone always know what's going on?

An invisible gag has been tied across my mouth. A gag with *BOY* written on it, under which I feel as though I am suffocating. I need AIR.

Outside the house, the air is cool and the sky is clear and the stars shine down.

And that sky—my beloved sky—I breathe it in.

I can hear Granmumma Heloise singing, chopping wood in the workshop.

I feel the sting of not having thought that this was a job that needed doing. That's how this night has thrown the balance: I didn't think.

The fourth Global Agreement: *We will all help one another.*

I am, I know, physically exhausted and cannot imagine anything worse than chopping wood right now, but if you know someone needs help… I open the door to Kate's workshop.

It is not a place that should exist, but it does. Kate can make all kinds of things because she learned when she was very young. At fifteen, she made her first coffin because there weren't enough people left alive to make one.

It was rubbish, Kate says, grim with the memory of it, *but it did the job.*

She soon got plenty of practice. She had planned—in as much as she had planned anything—to be a beautician, and instead she became a worker of wood—not just coffins, but also happier things: small and large pieces of custom-made furniture. All strictly unnecessary. All made in her own time. And the coffins? It was Agreed years and years ago that they should no longer be made. It is a waste of wood…but the granmummas like them, so there is still a steady, quiet trade to which everyone turns a blind eye.

Inside the workshop, I am at least relieved to see that the granmummas haven't yet started on the special, seasoned coffin planks. Careful to avoid the precious Triumph Bonneville, the vintage motorbike that belonged to Kate's boyfriend, they are chopping away in earnest at the winter's supply of logs. Plat and I only collected them last week. At this rate, they'll be gone in a night—or so my sinking heart says. Our house is already as hot as the sauna we have at the granmummas' house, to luxuriously roast out winter aches and ills. We will be seriously down on wood.

"Need some help?" I ask Heloise.

"Nope, got this," she says, as Granmumma Rosie tosses another log on to the massive pile and Granmumma Dora splits kindling.

"Well, just give me a shout," I tell her as Heloise smacks down the ax.

Granmumma anger fuels them.

I feel irrelevant.

I feel useless.

I feel agitated.

I feel lost.

I don't want to go back inside. Through the kitchen window, I can see the clattering bustle of the granmummas cooking.

Who cooks on a night like this?!

I wander out of the yard…and see the one job I can do.

Moon and stars shine down on hundreds and hundreds of spilt apples lying in the lane.

This is my job.

♀ ♂

Come dawn, I have filled every container I could lay my hands on. Even the tiniest plant pot is packed with apples, some still slippery with what came out of the XY.

It had felt soothing and purposeful, sensible, to gather up the apples. I did it, working undisturbed in the dark, with only the universe for company.

In the gray light of the day that's coming, it looks a little crazy: a lane full of pots of apples. One more crazy thing in a crazy world.

Boy. Him. His. Son. He. Male.

All night long, these weird words have sounded in my head. I could not shut them off. But now they are drowned out by the sound of a car—Mumma!—coming from the east and a helicopter—**A HELICOPTER!**—coming from the north.

Even before I get a clear visual on it, I know from the sound alone it's not a little Explorer like Akesa's. It's a **MERLIN**!

Wow! Wow! Wow! WOW!

WOW!

I've never seen one flying before!

WOW. WOW. OH WOW.

I look back at the house to share my excitement, and I can see Kate, Yukiko, and Willow peering out of Kate's bedroom window, Willow's face so frightened and Kate saying something over her shoulder. Yukiko nodding in agreement. If Yukiko, PhD Yukiko, is agreeing with something Kate is saying, there is big trouble ahead, my instincts tell me, because Kate is hands down the fiercest granmumma there is. (*I can't help it*, she says, *I'm a born troublemaker. A natural rebel. I'm what we used to call a total pain in the ass.*)

This sight would really worry me, but my mumma is the most calm, firm, fair, and reasonable person you could ever meet. That can actually be a little annoying, when you're convinced you're right about something and she gets you to see you're wrong, but today it's going to be just what's needed.

Mumma's car pulls up. Mumma gets out.

"AH! Do they have to land THERE?!" she exclaims.

The pilot of the Merlin has made a choice and is descending

on to the ha-ha-harvest field—a jumble of a garden, where the last cabbages and cauliflowers are still waiting to be picked among dying nasturtiums and marigolds and next year's broccoli.

I fling myself at Mumma, and she hugs me tight, as H&R people in jumpsuits (pilot's orange, doctor's green, camouflage browns) come clambering and crashing straight over and through the hedge with a ton of equipment.

"I'd really rather they used the gate," Mumma says quietly as Yukiko bursts out of our house, rushing past us all, crying, "False alarm! False alarm! Apologies! Everyone's fine! Kate's fine!" to the handful of neighbors who have already come running to the top of the lane to investigate this unprecedented spectacle. Among them I spot Lenny—Eleanor—who takes care of Milpy. Even in the mayhem, I flinch when I see her; she'll have cross questions to ask me about the even crosser horse.

The H&R people approach, offering hands of greeting, but the two in camouflage browns carry guns strapped across their backs—GUNS!—and some other kind of thing that looks like a weapon at their waists. There's a round of handshakes and kisses, and Mumma asks, "What on earth are you carrying guns for?"

She asks it calmly enough, but I know she must be as astonished as I am.

"It's only tranquilizer darts. Precautionary, as are the Tasers," says a camo-person.

I'm desperate to ask what a Taser is, but now doesn't seem like the right time.

"A precaution against what?" Mumma asks.

"Sometimes they run," says a camo-person. "If they've still got enough life left in them."

"Sometimes? How many XYs have you found?"

"Not so many," the green doctor says, pecking Mumma on the cheek. "Are you the representative?"

"Yes," says Mumma. "It was my grandmother who—"

"Is this where the XY is located?" another camo-person asks, pointing at the house.

"Yes, it's—"

And that's as far as Mumma gets, because the camo-people rush at the house.

The next few minutes go as fast as—faster than any—I have ever known. I run into the house with the green doctor and Mumma, and find the camo-people confronting a steel wall of granmummas in the kitchen. A steel wall and the sweetest of scents: a table packed with fresh-baked cakes, dozens of them, made in the night by hands too anxious to keep still.

"Unless we have clear assurance that the boy will be treated, we do not agree to hand him over," Yaz is saying.

So it's still alive?! I'm thinking, even as I realize Mumma is telling me to go and ring the bell. It's the alarm signal for the village, used just twice in my lifetime. The signal for everyone to gather at the school. "I don't want people to have to see this," Mumma is saying.

See what?! Are the granmummas…going to fight H&R?! As though sensing this could be a serious possibility, one of the camo-people releases her Taser from her belt.

"There really won't be any need for that," says the green doctor.

"I wouldn't count on it," mutters Kate.

"River! Go!" says Mumma.

And I go—*almost* straightaway. I should have looked last night. I cannot miss my final chance to see the first and the last of an XY. The magnet of the extraordinary weirdness of that makes me shove open the door to Kate's room for one last peek.

Boy. Him. His. Son. He. Male.

Unicorn. That's what it might as well be. A unicorn.

A mythical creature.

Boy. Him. His. Son. He. Male.

Window: wide open.

Bed: empty.

Unicorn: gone.

CHAPTER 6
ALARM

The granmummas wanted the bell. Everyone else just agreed because there was no reason not to, and because the granmummas wanted it so much. They were born when there was 999: a number you could call when something bad happened, and in the once-was, as far as I can tell, a lot of bad things happened *a lot*. It wasn't just a number for the fire brigade. If there's a fire here, we'd all deal with it, and we have equipment and key neighbors who are specially trained. A health emergency? Every single one of us is first- (and last-) aid trained to treat and triage. I cannot imagine the once-was world in which people would have to just stand by while someone could die in front of them because they didn't know what to do. We do what we can—and then we call

Akesa, if we need to—or H&R if she is out of range and we need to get a person to the hospital ASAP.

The bell, the granmummas said, should not be electronic. What if the electricity failed? (Which it used to, apparently.) The bell should be a proper bell. "For emergencies."

What emergencies could there be?

Emergencies that would require *the police*? This has always been the most baffling thing to me, whenever I have rarely had cause to think about it.

What were the *police* for?

Why would anyone need such a thing?

It's not that people don't do bad things anymore. It's not that people don't ever *steal*, for example. They do! It's just that the community deals with it. The neighborhood 150 Court sorts out wrongs with restorative justice. And if they can't, it'd have to go to the regional court. And if they can't, I suppose it'd end up at the National Council, but I've never personally heard of any issue that went that way. I've never, personally, heard of any problem a 150 couldn't deal with.

But when it came to the bell, everyone Agreed—even though no one except the granmummas could imagine what it could be useful for. It wouldn't do any harm. It could only do good— couldn't it? A signal the whole village could hear. A signal for unspecified and unimaginable emergencies…that would help the granmummas sleep more soundly at night.

Unspecified and unimaginable emergencies. Two of those in my whole lifetime! Once, years ago, when Hope's mumma thought she'd seen an adder in the Memory Garden (it was a slowworm), and once again, when there wasn't an emergency at all: there was just granmumma excitement and joy.

♀ ♂

The bell, salvaged from the crumbling church by Lenny, is housed in its very own Kate-built wooden shelter in the middle of our school "playground"—not that all that much playing happens; even the littler ones have their share of chores and duties. The playground is a once-was parking lot for the once-was *home* for "old people" that is now our school. It could never have looked or felt like any kind of home, but is just perfect as a school because the once-was bedrooms are now small, quiet study rooms. The wooden shelter the bell hangs in is Kate's most brilliant creation. We students love it. We love that we can hang out in it, breathing the weather, whatever the weather is doing. She didn't just make a shelter, she made…a pagoda; that's what we call it. Kate the coffin-maker didn't just learn to cut wood, she learned to carve, and to consider architecture—and to imagine… And, with Lenny's help, she made this.

Our pagoda.

Such a crazy extravagance of labor—and loved by all. The bell from the church hangs in the middle of it, sheltered by a wide, low-hanging roof on all sides. Enough to protect it from all directions of weather and provide a great spot for students to lounge or play. Even the naughtiest of the littler ones do not mess with this bell. They have all been shown how to ring it, and there are steps, built by Kate, to enable even the tiniest of the tiny to reach it.

I don't need to climb up the steps to ring the bell, but I do.

I somehow need to feel I have full control of the ringing of our alarm.

I take the rope.

It has such a pretty sound, that bell. It is sweet and loud—and frightening.

Everyone comes running. Of course they do.

My fright eases as the community comes to the pagoda—I register Plat's face in the crowd, am comforted—but still I keep ringing that bell. I keep ringing it until my mumma shouts, "River! You can stop now!"

And in what is probably just a moment but feels like an age, my fright wells up again in a different form. I rang the bell: What for? At this most inappropriate time, I feel my anxiety about public speaking clutch and clang me, fear whooshing in my ears, more deafening than the bell.

Mumma is conferring with Yukiko and Yaz.

"Students! In school NOW!" Yaz shouts.

That's me. That's me. That's me.

"River, you go inside," my mumma is telling me, and I feel my hands leave the bell rope. I've clutched it so hard with my sweating palms its imprint is upon them in vivid red.

That's what I'm looking at, staring at my own palms…and then I look up and realize all eyes are on me.

I am being bombarded by questions I can hardly even hear from the students who have gathered in the community studies room. It seems it's not just the *boy* that's roaming. There's a pack of rumors running loose too, none more crazy than the truth.

My brain judders into life. I'm not sure whether some kind of emergency decision has been taken *not* to tell the students—though that seems unlikely with the whole village frantic around us—or whether everyone is in such a state they forgot.

Either way, this is the weirdest and most exciting thing that's ever, ever happened, and the truth of it isn't even out yet.

"What's going on, River?" Plat asks.

My heart sighs with relief. I need Plat now more than I have ever done before, more than I have ever felt I needed anyone. I know Plat will help me out; I know that's why she is asking the question, to give me support and encouragement to speak…but I don't even know where to start, and the room is so hot with excitement I can feel myself starting to sweat.

"I don't know," I mutter.

"Liar!" Sweet, a littler one who's not sweet at all, dares to yell. "It's chocolate, isn't it?!"

Two years ago, the granmummas rang the school bell because they had CHOCOLATE. One planeload of unbelievably delicious Mexican chocolate shared across the whole region. It seemed like an outrage at the time, that they had rung the bell about it. Then people tasted it—and it was agreed that

68

if we ever got proper chocolate again, the bell should most definitely be rung.

"Of course it's not chocolate!" Hope says. "Is it?"

"What's H&R doing here?!" Jade asks, ignoring them both.

"I..."

These are my friends. Even Jade. These are the people I
have grown up with. But I'm so *out of it* right now, so wired with
exhaustion and weirdness, I can't form the words to explain.

"Tell us!"

"I'm not allowed to talk about it," I lie.

"Says who?" Jade calls me out.

"I don't *want* to talk about it."

That is definitely the truth.

"That's not fair," one of the littler ones whines.

"Is it...a *new sickness*?!"

Typical of Hope to ask that. She's always fearing the worst
about everything—and speaking it. She gives the littler ones night-
mares. Now she's managed to scare everyone: the hot excitement
in the room fizzles with terror. *Sickness* is a granmumma word for
the virus that killed the males. No one ever did find out where
it came from, and the possibility that an XX-targeted mutation
of the virus that would kill bio-born females could emerge gets
whispered in fright—usually by granmummas—every time more
than a couple of people get sick with winter flu or tummy upsets.
We tend to ignore their panic.

"Stop it! No!" I cry at them as Hope's imagination heats
others.

At least I don't think so, I'm thinking. *Surely if there was any worry any of us would catch anything from* ***it***... *No! What could we possibly catch from a* ***boy****?* I realize Plat is staring at me, so worried, too spooked by the sight of my whirling mind to help me out.

"You're withholding knowledge," tries Jade.

The fifth Global Agreement: *Knowledge must be shared.*

"I have no knowledge."

I'm not sure *every* girl in the room except Plat folds her arms in disbelief, but it certainly feels like it.

"Not any *real* knowledge."

Excitement, curiosity, terror...and now this: stonewalled.

Out of nowhere—but it's a nowhere that's vaguely Kate shaped—it occurs to me that this is my moment, when I could instantly become the most popular and important girl in the school. But this does not feel great, and I don't even know why. It's not a fear of the consequences of telling—after all, the truth of this is running loose—it's the telling itself. The words feel too big and strange for me.

"I found a boy."

And...it's going to be harder than I thought. Everyone is so hyped up no one even laughs at this ridiculous statement. Not even a snigger.

"As. If."

This comes from Hope, whose ability to imagine the worst and the weirdest has apparently just met its limit.

I don't lie (much). Everyone knows I don't lie (much). I'm not a seeker of attention—the opposite: in school, even after all these years, I am quite *shy*. They all know this. They seem to have all forgotten it. Even Plat is looking at me like she doesn't know who I am. Like I have gone crazy or something. Which is how I feel.

"I did! I found an XY! In the woods. It was sick. And now it's run away."

Stonewall. With an edge of utter disbelief.

I know—I do know—how the very idea of it is so preposterous as to be beyond shocking, but it could almost make me angry, their disbelief. They *know* me. They *know* I wouldn't lie (much).

"It's true! They're looking for it!"

As one, my friends' minds move beyond the room, making sense of the shouting that's been going on as everyone who can searches.

"A *him*?" Sweet says. If I've hardly ever thought about what *him* might mean in reality, the word itself is almost meaningless for Sweet. You can hear the disappointment in her voice, her hopes of an excitement she can understand—chocolate!—dashed.

"A *boy*?" says Plat. "You found a *boy*?"

"Yes…"

In the brief silence that follows, Plat's eyes meet mine. We have known and loved each other all our lives. "Oh, River!" she whispers, because Plat knows I am speaking the truth. And it's that, her whisper, her knowing for certain that I am telling the truth, that is all the convincing that's needed.

"I've gotta see this!" says Jade, reaching for her coat. "Who's coming with me?"

There's a roar of chairs scraping, a mass grabbing of coats, a battering of questions that come too fast for me to answer, even if I could. *Where'd he come from? How come he's alive? Is it really an XY? Is it going to die? Have they found a cure? Have the XYs been released?* I feel a hand hold mine—Plat's. It's shaking. Her eyes are wide with utter amazement. And in the midst of the madness of there being a *boy*, this is what feels good: me and Plat.

"WE'RE NOT SUPPOSED TO LEAVE HERE," Hope, predictably, points out.

Jade, predictably, ignores her. "If there's a *boy*, I wanna see it," she says. "IF."

It seems not even Plat's certainty that I am telling the truth can convince some people—and I don't blame her. I can hardly believe it's the truth myself.

Jade runs out, girls scrambling after her.

"No! No! Wait!" I shout at deaf ears. "It might be dangerous!"

Should I even be saying this? Why didn't Mumma or Yaz tell me what I should say? I do not want to scare people, but I want to tell the truth!

It doesn't matter. My words are heard only by the creaking door of the community studies room and Plat and Hope. Everyone else has left.

"The XY is dangerous?" Hope asks, eyes wide with fear. "That's what the mummas always say!"

"No, they don't," says Plat, gripping my hand harder. "*Some* XYs were dangerous. That's what they say. You haven't been listening properly."

"The granmummas say it too," breathes Hope. I dread to think what the terror in her mind is constructing—I dread to think it because my mind could construct it too. I see the **boy** in my head, admiring my knife, talking of killing.

"*Some.* They all say *some*," says Plat. Her grip on my hand tightens. "And they mean men, not boys. It was a *boy* you found, River?"

"Yes." I know what Plat is trying to do—calm Hope. It works, but the effect is not what you'd want: Hope snatches up her coat.

"They shouldn't be doing this," she tells us as she pelts after everyone. It seems even Hope is too curious to miss this spectacle.

I feel Plat's grip on my hand loosen, but I am still gripping her hand tight. She turns to face me; in her gaze, I become aware of myself—that I am filthy from the night that has passed and that I am shaking: cold, fear, exhaustion? All.

"River?" she says to me, her sweet face frowning deep with concern. "Is it dangerous? Is the boy dangerous?"

In my mind's eye, the blade of my knife glints. *I swear to God I'll kill you.*

"I think it could be. I think it is. It hurt me and—"

"*Why didn't you say something?!*"

It is not a question. Plat knows me. Plat knows me inside out. Plat thinks fast—and she feels fast too. She already knows, from the grip of my hand alone, what I hardly even know myself at this moment: that I am too traumatized to speak clearly. I would have trouble coping with speaking in public on a normal day. On this day—

73

"Go home and stay home!" yells Plat as she runs out of the community studies room.

And so I am left alone there. I am left alone, stunned, bewildered, and numb. I can hear the excited shouts of the boy hunt all around the village, but I am alone in the room in which, every Friday afternoon, the whole school comes together to discuss our world. We talk about school issues, we talk about village issues, we talk about 150 issues, we talk about regional issues, we talk about national issues, we talk about world issues. We don't *ever* talk about boys.

I have no coat to grab. I wish I did. I am now freezing; the cold of fear has grabbed deep into my very bones—and I think of Kate, and about how she always complains of being freezing, even in the height of summer, and I think of her now, out with all the granmummas searching for this boy. Out searching for the past in the cold and damp.

And she will have forgotten her inhaler.

That thought snaps me into instant action. I run.

I run down our lane. I burst through our front door. I burst into Kate's empty room—the inhaler is not where it should be (of course!). I burst into the kitchen: there is Kate, calmly making a pot of tea. She turns to me with a most unexpected look on her face: stern but with a twinkle of excitement in her eyes.

It is the look she had when I told her I'd hit Jade. I was thirteen, I was way, way, way beyond the age when anyone would resort to violence, but when Jade said the only reason I'd been admitted to the 150 was because my mumma was a National

Representative, I punched her. I did do that. I punched her not for me, but because I was so angry for my mumma. My mumma works SO hard.

And then Jade punched me back, and I punched again.

In front of Mumma, Kate was stern, but with that same twinkle, and then she later drew me aside and quietly said that if I were ever to hit someone again, I should get it right: throw the first punch hard as you can, because you do not want your opponent to get back up. *If you're going to get into trouble, make sure you really get into it*, she advised.

I have no idea what the particular twinkle in Kate's eye means; it is disturbing to behold—and then I hear Mumma's voice upstairs, and a tiny smile of triumph joins the twinkle.

I go upstairs.

This is when my life as I know it stops.

Akesa is in my room. So is Mumma, standing there reading my account.

"Hello, River," says Mumma.

It's in my bed.

CHAPTER 7
XY

I sit, aghast, at our kitchen table with Mumma and Kate.

It is an enormous table, ridiculously large to accommodate those who come from all over the region to talk to Mumma and prefer tea and a warm kitchen to discuss concerns. Or, like the Cornish fisherwomen, come in such number they cannot fit into Mumma's study—the once-was sitting room. It is a place where people come to be listened to, anticipating fairness and justice, which my mumma always delivers.

We have just come back from a Community Meeting. Not a 150, but *everyone*—even the grumbling littler ones, who were rounded up to spend the day in school lockdown—got dragged into the community studies room to hear the H&R crew declare the outcome of the day's boy hunt: the boy is dead. Casey, who'd hunted along the shoreline of the estuary, produced a muddy, cloven-toed shoe. He must have tried to swim for it; that was the conclusion. And if he tried to swim for it from that part of the shore… Not a single one of us doesn't know how that tide rips. It pulls—hard—one way on the surface. It pulls—hard—another way below. Its pulling makes the water bounce and tear and foam. There are few rocks below, only constantly rearranged sandbanks, but still the water madly dances in a frenzy of certain death.

Sweet wanted to plant the shoe in the Memory Garden, the mini-arboretum the granmummas keep to remember their lost boys. Hope's mumma wanted to put a lock on her door. Just in case the XY—

"I think we can safely assume that the *boy* is dead," my mumma said.

The H&R crew, a long, tiring day behind them, agreed. The granmummas agreed—and it was their agreement that put an end to it all. I looked at my boots to avoid looking into Plat's eyes. When she came pushing her way through the villagers headed home to reach me, I saw Kate glare at me, and so I just hugged Plat, soaking up her very being.

"*Are you okay?*" she whispered.

"*Yes,*" I told her.

And then Kate pulled me away, and I…I played my part. I slouched away, as though I felt the same way as everyone else. Exhausted. Defeated. Sad.

But I do not feel the same as everyone else. I feel angry—and very confused. What happened—what is happening—is a violation of *everything*. That's what it feels like to me. Everything that makes the village work. Everything that makes the *world* work…though it occurs to me that there is no specific Agreement about lies or truth or trust. Does everything need to be written to be Agreed?

"I know this…must be a bit of a shock for you," Mumma says.

I manage one small nod because that's true, but what has happened to truth this past day?

"And it is shocking to us all in its own way."

"In every way," says Kate with unusual, quiet sincerity. She's got the apple brandy out and pours a shot for Mumma—who doesn't drink—and for herself. "Want one?" she asks me.

I manage one small shake of my head.

"I am shocked myself," says Mumma, and she takes a sip from her glass, wincing as she swallows.

The fire in the stove, softly hissing, is still stoked up high. The kitchen door open. And upstairs, Akesa sitting next to the bed that is not occupied by me, Mariam and samples from the XY dispatched in the helicopter along with yet another lie: that Akesa had left too. Akesa wouldn't leave the community unattended. She must have said she was sick, got someone to cover…so that's another lie told. It's worse than the virus, how fast these lies are spreading. I am baking alive in the heat of this kitchen, waiting and watching Mumma and wanting to understand—because there must be an explanation I can understand. There has to be.

"Go ahead, big shot," says Kate again, *gently*.

"River, this is hard for me. I am, as I said, shocked myself—"

"Just tell it like it is," says Kate, taking a slug from her glass. "Kid needs to go get some sleep."

Mumma takes another wincing sip.

"Tell her," urges Kate. "It'll be good practice for when all this really kicks off."

Mumma looks at Kate.

"Y'know. I mean, it's bound to, isn't it?" says Kate. "Okay, I'll just shut up."

Mumma clears her throat, composes herself, looks at me—ah! Such a look! I find myself trembling. What—WHAT—**WHAT** is about to be said?!

"No XY—"

"No *boy*," Kate chimes in. She has shut up for approximately two seconds.

"No *boy* has survived outside a Sanctuary for sixty years," she says, her tone serious and thoughtful, like she was speaking to the National Council itself and not just to me and Kate.

"That we know of," says Kate.

"That we know of," Mumma says, frowning.

"It's a thought though, isn't it?" says Kate. "I mean, what if—"

"As far as we know, no boy has survived for more than a day," says Mumma, shutting Kate down. "This boy *has* survived for five days—six now…with help. If he regains consciousness—"

"When," says Kate, her fist clenching around her glass.

"It would be the first opportunity we have had—"

"In *sixty* years," says Kate.

"—to find out—"

"What the hell is going on." Kate takes a slug of her apple brandy. "Let's face it: you don't know. Do you?"

"We've been through this. No one does. No one could have known. The Sanctuaries have always told us—"

"That everything was *fine*."

"Yes! Yes…"

"And you believed them? Everything about this boy says nothing is fine in the Sanctuaries! The fact that he would even run away when he knew the outside might kill him. I've got news for you," Kate says, taking a gulp and topping up Mumma's glass, "men are quite capable of lying."

And so are we, my muddled, exhausted, shocked, heat-dizzy head thinks. *You've lied today. Mumma has lied. We all have.*

"We could hardly go into a Sanctuary and check, could we?" says Mumma.

That *is* true. No one from the outside has ever entered a Sanctuary since…ever. No one could… Contact with an XY would result in what's lying upstairs. A person from the outside could bring viral contamination. Sickness. Death.

"We gave…the survivors…to *those* places," Kate says, cutting a fat slice of cake. She cuts so hard the knife bites the plate with a hard scrape. "We thought we were helping them."

"You *were* helping them," Mumma whispers.

I know what my mumma is thinking of: the story that's been told so clearly and so painfully in the past. It's as though it was

80

happening again in front of us—Kate reaching up, pleading, baby Jaylen in her hands. The baby lifted into the plane. Her hands falling free. The burden of keeping him alive taken from her, and in exchange, her heart wrecked forever. Kate's boyfriend didn't get on the flight. He knew he was already sick. He died before they even got back home. In a field, by the side of the motorway, writhing in agony, and Kate unable to do a thing. All she could do was crouch over his body, stroking his hair, watching her first and last boyfriend die.

Her hands needing a hard task to escape her feelings. Her hands becoming coffin makers.

"I don't really understand," I dare to say. "I mean…XYs are really precious, aren't they? Shouldn't we just hand him back?"

"Have you not listened to a word of this?!" Kate says.

"**Yes!** Of course I have!"

The coffin maker taught me to use my hands—and to speak up.

"The thing is, River," says Mumma, holding out a piece of cake to me, which I (reflex) take with a courtesy thank-you nod, "he *can't* go back."

The slice of cake in front of my nose smells impossibly good. I'm so tired and so hungry. I take a bite, and it IS good: apple cake with precious cinnamon and a crunchy beet-sugar crust. My whole body is instantly greedy for it, and I stuff more into my mouth as I wait for Mumma to explain why *he* can't go back right now.

"He can't *ever* go back to a Sanctuary because he's

contaminated—with our bacteria…and with the virus," says Mumma.

That can't be right. Even though I've never really listened closely in community studies—least of all in men's week (why would you?)—and I've only half listened to the granmummas, there is one thing we all know: XYs cannot survive in our world. The virus still exists. The virus kills them. Five days alive would seem to be some kind of record, but even the *boy* knew how this goes: they run; they die.

"But he's going to die, isn't he?"

"Nope!" says Kate, taking another slug of apple brandy. The twinkle, that exasperating twinkle, is in her eyes again, accompanied by its friend: a smirk of triumph.

"It seems not," says Mumma.

"What… Are you saying that he's *immune*?"

"It's weirder than that, kid." Kate smirks.

"Akesa got the first results back," says Mumma. "He has the virus, same as us. His body has not reacted. The virus does not affect him."

"Same as us," breathes Kate and clinks Mumma's glass in toast, even though Mumma has not lifted it.

I can't get enough spit to swallow. I grab my mint tea—cold now—and swig.

"He is NOT the same as us," I manage to say.

My mind is reeling. The granmummas always speak as though the XYs will come back, as though, after all these years, some kind of solution will be found. The mummas never speak like that. Though I never listen closely, *until a solution is found* is a phrase I know well. I understand it, but I never attached much meaning to it. It is the mummas' polite way of acknowledging the granmummas' heartfelt desire for the XYs to return, spoken, always, before whatever proposal relating to XYs is Agreed— that they should be supplied with new tech; that they should have their own air-transport service for the purpose of moving XYs between Sanctuaries. These are things I've heard. These are things I've heard and not paid attention to, because they were prefaced by the phrase *until a solution is found*. *Until a solution is found* means that whatever follows does not apply to me.

I feel not an eruption, but a huge *landslide* happening in my head.

"If *the boy* is able to survive...does that mean all the XYs are coming back?"

I try to imagine a world full of Masons. I cannot. I will not. It's horrible. It cannot be. Why would the granmummas even want this?

"We don't know yet," my mumma says at the same time Kate says, "Yes!"

"We don't know," Mumma says. "So, River—"

"We gotta keep a lid on this," says Kate.

We don't "keep a lid" on anything that I know of. A secret— one like this—is the same as a lie.

"But...*why*?!"

"Kate's view is that—"

"They're not getting their hands on him. If we'd followed

83

the damn protocol, he'd be dead already. Until we find out what's been going on and where this boy has even come from, he's going nowhere."

"Mumma?" I cannot believe she is agreeing to this, that my mumma, a newly elected representative, would even dip a toe into all this lying—and, in any case, since when did Kate and the rest of the granmummas have the final say over something that is so clearly of national—international!—importance? This cannot be right!

"I have listened to the granmummas' concerns," Mumma says, "and I have listened to Akesa. She seems confident that the boy is indeed recovering—rapidly. I am prepared to allow him to remain here until such time as we can speak to him. After that, any decision regarding his future and our position regarding the Sanctuaries will be a matter for the National Council."

"Over my dead body," says Kate.

My mumma does not respond to this. "So, for now, we're keeping it." She sighs.

"Him," corrects Kate.

"*Excuse me?!*" I manage to get out. It's a phrase I learned from Kate. You say it when you have heard perfectly well what the other person has just said, but you do not want to believe it. The mental landslide piles down on me and I—

"*What do you mean, we're 'keeping' it?!*"

"He's not some kind of pet!" says Kate.

"That's right," says Mumma, who knows hardly anything about pets (apparently people used to have tons of them) and even less about XYs. "It's not some kind of pet."

84

"*He*—*he*'s not some kind of pet," corrects Kate, cutting free a new slice of cake. "He! He! He!"

"Oh—yes—*he*. It's just so hard to remember."

"Try."

"I am!"

HELLO?! I'm thinking. Another Kate-learned phrase. *It hardly matters what **it**'s called, he or she or… What matters is that it's in our house—and, specifically, IN MY ROOM.*

"Where am I supposed to sleep?"

"Don't start getting antsy," chides Kate.

"You could come in with me," says Mumma.

"Or there's always the utility room," says Kate.

The once-was utility room: tiny and cold and packed with junk. Or sharing Mumma's big, warm bed. "Fine, I'll sleep in the utility room," I say coldly—colder than I know that room will be.

"Oh, River," Mumma says.

I look up, wanting to catch Mumma's loving warmth and see Kate shaking her head at Mumma. If there are already a thousand things I do not like about this situation, this—Kate and Mumma *siding* together, *working* together—is number 1,001.

"You can always change your mind later," Mumma says.

"Later? How long are we keeping…*him*…for?"

"We don't know yet."

I rest my elbows on the table and squeeze my fists against my head, squishing the landslide inside it. One thought is forced to the surface:

"What if it's dangerous?"

85

"Oh, stop now," says Kate.

"It said women rape and kill, but that's what men did, isn't it?"

Mumma darts a look at Kate.

"Get a grip! Both of you! Where did you even hear that kind of thing?"

"School," I say, shrugging.

"Oh, for crying out loud! That's what they're teaching you?"

"It was mentioned during a discussion last Men's History Week."

Kate rolls her eyes.

"But there's truth in it though, isn't there?" says Mumma. "Didn't there used to be prisons full of men?"

"Violence! Wars!" I nod encouragingly at Mumma.

"Stop!" Kate stares us both down. "He's a boy," she says. "He's just a boy. He's no more dangerous than…River."

I, nondangerous River, slide my chair back. It makes a long, slow groan.

"Just remember: you can't tell anyone about this," Mumma says.

I shake my head in disbelief and confusion.

Kate scrapes back her chair in a fast shriek, leans across the table to eyeball me.

"Have you told anyone about what the boy said?"

"**No.** Only that I found him. And that he was sick. **No.**"

"You tell no one," she says, voice pointed hard as her shaking finger—right in my face.

♀ ♂

I am in so foul and disturbed a mood I do not bother with washing my face or brushing my teeth or even getting changed for bed. I shove the creaky, old folding cot up against the utility-room window, so I can see a snippet of sky. Clouds have come in, but still I place the stars and the planets beyond them. I know they are there.

This is what happens when you see Mars: a single tiny scrap of light that might have taken millions of years to reach Earth hits the back of your eyeball, and your brain grabs it and whispers, *Planet*.

Is that not amazing?

It is only you who sees that. You are the only person on Earth to receive it. You are the only person in the entire known universe to see that scrap of light at that second, which will never be repeated again. Only you.

CHAPTER 8
GEOGRAPHY

It is worse than I thought it would be.

It is supposed to be the first day back at school after the ha-ha-harvest break, which should have been yesterday, but yesterday got canceled.

I wish today were canceled too—what's left of it.

It is very hard to sleep when your world has been turned upside down (along with half the village). It is also quite hard to eat breakfast, even though you're starving because you've slept so late it's lunchtime already, when there's Mumma's huge map lying on the table and you're immediately asked to point out where you managed to be unlucky enough to stumble across a boy creature.

"About here," I mumble, jabbing at the map.

"You need to do this properly," says Kate.

"I am." I really am. On the map in my head, which is more accurate than this one with all its once-was features, I know exactly the place. "Here." I press my finger down on the spot, amazed at how filthy not just my nail but my whole hand is. It leaves a grubby mark on the map.

"Thank you," says Akesa. "Well, the fact that he was on the road complicates things a little. What did he say again, River, about how fast he could run?"

"He didn't."

"He did," says Kate. "He said he could do a mile in…"

"Six point eight." It horrifies me that I can remember every word of that weird, nightmarish conversation. It horrifies me even more that I feel as though I'd be remembering it even if I hadn't had to write it all down; it feels like it's going to be burned into my brain forever, taking up precious space where information that is more useful to me could go. I calculate how fast six point eight is. "He couldn't run at that speed."

Mumma shrugs. She wouldn't know. Sports used to be a big thing, apparently, and there's talk about it happening again in some sort of large-scale, organized way, but it's the same as all kinds of once-was entertainments, such as television; there isn't really enough time or resources for it—or enough interest.

"Plenty of people could run that fast," says Kate. "And those shoes he was wearing, they're runner's shoes. It is possible…"

"But how long could he keep that up for?" Mumma asks Akesa. "If he was sick too, how long?"

89

"I really don't know," Akesa says.

"People used to run marathons," Kate is saying, explaining how a person could run twenty-six miles in not even a whole day with breaks, but in one go, in just hours (!!!), as I scrape leftover porridge out of the pan, pile leftover eggs on top, pour myself the last of the sage tea—so strong it makes my mouth crinkle—and scoop a seriously enormous spoonful of honey into it.

"Go easy on that honey, *honey*, and get a move on," says Kate. "Have you seen the time?"

I am stunned. She can't mean it. "I've got to go to school?"

"Yup."

"No one could run that far, every day, for five days," Akesa is saying.

"And not if it was sick!" Mumma says.

"But perhaps if *he* was desperate enough," says Kate, looking hard at Mumma.

Akesa ties a piece of string around a pencil, measures the string against a ruler.

"Mumma?" Even before the question that follows leaves my lips, I know what Mumma will say: school. School, school, school, school, school. Kate isn't strict about it at all ordinarily, but Mumma... "Do I really have to go to school?"

"Yes, of course," Mumma says without even looking up.

"What did I tell you?" says Kate.

I do not like this. I do not like this at all. Mumma and Kate agreeing...like last night. Like this whole *keep the boy* idea.

A thing has been happening to me sometimes lately. A thing

Kate calls "hormones"—and when she does, it is guaranteed to make the THING worse. This seriously bothers me in every way. When Kate loses it, that's just Kate being Kate. Now, when I lose it, it's hormones. Not River. Hormones.

The thing that bothers me most is I sometimes think it might be true—and I don't like it. I liked it when I was just me, and not hormones. Although sometimes, like right now, I feel like changing my name.

Hormones scoops out another spoonful of honey and—

"I said that's enough," says Kate. She hasn't even looked up; she has a sixth sense when it comes to Hormones. *I could be a terror when I was your age*, she says, forgetting that she's still a terror.

Akesa has drawn a circle on the map, finger where mine was, string pulled tight.

"Maximum distance," she says.

Mumma gasps.

"As the boy flies," murmurs Kate.

I can't help myself. I have to look. The circle covers a huge, huge swath of land; it's got to be several hundred miles in area. It stretches down as far as the north of Cornwall. It stretches into the sea—and across the sea. It stretches as far as the south of Wales.

"How in the hell did he get here?" says Kate. "I mean, think about it: Where is the nearest Sanctuary?"

"That's not supposed to be public knowledge. You know that, and you know why."

I know it and know why too. The location of the Sanctuaries

was kept secret to begin with because, globally, there were sky-high levels of fear and mistrust. It's not really a secret anymore, at least not in most former countries. It couldn't be: Sanctuaries must be serviced with food and supplies. The women who travel to them to give up boy babies in cesarean sections see where they are going if they choose to look, but the precise location of the Sanctuaries is still not shown on maps. They have no official addresses.

"I mean…Wales? Or Cornwall? They'd be the closest," Kate persists, ignoring Mumma. "Because you're not trying to tell me he ran all the way from—where else is there? Northumbria, Galloway, John o'Groats. Orkney! But wait. Maybe he came from Iceland? We've got boys there, too, haven't we? Maybe he floated here on an iceberg."

No one is going to figure out where this boy came from or how he got here. Unless he tells. That's what's apparent to me—very, very clearly. That circle is huge, but there is nowhere within it that he could have come from. Nowhere.

"Did he say anything else to you?" Kate asks me, shaking her head over that circle. "Anything you forgot to write down."

"No."

"Anything at all?"

"No!" I glance at the kitchen clock. Unlike my notebook, it's not always right. It's got a wind-up mechanism. Nevertheless, I am, approximately, five and three-quarter hours late for the start of school, and despite the prospect of facing yet more questions about the boy, I'd almost rather be there right now. Almost, but not quite…because at school I know I will be asked more questions. I won't just have to speak in public—I will have to *lie*.

Kate looks at the clock too. "Better get a wiggle on," she says.

"There's only forty-five minutes left!"

"You need to go," Mumma says.

Yes, that's what she would say. That's how it goes, isn't it? A student has got to be screaming for the death pack before she has any excuse to miss even forty-five minutes of school. We ARE the future. We know that. But seriously?

I try one last pleading look at Kate—

"You just need to show your face," she says. "And don't worry. I've squared it with the brain boxes: no one's going to be pestering you."

Kate has never quite *squared* it in her own head that it's not just Yaz and Yukiko who are "brain boxes"; this whole community is dedicated to fast-track study. We're a tech village. Kate calls it Nerd City. She says there's no one dumber than a smart person.

I shove my bowl of cold, disgusting breakfast away from me. Hormones would like to shove it harder—perhaps so hard it skitters clean off the table and shatters on the floor—but I am River. I don't do that kind of thing.

"And take a shower!" Kate speaks to my back.

My back turns around, so my face can handle the situation.

"You're gonna make me go to school for thirty minutes?"

"Yup."

"I need clean clothes."

"Obvs," says Kate, back to studying the map. It's teen slang from her day. It means "obviously."

"Well, *it*'s in my room."

"She's unconscious," says Akesa, tracing her finger over once-was towns.

"*Him*," corrects Kate. "*He*'s unconscious. How many times do I have to tell you people? Now, what about Plymouth?" she says, jabbing at the map. "I've always had my suspicions about Plymouth. What if there was a *secret* Sanctuary—"

"There are no secret Sanctuaries," my Mumma says. "There are no secrets!"

"Sure about that, are you, big shot?"

"This isn't the past. This is now," Mumma states, flustered and tired. She was up all night in her study. *Researching*, was what she told Kate. *As long as it wasn't snitching*, Kate growled back.

"It had better be," says Kate. "And it had better not be *yesterday in a skirt*."

I don't know what Kate means, but I don't like the way she says it. I shut the door on them in disgust. Hormones would like to slam it.

I shower, gloomily watching a surprising amount of filth come off my body. So much filth, in fact, I decide I will wash my hair after all. More filth. And the odd twig.

At least you're clean, I swipe across the steamed-up mirror to tell myself as I brush my teeth. *Isn't that better?* I can't even manage a smile.

My mumma has left the pointless kitchen conversation and is washing her armpits at the sink. She nudges me out of the way for a moment and smiles tenderly at me. I love her love just as I love Kate's love, but maybe in a slightly different way. Like most mummas around—or rather, not around; they are always so busy—she has little time to express her love in the way that a teen or a littler one or even the gruffest granmumma (like mine!) would…but I am very sure of it. The mummas' love is a hard-working love. A love that has rebuilt the world.

"This will be okay, River," she says. "Be patient. This will be okay."

A smile from her is a jewel. A jewel that is so shiny and precious it makes me not even want to ask *how* this will be okay. My mumma knows how things work. My mumma knows about politics and disagreements and how to resolve problems, and even if this situation must be as strange and alarming for her as it is for me, my mumma *will* sort it out. Because that's what mummas do.

Knowing that, I smile back, basking in the intelligent brilliance of her love.

I have to go into *my* room to get clean clothes with the *creature* lying in *my* bed. It is too alarming. It is too weird and horrible. My room smells wrong, chokingly wrong—disinfectant cannot quite mask the stink of the beast. The creature lies creepily quiet as I dig out my clothes. Every second of hunting for what I need, my eyes keep darting looks at it. Darting, because they refuse to outright STARE at it.

Thing. Creature. Boy. Sweat flow reduced to a sheen. Breathing steady.

It almost looks human. Really, I could even laugh when I think about it. Almost. Though I've told Mumma and Kate and Akesa in great detail how this thing behaved, it's as though they haven't really *heard* me. It's as though they're thinking this thing is going to wake up and sit calmly at the table having a polite chat over a cup of mint tea and a slice of cake. It's madness. This whole thing is madness.

I come out of my room with a pile of my clothes, and—

"Jesus! River!" Kate says.

"What?"

Really: "WHAT?!" From the way she says it, I think some new dreadful thing has happened.

"Oh my God!" Kate says, as my mumma comes out of the bathroom to see what's going on. "Get back in the bathroom, both of you!"

"Here!" she says, shoving towels at me and Mumma. Us both baffled.

"I'm all dry," I tell Kate.

That's how it works. *Tread lightly*, i.e., you don't use any more of anything than you absolutely have to. I only ever use one small towel. It's how I was brought up—it's so the way of things. Who'd even think about it? More towels = more laundry = more resources wasted. That's how it goes. Anyway, the specifics none of us think about: you just don't use anything unless you have to.

I'm still thinking there's something really wrong happening. Kate holding out the towel, me not getting why, her seeming… upset?

"You need to cover yourselves," Kate says.

"Huh?"

"Just cover yourselves up!"

"Kate?" says Mumma.

"We'll…we'll talk about this later," Kate puffs at us, asthma attack threatening.

I look at Mumma, and I can see, from the look in Mumma's eye that she also has not the slightest notion of what this is all about…except that, presumably, it has something to do with the *boy*.

CHAPTER 9
POO

"I don't want to deal with the sewage on a Thursday," Hope is saying as I creep into the community studies room. Everyone turns and stares at me, but it's only Plat I see. Her eyes shout *River!* and mine shout *Plat!* back. And then I remember, and it hits me all over again how hard it's going to be not to tell Plat about the boy. I plonk my despairing bottom down in the only free seat, next to Hope.

"So, about the poo?" Jade says, wanting to hurry Hope along.

Poo. At last there's a conversation happening I can understand. This is what I'm late for. It's what we do after every school break: spend the afternoon sorting out who's doing what and when. It usually takes hours, as the whole school is involved, us teens and the littler ones, and everyone is bound to have some kind of gripe. We're pretty much expected to; it's supposed to be good preparation for the future, us learning how to discuss and agree.

We all know why Hope doesn't want to deal with the sewage. Over the past year, we've had a lot of new import food coming in; more food than there has been for YEARS. It's delicious—it's brilliant!—although Kate says it's nothing compared to what you used to be able to just walk into a once-was supermarket and BUY. (I don't pay much attention to the stuff Kate says about the once-was world, but hearing about supermarkets and takeout? I love it! It's AMAZING.) In any case, everyone knows what the ultimate result of the import food is: more poo. *Import, excrete,* Plat jokes, but it's true. After the weekend, on a Thursday morning, we've all noticed it—more poo. I've been so stuffed full of food I poo more. Everyone cleans the toilet after themselves—who would not?—but someone has to make sure the flow from the tanks into the reed beds is...*flowing.*

"So what's your solution, Hope?" says Plat, trying to keep everyone on track.

"We should randomize the rotation," Tamara, one of the older teens, jumps in.

"Agreed?" says her partner, Silver-Moon.

The whole room nods.

"I suppose that's my job?" grumbles Hope.

No one answers because everyone, Hope included, knows the answer. If you see a problem, you're expected to at least try to think of a solution, and you'll almost certainly need to be involved in implementing it.

"So that's everything pretty much sorted out then?" Jade asks the room, then, before anyone can point out that that isn't pretty much everything, "I mean, with everything else, we could just run with last term's arrangements, if everyone is happy to Agree with that?" she says.

In the middle of the enthusiastic round of nodding that follows, Sweet starts up with, "Well, I think—" An older littler one nudges her and whispers something in her ear. "But I don't want to talk about the *boy* again," Sweet "whispers" back, loud as a shout. "It's boring me now!"

Plat's eyes are on me, silently offering support. Both of us knowing this moment is unavoidable. Of course it is. A thing that has never happened in our lifetimes has happened—and if it hadn't happened to me, I'd also be itching to get the school business Agreed so we can talk about this extraordinary event.

My head, hurting, hears people saying again what they'll already have said to anyone and everyone: how they thought they saw the boy in the woods (*It was a deer!*), in the estuary (*It was a log!*), how they heard strange sounds in the night.

"Did you speak to the XY?" Jade cuts across the babble.

My stomach flips. Uh. Here I am again. All eyes on me.

"Y&Y said not to do this," Plat steps in. "They said to leave River alone. She's had a shock. We all have, haven't we?"

I could melt with gratitude. Plat gets up, stands next to me, and puts her arm around my shoulder.

100

"We only want to know if the boy said anything," says Tamara.

"And how dangerous it is," says Hope.

"How can it be dangerous? It's dead," says Plat.

"No one found a body though, did they?" says Jade.

A shiver of possibility runs through the room.

"And no one ever will," says Plat. "It went into the estuary."

"So did you," says Jade.

It's true, and the whole school knows it. Me and Plat, we are legends. Two summers ago, we swam out too far—when we just "happened" to have a raft with us. We just "happened" to pick the tide right. We'd planned the whole thing, of course. We ended up in Gloucester. We got such a talking-to. It was worth it.

"It could still be alive," says Hope. "Alive and *dangerous*..."

The room stills. The mood swings from thrill to—

"Did it seem like it could be dangerous?" asks Silver-Moon.

YES. He grabbed me; he hurt me; he threatened to kill me. I was scared out of my mind. Who knows what...

MAN

MEN

KNIVES

MURDER

RAPE

GUNS

WAR

KILL

DEATH

...he might be capable of.

I cannot reply. Tears of a whole new kind well in my eyes. Tears so new I don't know what they mean—and nor does anyone else. Through blurry eyes, I see them all staring—not curious anymore. Concerned. Baffled *concerned* concerned. That's the only way to put it. Concerned in a new and unknown way.

"I heard things in the night," Hope is saying quietly.

"Shut up now," Silver-Moon is telling her, granmumma-style.

"Did the *boy* HURT River?" Sweet speaks up.

Small, brilliant, troublesome Sweet. Five words speak what the concern cannot.

"Whoa," says Jade, super-slowly, and just as super-slowly, she turns to look at me, her concern burning brighter than even her pushy curiosity.

I feel Plat's hand massage my shoulder: *I am here. Are you still here?* she is saying. I also feel the doubt in it: *I am here. Did you get hurt?*

But it's as though I see, not my school friends, but Mumma and Akesa and Kate and the rest of the granmummas sitting in front of me. And the *boy*—his phantom version—slumped in a chair at the back, so sick. The secret I have been asked to keep is here. It is right here in this room.

"Look, I'm fine," I hear myself telling everyone. "I'm just really, really tired."

The concern grabs hold of that statement and hugs it tight.

"The boy is dead," says Plat solemnly, to the littler ones. "It's very sad, but the boy is dead and swept away to sea."

One of the littlest of the littler ones snuffles sadly in the silence.

"Perhaps we should just all go home now? I mean, it's about that time anyway," says Tamara. Tamara: Queen of Solutions.

"Agreed," says Plat, Queen of my Heart and, sometimes annoyingly, Queen of Sensible. *Okay, mini-mumma!* I joke with her sometimes. She's that sensible. That *diplomatic*—an old word, but a good one to describe Plat. She's courtesy with brains.

I feel Plat's hands grip my shoulders and practically lift me out of that chair.

"Let's talk," she whispers in my ear as we walk down the corridor.

I want to talk to her so much, but...I mustn't.

"I'll miss English lit," she offers.

We don't miss classes. No one checks up on us, as Kate says happened in her day. Now that we're teenagers, we're free to study what we're best at or what we need to study in order to do best at what we're best at. In my case, that's math, physics, and chemistry (my need-to-study subject—I find it quite difficult). Those are mainly daytime subjects, but I get up at all hours for online seminars in aeronautical engineering. That's my direction; that's my love. Plat? She's justice, economics, history, and literature (her she-doesn't-really-need-to-study-it subject; it's not exactly relevant, is it?). She studies global literature because she says stories can tell us more about ourselves than history does, although even she sometimes struggles to understand them. She is going to make a brilliant representative, and everyone knows it. Though Plat herself says representatives, like my mumma, are just that. You can't represent anyone unless you listen to them and unless they vote for you. People will vote for Plat because Plat thinks and Plat listens.

"I've got *Tess of the d'Urbervilles* at five," she says.

"Huh?"

"My thoughts exactly. Come on. Let's talk."

We take a walk. I know I cannot talk to her, but my need to be with her is so great right now I go anyway. Without either of us saying a thing about it, we take *our* walk. Our walk is up, up, up through the woods, crisscrossing. Everyone has their own route through the woods, everyone thinks their own route is the best. No route is so well trodden it seems like the "right" way, though certain paths are preferred. So we part, meet, part, and meet again. It makes us smile; even in the pitch-dark of a winter night, when we cannot even see each other and only hear the crack of a branch or the squelch of a muddy hollow. On this autumn afternoon, we can see each other under the canopy of trees that are only just thinking it's time to let go of their leaves, making a big show of amazing colors.

"You're not going to tell me, are you?" she says, as we lie on the smooth, sun-warmed rocks at the top of the hill. The woods thin out here, turning to scrub, then moor. The view is huge and inspiring.

"There's nothing to tell," I say, reaching for her hand.

"I know that's not true."

I find her hand. I hold her hand. I feel our lives pulsing.

"What does 'yesterday in a skirt' mean?" I ask her.

"Ha! River! Since when did you start taking an interest in history?"

"Since never. What does it mean?"

"It was one of the last things the American president said on social media before he died. 'We are now facing a new tomorrow. It looks like yesterday—in a skirt.'"

Plat's so good at doing historic voices. She gets picked time and time again for lead roles in our plays for the granmummas because she is so excellent at making voices that are supposed to be XY come to life—even now her rendition makes me grin, but—

"What does that mean?" I ask her. It doesn't make any sense to me at all. I know what skirts are, of course, though people—even Granmummas—tend not to wear them much, unless we're dressing up for fun. They're not practical for most of the year. I've worn them in summer—loose things are great when the weather is hot.

"I think," Plat says, "he was trying to be nasty."

"A president would do that?"

"This one did. Although he didn't often make that much sense. I think he was probably trying to say that he thought the world was going to take a step backward."

"You're kidding!"

"No, really…I think he just wasn't capable of imagining what the world would be like—you know, without men."

"I can't imagine what the world would be like *with* them."

105

"We don't have to, do we?" says Plat, gently squeezing my hand. "It's just a dream, isn't it? A granmummas' dream."

I squeeze her hand back tight. "Let's move into one of the empty cottages!"

It's *our* favorite dream together. It would be a realistic plan—Tamara and Silver-Moon have already got their own place, and last summer, some of the oldest of the littler ones tried out living in a tumble-down cottage for a whole impressive month before Sweet tried to move in too and gave them all an excuse to go back home. But what keeps it in the land of daydreams is Kate. She doesn't want to move into the granmummas' house (it is mutual), and with Mumma away so much...I just couldn't leave her—even though next year, I'll have to, at least during the week, because I'll be old enough to be on an apprenticeship at the training airport. I'll have to leave Kate and the village...and Plat.

"This is hurting my feelings, River," Plat says abruptly, then kisses my hand. "You're not telling me something, something important, and I don't understand why."

It's hurting my feelings too, I want to say—but I don't. I feel all crunched up inside looking at her. I thought it would comfort me, just being with her, but it's all so wrong. She lets go of my hand and gets up. I look up at her from where I lie on our rocks. I look up at her with a plea in my eyes, hoping she'll guess, so I won't have to say.

She doesn't guess. How could she? How could anyone even think this thing could be possible?

"I suppose you'll tell me when you're ready," she says, her

face crinkling with pain because we don't do this. We don't not tell each other things. We have all kinds of disagreements about things—we always have; we always will. Some of our disagreements have rumbled on for years: Plat thinks I should care more about our community, about local and national politics. I think Plat should concentrate on international issues and specifically the undeniable fact that we need a new satellite. *Don't sweat the small stuff*, Kate always tells me. Plat says the local is the international—about which we then disagree, when we can be bothered to. We are too close to let such stuff come between us.

She leaves. Plat leaves me. Without her, the rocks themselves feel miserable to me: hard and cold and lonely.

♀ ♂

And so it comes to be that the first official casualty of the boy-keeping situation is my <u>sanity</u>. Although I have felt as though either the world around me had gone mad or I had from Day One, it is the loss of Plat that truly threatens my mental health. Plat is my true sanity. I knew it before, when the world was normal, and now that the world is not normal at all, I really, really, really know it. It is a whole new agony in my life not to be able to tell her about the boy.

I walk back down through the woods alone, on my own path.

♀ ♂

Kate is in the kitchen, still poring over the map.

"Is it dead yet?" I ask her optimistically.

She looks up. "*He*. Nope." She goes back to the map. "The old gals have set up a care rotation; Casey and Willow will be here at nine."

"Where's Mumma?"

"Taking Akesa home. She should be back any minute, then we can *have a chat* over supper."

"I don't really want any supper."

"You mean you don't want to have a chat."

"Both."

"Too bad."

"Well, can I at least get stuff from *my* room?"

"It can't be helped, River. You'll get your room back soon enough. Probably."

As my mouth opens to express outrage, Kate looks up, grinning.

"You *will* get your room back." She smiles at my most unamused face. "You're just going to have to wait awhile. Go ahead, get what you need."

I trudge upstairs and I walk into my room, averting my gaze from *my* bed because I have one mission here and one mission only: the location of my snuggliest pj's.

And I find them and I grab them and I turn and—

It closes the door with a quiet click. It's standing there

wearing my pink satin bathrobe, a *Now THIS is the kind of thing girls used to wear!* gift from Kate. The bathrobe is unbuttoned, and *it* is very naked underneath.

"*Brother!*" it hisses.

CHAPTER 10
CODE OF HONOR

It advances up on me. With one hand, it takes hold of my arm. The other hand lays itself over my lips.

Even in this moment, a part of me thinks, *Oh for crying out loud!*

But most of me is just *freaked out*. Fully, completely, totally, and utterly FREAKED OUT.

Its face—breathing stinking, sick breath straight into my face—looks ashen, shaky, sweaty as it listens for a moment to the silence of the house. Me just standing there, holding my pj's, trying so hard not to think…

MAN

MEN

KNIVES

RAPE

MURDER

GUNS

WAR

KILL

DEATH

It drops its hand from my face.

"*What the hell are you doing here?!* Jesus! Listen to me, kid: there's *wimmin* all around here. Not a word of a lie: the place is *swarming* with them."

The hand leaves my mouth to wave wildly at the window, then swoops back to clutch my other arm. "You've gotta get out of here!"

The stench of its breath gusting into my face as its crazy eyes stare into mine.

"You know what they told us in unit—wimmin will rape and kill you. Better to die in the jungle than here!"

I am…rigid with terror.

"Snap out of it, brother," it gusts, shaking me. Then suddenly, it stops and grabs its arms right around me. A tight, brutal squeeze—of a hug.

One single strange cluck chokes in its throat. *Is it going to be sick on me?* I'm thinking as it swallows the cluck down. It releases me.

I've just been bear-hugged by an XY.

"Don't you worry. Don't you worry now," it says, stepping away, methodically buttoning the way-too-tight bathrobe with shaking hands. "We'll figure this out. We'll get you out of here," it says, looking up at me, alien XY tears in its eyes.

Was that what the cluck sound was?! Crying?! Crying because—

"You're scared?" I speak my thought in uptalk; my thought is too strange.

It swipes the back of its fist against its eyes. "Takes more than this to scare Mason," it whispers—then cringes, backing away from the window. Despite shut, double-glazed panes you can hear the village: the littler ones shrieking in a new hunt-the-boy game, Hope's mumma calling out, "Hope? Hope?!" And I wonder if *I* shouted right now, what would *it* do?

"But I ain't gonna lie to you, brother, this is what you'd call a *bleak* situation. Know what I mean?"

I nod.

"We're talking *maximum* bleak here," it whispers, looking anxiously at the window. "Maximum bleak."

"RIVER!" Kate yells from downstairs.

The creature stares wide eyed at the door, then swivels its head to look at me. A *shush* finger creeps up to its mouth.

"RIVER!"

Oh no…oh no, oh no, oh no.

"DO YOU WANT A CUP OF TEA?"

What a fine, what a just perfect time for Kate to suddenly remember that I exist.

The creature pads silently over to me. It lays its finger on my lips.

112

"There's actual wimmin in this unit," its sick breath whispers, stinking, into my face.

My heart is pounding so loud I'm worried it will hear it. I'm even more worried that—

"RIVER!" Kate calls.

OH. NO.

I hear her heavy tread stomp up the stairs. One two three—

"I'M JUST COMING!" I shout, from behind the finger of the thing.

Three-two-one. That's Kate, back in the kitchen. Waiting to give me a talk about Hormones, I expect.

The thing pants into my face.

"What the hell is going on here, brother?" it whispers.

My brain is spinning. I've got to protect Kate, protect me—*this is supposed to be important*—protect the future of humankind?!—protect Mumma, protect the granmummas, protect the secret. How do I do all that? How do I do any of that? All I've got is:

"She called me. I had to answer."

The truth. That's the truth.

It stares into my eyes. Its finger pushes hard into my lips, then whips away.

It throws a slap at its own face. It slaps itself again—so hard I flinch.

"I ain't right," it whispers. "Get me some of that water."

There's a jug of water by the bed, and a glass. I pour a glass, feeling the weight of the jug. It's a heavy jug. You could hit someone with it if you had to. I offer the glass.

"No," it decides. "Could be drugged. Don't you drink that neither." It rakes a shaking hand through its hair. "River? That *your* name, is it? River? My God. I mean. My God. They're calling you by your name?"

It paces, padding silently, sick face screwed up tight.

"I'm gonna get you out of here, River. I'm gonna get you out of here," it mutters.

I take *one* step toward the door.

Lightning fast, it blocks my way.

I think I might just scream because every scrap of calm I've got is failing me. It looks agitated and sweaty.

"There's no need to be scared," I tell it. "No one wants to hurt you. Everyone wants to help you."

Womf! It slaps itself.

"See, now, River… So just let me ask you a thing. I wouldn't want you to take this the wrong way or anything, but, see, River…" It screws its eyes up and rubs its palms hard against them. Then they slide down its sick, sweaty face. Its fingers dig into its cheeks, and it stares at me. "Are you some kind of girl?"

I cannot move. We just stare at each other.

"As I live and breathe," it says. "You're a goddamn *girl*?"

Thoughts are getting thrown about every which way in the swirling panic of my brain. So, truth:

"Yes."

It can't seem to speak.

Kate can. "RIVER!" she yells.

Oh, and she really IS coming up the stairs this time. *NO. NO. NO. NO. NO.* I see fear surge into its eyes.

"Please don't hurt me," it says, tensing.

The door whips open; Kate glares at me—then sees the empty bed, then sees it, and clutches her chest.

"This is my granmumma," I tell it. "She wouldn't hurt a fly."

No, she would not. The fly would feel no pain. It'd just be smashed to death. Obliterated in an instant.

It strides across the room straight past me, grabs the jug, raises it, and—

"NO!" I scream at it, grabbing its arm. "NO!"

NO. And I am stronger than it—when I grab that arm, yanking it down, the jug smashes onto the floor. Fear and desperation are fast to act; this is what I learn for sure in this moment. My fear and desperation made me stop it. The boy's fear and desperation, so much quicker, make it snatch up a fat shard of glass and wave it.

I...FLIP.

"We saved you!" I yell at it. "I saved you!"

"She damn well did," pants Kate, "so just get a grip."

It falters. Staring at me with its crazy-killer eyes.

"You only saved me so you could rape me," it says.

"FFS!" shouts Kate—it's Granmumma speak, but the creature seems to know it, is distracted by it. "You *really* need to get a grip!" Kate wheezes at it.

I nod ferociously—it darts a look at me.

Confused, it waves the shard at both of us. I launch myself at it and fell the creature in just one go, pin it underneath me—*WEAK! IT'S SO WEAK!*—grab its wrist and bash-bash-bash that shard out of its killer hand. Bash-bash-bash—BANG! I hear the front door slam.

"STOP!" Kate is yelling. I'm not so lost in the fight that I can't hear her breath failing.

Mumma running up the stairs, straight into the room.

"***River!***" Mumma shrieks.

I've got it pinned. It's going nowhere. "Get her inhaler!" I shout at Mumma.

Mumma runs straight back down the stairs.

"I saved you. I sure as hell saved you," I'm hissing into its ear.

Kate is gasping. "No one's…going to hurt you…" Her breath falters totally.

"Code of Honor," it tells the floor.

"I'll freaking hurt you if I have to," I spit into its ear, my heart bursting with fear and anger at the sound of Kate's failing breath.

"Code of Honor!" it cries.

Mumma comes stomping back. I hear Kate shoot a dose of her inhaler.

"I'll call H&R," Mumma says. I glance up, see Kate grab Mumma's arm even as she takes another shot.

"Let him go," Kate pants at me.

I feel the creature's weakness but also its fight-or-flight tension beneath me. It's a tension I recognize from the catching of wild things—even an estuary-netted salmon, helplessly drowning in air, is prepared to thrash and snap for life.

"Mumma, we can't trust it," I growl.

"Code of Honor," it speaks to the floor.

"Shut up," I snarl at it.

I look up, Mumma and Kate just standing there—I'll never forget how they look: Kate, still trying to catch her breath, eyes burning with once-was; Mumma, perhaps more frightened than I am and certainly more confused. Mumma, caught between us, between the once-was and the now.

"What does that mean, 'Code of Honor'?" my mumma speaks to the boy.

"It's obvious, isn't it?" Kate manages to get out—third shot now. One more and we'll be calling Akesa back whatever happens.

"Not to me," Mumma says. "What does it mean...*Mason*?"

It sounds so weird to hear my mumma call the thing by its name.

"I owe her my life!" it tells the floorboards. My hand is on the back of its skull. My fingers grip its scalp through its stinking, filthy hair.

"I still don't..." Mumma says.

"It means he's not going to hurt anyone—are you?" Kate says, her voice soft, and not from the breathlessness.

"Correct, sir," the creature speaks.

"Code of Honor," Kate says, and I feel the creature try to nod under my grip.

"Code of Honor," it rasps. "Code of Honor."

"Let him go," Kate says.

I strain to look up; I've got to see Kate speak the words I can't believe I'm hearing. *This is insane*, blasts into my head. *This is totally crazy.*

Mumma looks at Kate, then turns to me. "River, let him go," she says.

I release the beast. I scramble to my feet and stand over it.

"I owe you my life," it says and cranes its neck to look up at me.

It tries to peel itself off the floor, but whatever surge of strength it managed to dig out has left it; it passes out. Once again, I am concerned that I might have killed it.

Me and Mumma lift it back into bed, and under Akesa's remote instruction, Mumma reinserts the cannula into the back of its hand, chemistry and biology hanging right there, in a bag of clear fluid that is dripping life into its veins.

"*I told you it was dangerous!*" I hiss at Kate and Mumma over its unconscious body.

Mumma looks at Kate.

"He's not dangerous," Kate says. "He's just…scared."

"Scared?" Mumma asks Kate.

"Yes! Scared! Fear makes people do all kinds of things. Trust me, I've seen it. I've seen it *plenty*. He is just scared."

"What would he be scared of?"

"You heard him. He thinks he's going to get raped! He thinks he's going to get raped or killed. Wouldn't you be scared?"

"I don't know," my Mumma says. "I mean…yes…but I can't imagine—"

"Well, try!" shrieks Kate.

"Shh!" I hiss because the creature is twitching. "Mumma, call H&R and get it taken away."

"She's not going to do that," says Kate.

"He's dangerous!"

"He is not!" snaps Kate.

"Mumma!"

"Every child is our child," Mumma whispers. Global Agreement No. 2.

"Damn right," says Kate. "Goddamn right."

*Not if it's a **boy**, surely?* I'm thinking.

♀ ♂

For the whole of the rest of my life, I will never forget the look it gave me, craning its neck to look at me as I pinned it to the floor.

And I didn't even understand what it was. I didn't even understand.

I think, perhaps, I do now…but it is not a look I ever want to see again on any person's face. It is not plain-and-simple gratitude. It is not the non-look/terrified glance of a creature set free, checking the hunter isn't coming after it. It's the worst thing you'll ever see in your life: a person who feels grateful just for being treated like a person.

Bad enough.

The twist?

Deep down, they know no one should have to feel grateful for that. And you know it too.

A BOY ON PLANET GIRL

CHAPTER 11
NOT NORMAL

Not Normal is not being able to tell your best friend in the whole world what is going on. Not Normal is eating alone. Not Normal is having to stop chewing midmouthful so you can listen, in case there is something happening upstairs. Not Normal means a stomach so tight with anxiety all you can do is pick at your food and listen, pick and listen.

Pick, listen, and realize Not Normal is not contained. Your own kitchen has been invaded by it. Savory smells, sweet smells, delicious smells, all cocooned in extremely toasty kitchen warmth, but all your nose tunes into is wafts of weird cleanliness, disinfectant, and sickness. A distinct, bad-breath stink is in your house.

Not-Normal must be kept warm. I drag myself out of my

seat and yank open the kitchen stove and shove more precious wood in. Behind the iron door, I hear wood that wasn't quite ready to burn hiss, and that is exactly how my thoughts are: *hissing*. Not quite dry enough. Not quite ready.

The wood spits. Even behind the iron, you can hear explosions of fury, pockets of moisture, superheating too, too quickly. And I sit back down and for a moment, the stove spluttering, the shutters drawn, curtains pulled across. I can almost imagine winter has come.

When the sputtering stops, I hear their voices. Mumma's. Kate's. *Its*. Low, murmuring, but I hear them. So I haven't killed it. Seems like it's not that easy to kill an XY—or at least not this one. Not even accidentally. I shove away the plate of delicious food I have only picked at and go upstairs.

"Ah! Here's River!" Kate says in a gentle, happy (i.e., weird) voice as I stride in, ready to fight.

The boy's gaze swings my way and locks on.

"We were just explaining to Mason," Mumma says, "how there's really nothing to be afraid of here."

*Except for **him***, my brain adds. The creature—he's awake!—and the way he's looking at me. What is that?

"Isn't that right, River?" Kate asks in that weird lullaby voice.

"Suppose so."

Kate gives me an un-lullaby glare.

"I mean, yes, of course."

It clears its throat, sniffs. "I wanna see for myself," it tells me—me, not Mumma or Kate.

"Oh, I'm not sure that's such a good idea right now," says Mumma.

"There's always tomorrow," Kate says. "Don't feel you have to push yourself."

"I wanna see," it tells me, reaching to pull out the IV.

"No! Don't take that out!" says Kate.

"It's what's making you better," says Mumma.

It looks at me. "It's true!" I tell it. "I mean, *for crying out loud*, all we're trying to do is help you. Just keep the *damn* thing in, can't you?"

It's the tension that's making me speak like that, a thing I am for sure going to have to explain to Kate and Mumma later, because I am very much aware that they are staring at me in tight-lipped shock.

The creature eyes me, then gives a curt nod. It shakily maneuvers itself out of bed, still buttoned into my too-tight pink satin bathrobe (that I am so never going to wear again). Mumma goes to offer it a helping hand, but the creature recoils.

And I deduce a thing that further observation will teach me is right and true: it is afraid of my mumma. You'd think it would be afraid of me, for pinning it, and anyone with any sense would be most afraid of Kate, who is truly fierce. But Mumma? It's afraid of my firm-but-fair, reasonable, sensible Mumma.

"Give the guy a hand," Kate tells me.

Boy. Him. His. Son. Male. *Guy?!* I don't think I've ever even heard that word before. What exactly is a "guy"?

The creature darts a look at her like it has heard that word. Like it knows that word.

"I'm good," it mumbles at me.

I know what that means—it's granmumma-speak for "I'm okay, thank you." The creature doesn't seem okay, but I don't want to help it—I don't want to touch it—so I don't. Instead, it curls a fist around the coatrack, which becomes a giant walking aid for the tour.

A *tour*, that's what it feels like. I know because I have been on a tour to Birmingham. The whole school went. I was raging mad about it because I'd be missing two live math classes and my first dynamics seminar. I was raging mad on the train, and I was raging mad until we got there. Then my jaw dropped. So many things I'd never seen before: high-rises, tons of roads, an escalator, tons of people—I mean every kind of people—a museum packed with art, including *religious* objects, that was just incredible to me…and the National Council.

That part became boring because, after I'd studied the quite interesting building adaptations, all that happened was talk—and as they talked, I remembered: *I am missing very, very important classes for this.*

The creature, though it tries to hide it, seems shaken by all it sees. It hides it very badly, I decide. *This is my room,* Mumma says. The creature won't even step inside. It backs away. *This is the bathroom,* Mumma says. The creature—it cannot seem to help itself—shambles in. Our bathroom is normally such a mess. Thanks to the granmummas' anxiety, it is sparkling clean and super-tidy. The creature moves straight for the bath.

"This is a bath," it mutters.

"Yes," Kate answers, Mumma and I being speechless. "You can have one anytime you like."

WHAT?! No, you can't! I'm thinking. Who takes baths?! No one takes baths! I mean, even the grumbling granmummas have gotten used to not taking them! Baths are for emergencies—and birthdays! Baths are special!

"And when you use the toilet, put the seat down afterward," says Kate.

Me, Mumma, and the creature all look at Kate: *What?!*

Kate draws so deep a breath I have thoughts about her inhaler. "I'll explain later," she says.

"Would you like to go back to bed now, Mason?" my mumma asks.

It looks at me.

What does it have to look at me for? I shrug an up-to-you shrug.

It slinks out of the bathroom, me in front—just wishing it'd go back to bed and we can nail the door shut and all get some sleep—Mumma and Kate hovering behind it, like it's a first-steps baby about to fall. And then it pauses and looks down the stairs.

"Do you want to see downstairs?" Kate asks.

Please, I'm thinking. *NO!*

"Or just wait until tomorrow?" Mumma says.

Apparently, the "guy" wants to see right now.

As it starts down the stairs, hand on banister to steady itself, Mumma darts past. It's what you'd do with any shaky first steps: get in front to catch a fall. With Mumma ahead of him, the creature stops.

"You need to leave him be," Kate says from the top of the stairs.

"But—" Mumma says.

I mean, really, that creature is going to tumble, and though I know nothing of XYs, I'm pretty sure their necks would break just like ours.

"Back off," Kate tells Mumma and elbows me. "You help him."

I frown hard at her. *No!*

She frowns harder—GRRRR!—back at me.

I feel the creature flinch as my arm links through its arm. And it looks at me—and that look, the fear in it, makes me know it isn't just afraid of breaking its XY neck; it's afraid I might shove it. ARGH! That's a horrible, HORRIBLE, **HORRIBLE** thought. And I realize: I have done what it did to me. I threatened to hurt it, didn't I?

"It's okay," I tell it. "You're good," I say, as it takes another step, and so I help it down the stairs.

It feebly pulls its arm away from me as soon as we're down.

Kate descends behind us.

"So what we've got here is my room." She shoves open the door to a mess so complex and long established that not even the granmummas' anxious hands could clean and tidy it.

"We put you in here first, when River found you. Do you remember?"

It looks at me.

"After I brought you home in the cart. Do you remember that?"

It shakes its head a little.

"And this is Mumma's study," I tell it. The door is open, I flick on the light.

I love Mumma's study. It's packed with amazingness. It's got all kinds of sculptures and paintings and books, books, books, floor to ceiling.

It turns away immediately and—

"This is the front door," Mumma says, opening it just a little to let in a blast of chilly night air. The creature shivers immediately, and she shuts it again.

It plants a steadying hand against the wall.

"Do you need to sit down for a moment?" Mumma asks.

"Think you can make it to the kitchen?" Kate says. "River, go get the door."

I head for the door, the creature shuffling rapidly after me, and when I open it, the shock on its face is a thing to behold—for a moment, its astonishment is beyond disguise, and it sways in the grip of it, so I steer it to the table and deposit it in a chair.

♀ ♂

And so it comes to be that Mumma and Kate are sitting at the table having a polite chat with the creature over a cup of mint tea and a slice of cake. And me—I'm there too because Kate whispers, "You've gotta stay. I think he trusts you!" when I dare to suggest that I might just head off to bed.

I don't feel trusted. I feel watched.

Of course, when I say "having a polite chat," I mean Mumma and Kate are trying to explain what's what to the XY, and when I say "over a cup of mint tea and a slice of cake," that's what Mumma and Kate are having. Me and the creature sit in brooding silence, not touching a thing. Though I do keep looking at the array of cakes—and I keep catching the creature doing the same thing, its nose flaring with those enticing, sweet scents, then looking at me. It's cake—creature—cake—creature—cake. A disturbing combination.

Meantime, Mumma and Kate in the background, delivering lines as though they're in one of the plays we put on for the granmummas. We've done tons of them: *Twilight*, *High School Musical*, *Hamilton*, and even a disastrous production of *Les Misérables*. Anyway, anyone could deliver lines more smoothly and convincingly than this:

Mumma: We can explain all this again tomorrow—

Kate: Or whenever—

Mumma: But the thing is…

Kate: Yes, what is the thing?

Mumma: I'm getting to it.

Kate: Well, hurry up and arrive, because this boy is in no fit state to listen to a speech right now.

Mumma: The thing is…

Kate: We're very happy that you're here.

Mumma: Yes!

Kate: Everyone is.

(Kate kicks River under the table; River smiles ice at Creature; Creature stares back with shark eyes; River stares at a cake instead; Creature does the same.)

Mumma: Won't you please have some cake?

River *(thinking)*: *Sharks don't eat cake.*

Kate: He's just come out of a coma.

Mumma: Yes. Yes, of course. So, *Mason*, the thing is…

Kate: If you need me to handle this, just say the word.

Mumma: No. I just need a moment to…

Kate: Also, I actually think I might be better at it.

Mumma: Are you sure?

Kate: Sure I'm sure!

Mumma: It's just really important that—

Kate: Listen up, mister—

Boy. Him. His. Son. Male…Guy. Dude. *Mister*.

Mumma: Oh, Kate, I really—

Kate: Do you want me to do this or not?

Mumma: Perhaps you should.

Kate *(to the creature)*: See, now, I'm guessing this is pretty much as weird for you as it is for us.

(River opens her mouth, then shuts it again at Kate's raises "SHUT UP" hand.)

Kate: And this is VERY weird for us. We haven't seen a boy in sixty years.

Mumma: Well, we haven't seen an *XY* boy.

Kate *(to Mumma)*: Not now.

Mumma: But—

Kate *(to Mumma)*: Not now.

Kate *(to ~~shark creature~~ Mason)*: Scroll back, eh? This is my granddaughter, Zoe-River—

Mumma: Kate adopted my mother when—

Kate: Not now. And this is my great-granddaughter River. The one who found you.

River: Saved you.

Kate: Not now. We…would really, really like to know a little bit about where you come from.

(Creature looks at River.)

Mumma: And why you left the Sanctuary.

Kate: NOT now.

Mumma: No one will hurt you here. No one is going to… *rape*—

Kate: NOT NOW.

Mumma:—or *kill* you.

Kate: No one does that kind of thing. Not around here. Not ever.

Mumma: Well, very rarely.

Kate: **NOT NOW.** So we were just wondering, where have you come from?

Mumma: Yes! We've got this map here—*(Slides cakes aside to place map in front of creature)*—and…perhaps you could show us?

(Creature looks at River. Creature looks at map, a slight frown on its hairy face. Creature looks back at River.)

Creature *(to River)*: Where even is this?

I think the next part would be too hard to do onstage, at least with our school's drama skills. I'd describe the scene as quiet confusion, leading to quiet uproar. Creative English is no more my thing than BASIC GEOGRAPHY is the creature's.

"This is the southwest of Britain," Kate says.

"And we're right here," Mumma says, pointing out the village on the map.

I don't know what she thinks it's going to say—*Ah, yes! Now I see! And I'm from right here! A charming little secret village full of furry faces just outside Ilminster!* perhaps—but it doesn't say a word.

"River, run and get the globe," Kate tells me.

"But…that's so out of date!" I can hear Mumma saying as I grab the globe from her study. "The scale! The countries, the divisions don't even apply anymore!"

I know Kate suspects something, something Mumma and I can't even quite imagine, but can almost, almost suspect too. The way the creature looked at that map… Is it truly possible that it does not recognize a huge chunk of Britain?

When I plonk the globe in front of it, that thought escalates.

It stares. Though the stove is still hissing hard, I hear the softest gulp in its throat. Though the heat in the kitchen is crazy, I see a new bead of sweat trickle into its wispy beard.

Is it truly possible that—

Kate's thinking must be escalating too. "So…this is the world," she says, turning the globe. "This is Britain"—her finger jabs—"and this"—her nail traces out a minute section—"is what is shown on this map." And she taps the map, just in case there is any doubt at all in the creature's mind—and I have the feeling there's a lot of doubt. Dark bands of armpit sweat are SOAKING down MY bathrobe.

"The southwest," my mumma says, as though she's still expecting the creature to go, *Oh yes!* and point out Ilminster, most probably, or somewhere, or anywhere.

"Mason, have you ever seen a map before?" Kate asks.

"I've seen maps," the creature tells me. "Games got maps."

"Uh-huh, but of *real* places?" Kate asks. "This map is real."

"This is where we are," Mumma says. "This is where you're living."

In my room, I think.

The creature—it suddenly seems overwhelmed. Physically? Mentally? I don't even know. I am supposed to be up at 4:00 a.m. for a thermodynamics seminar, and I am *impossibly* tired. I grab cake and stuff it into my angry face, watching the creature.

"I ain't staying here," it says.

CHAPTER 12

BOYS DON'T CRY

I ain't stayin' here.

What brilliant words! I could applaud it: YES! GO! JUST GO! I WISH I'D NEVER FOUND YOU! I DON'T CARE HOW PRECIOUS AND IMPORTANT YOU ARE! YOU SCARE ME, **AND** YOU ARE WRECKING MY LIFE. GO!

There is the most awkward of awkward silences. Mine is particularly awkward because I am trying to suppress glee with cake. I stuff cake into my face to hide the grin that's desperate to appear on it.

"You can go anytime you like," Kate tells it.

"Oh, Kate, I—" Mumma says.

"Do you want me to handle this or not?" Kate blasts at Mumma. "Mason, that front door is never locked. You can just go. The question you've got to ask yourself is where would you go *to*. You can't go back to a Sanctuary. You're contaminated now. You've got the virus."

"The running dead," it says. Not even a shark's cold grin.

"Only you're not dead, are you?" Kate comes back at it. "Do you know why?"

"Are there others like you?!" Mumma says.

"Not now," says Kate.

Mason, oozing sweat, raises a hand to his head. It doesn't move any farther. His fingertips turn white with the pressure they're poking into his XY skull.

"Don't really get what you're saying here," he mumbles.

"So…there's a virus that should have killed you by now and—" Mumma tries to explain.

"I know about the goddamn virus! Who doesn't know about the goddamn virus?"

Well, I'd say that's about the first thing we all have in common. On the whole planet, who, indeed, does not know about the *goddamn* virus?

"You're infected, and you're still alive. We don't understand why you're still alive, but we want you to stay alive," Kate says. "We'll do everything we can to help you. And no one—hear me—*no one* is going to hurt you."

She finds her inhaler on the table and takes a shot.

"You can run on out of here anytime you want," she says, tight breath, shot held in lungs. "Your choice, dude," she says, exhaling. "Door's there. Or sleep on it."

"You're gonna snitch!" it snarls.

Kate slams her fist down on the table.

"DO YOU KNOW HOW OLD I AM?" she roars. "*I SAVED YOU. I SAVED YOUR DADDY'S DADDY. I MEAN HOW IN THE HELL DO YOU THINK YOU EVEN CAME TO BE HERE?!*"

There is a terrible silence, in which…well, honestly, I grab and stuff more cake. At this rate, Kate's going to be telling it to clear off herself. Hopefully.

"Um, she's right. Really, in a way, she's right," Mumma says. "No one here is going to hurt you. Or…*snitch*. We haven't told anyone you're here. And we won't."

"The unit will come looking," it mutters, wild eyes darting. "The unit will send people. They got operatives."

"*Operatives?*" says Mumma.

"Wimmin working for the units. They'll send them. They'll get me."

Kate shoots a fierce look at Mumma.

"That team was from Help and Rescue!" Mumma says to her.

"Look, Mason," Kate says. "People came for you. We hid you. They think you're dead. Everyone thinks you're dead. Everyone except us and the damn doctor."

I open my mouth to point out that that is not quite right, but Kate is on it: "Plus, there're the old gals. You've seen them, I'm guessing. You *know* who wiped your forehead and your butt. Who stayed up all night. Who gave you the drugs. Who tended to you like you were *their own son*. If you think a single one of

137

them old bitches is snitches then, yeah, you had better run. Now—and fast. But I'm telling you: every boy or man there is owes us his life. Code of Honor? No. We don't expect anything in return and we don't like to go on about it. In fact, we hardly even ever talk about it. And we don't EVER snitch."

WHOA. Teen Kate is on the loose. Teen Kate is *rampaging* with pure, red-hot, righteous rage.

"We'd really like to help you," says Mumma.

Well, I wouldn't, not particularly, I'm thinking. I'm also thinking, *NOT NOW, MUMMA*, because Kate just sounded so fierce who *would* want to be helped by her?

"We'd like to help you and all the…*boys* in the…*units*. We'd like to know how things have been for you."

The creature snorts.

"But to start with," says Kate, "just where did you come from?"

The creature shuts its eyes.

"I can't tell you where I come from because I don't know," it says. Its voice—it's tiny now—and for a moment, I feel for it. I cannot exactly imagine what it must feel like, almost dying and then being told that you wouldn't die but that others are convinced you are dead, but I do imagine that cannot be straightforward news. You'd probably struggle to believe it.

"Come on now!" says Kate, her patience totally lost.

"That's enough!" says Mumma.

"Not a word of a lie," the creature breathes at me. "We never went outside."

"But you did. You ran."

It's Mumma who says this, and I'm amazed that she does; it seems too aggressive right now. Too much of a challenge.

"Not from the unit," it says. "Not direct."

"Then from where?" says Mumma in a gentler tone.

"This is an in-terror-gation, ain't it?" the creature says to me.

Pretty much, I want to say…but I say nothing.

"If you're gonna start with the beatings, you'd best get on."

The terrible, terrible thing is that it does not appear to be joking.

"You get on and beat me all you like. I ain't tellin' you nothing."

And that is how the long, Not Normal day that became night that has now become morning ends. I help the creature back upstairs. I am raging annoyed with Mumma and Kate that they leave me alone to do the job—because what if it is dangerous?—but I also (reluctantly) instinctively get it. Instinctively—and not with my brain—it seems to me that the world is more strange and confusing to the creature than *it* is to me.

"You can switch this off if you want to," I say, demonstrating the switch on *my* starry night sky celestial globe as it slumps into bed, eyes rolling with exhaustion and who knows what emotions.

"You ain't really a girl, are ya?" it asks.

"If you need anything else, just shout."

That's courtesy. That's what we'd say to any guest.

"You don't look like one," it mumbles.

"Well, good night then," I say politely, as you would with any guest.

I turn off the main light. Then I snap it on again, just for a second.

"I am a girl."

Why would I even say that? I do not think I've ever said that in my life before.

I snap off the light and shut the door.

Despite all the appalling hints of untold horrors I've just heard…I can't help myself: I really, seriously, hope it does run away in the night.

♀ ♂

I can't sleep. I feel small. Small and shrinking. Brain flaming. I want my mumma.

It's been hours since she and Kate went to bed. *Years* since I last crept into her room for a cuddle in the middle of the night, but the urge to now—it's overwhelming. I extract myself from the creaking pit of the cot and creep up the stairs…and I hear him. I hear him crying.

It's a hard, choking thing.

So I knock quietly, and when he doesn't answer, I open the door.

"What the *FUCK* do you want?!" he snarls at me through the darkness.

"I heard you crying."

"I wasn't *FUCKING* crying."

I do not know how to deal with this.

I shut the door.

I breathe on the other side of it.

I hear *him*—for a moment, him listening, hearing nothing.

Then the next sob grabs him. He *is* crying.

If a person is crying, you go see them. You go see what's wrong. Even if you cannot help them (or don't want to or can't), it's the way it is. Even if you caused the crying, you go sit with them.

I sat with Jade after I'd punched her so hard her nose bled. Though I was crying too, so maybe she was sitting with me?

All my life, I've never left a person crying. Now? I tiptoe away.

"Mumma?" I let myself into her room.

"River," she whispers. "Come here."

I clamber straight into her bed and she folds the duvet over me.

"What's wrong?" she says, stroking my topknot of dreads. It's my own creation, my hair: I twiddled and fiddled with it, then got Plat to shave off the sides. Kate says I look like a sea anemone, but I like it.

"He's crying," I whisper. "But he told me to…go away."

"Oh dear. What kind of crying?"

I think, I feel. I reach down past my own feelings to get to it. "Despair," I say.

"That's a serious word."

"He's sad…and frightened," I tell her, knowing it in my guts. "Should I tell Kate?"

I don't exactly want to, but I will. She's the only one who might—*might*—know what to do. I hear my mumma breathe, thinking. I'm thinking it too: Kate is exhausted, done in.

"And he really told you to go away?"

"Mmm-hmm. Mumma? He's so...*different*. He scares me."

She is silent for a moment, still stroking my hair.

"He scares me a bit too," she says.

And that's how it comes to be that Mumma and I creep down the stairs. We pause outside the boy's room—*my* room—and my mumma hears the gasping snorts of tears.

We knock softly on Kate's door.

"Come in!" she calls immediately, like she's been waiting.

We go in. Kate is sitting up in bed, light on, awake, when she should be asleep.

"Oh, it's you," she says.

"He's crying," Mumma tells her.

"He told me to go away," I tell her.

Kate, as soft as she is hard, lifts her duvet aside. Mumma and I, we get in with her.

"Surely we should go to him?" my mumma says.

"It'd be best to leave him," Kate says.

"But—"

"Boys are not like girls," Kate says.

"That's absurd," my mumma says. "Crying is crying."

"Not when you're a boy. Not when you've been brought up the way I think he's been brought up."

"We don't understand," says Mumma.

"No." Kate sighs. "How could you?"

How I feel won't let me lie comfortable in this bed.

"Turn out the light," says Kate.

Mumma turns it out.

Seems as though Mumma can't lie easy either.

"I need the curtains open," she says.

"For crying out loud," says Kate.

We know that tone. It means, *okay*. Mumma gets up and opens the curtains.

I wish she hadn't. With what feels like perfect meteorological timing, a storm is rolling in. This, the weather, so unpredictable and so wild, has been, as far as I'm concerned, the only consequence of the once-was that has seriously continued to affect not just my life, but every form of life on Earth. The weather is wilder than a granmumma and will be wild long after the granmummas have gone. The weather has a loooooooooooong memory.

"For crying out loud," Kate mumbles, and rolls over.

CHAPTER 13
SHE-WOLF

Only Kate could sleep through thunder and lightning.

When it's done, my mumma stops stroking my hair and falls asleep too.

They are both snoring. And I am staring, curtains open to a sky that's clearing, stars popping in the inky night.

I creep out of the room. I creep upstairs. I pee. I don't even know for sure that I exactly mean to, but I go to check on *him*. I listen at the door, and when I can't hear a thing, I quietly open it.

"FUCK. OFF." It speaks at me through darkness.

I close the door.

I check my feelings. My feelings are…INDIGNANT. That means I should probably walk away.

I open the door.

"Why are you so rude?" I ask him.

He rolls over and switches on MY celestial night-light.

"What happened to the freaking knocking thing? FUCK. OFF."

He's lying in bed—MY bed—looking like a puffy-eyed zombie ghost boy in the dim light.

I shut the door behind me.

"Are you deaf?"

"No. *Why are you so rude?*"

"Rude," he says, and he laughs—he actually laughs. A dry, hollow rattle of a laugh. "What the hell is 'rude'?"

"You're impolite. You're not courteous at all."

"IM-polite. Not *cour-teous*."

"You're doing it now. You're *being rude*."

"Oh, wait. I get it. You think I'm an asshole."

"I didn't say that."

"Think it though, don't ya?"

Pretty much.

"I just think you're being somewhat unnecessarily aggressive in your language"—*and your behavior*—"and that there really is no need for it because—"

"Christ, kid." He sighs. "Don't be vexing me now."

I know what *vex* means. Kate says it. What I would never dare to say to her, I say to him: "Or what?"

Behind my back, I've got my hand on the door handle—a hand that's wondering what my mouth is up to, risking provoking this dangerous boy.

145

"Or nothing," he says after a time—and then he groans, a strange sort of agonized beast moan of a groan.

"Are you sick?!"

"Only in the head. This whole thing…sucks."

I don't know exactly what *he* means, I just know how I feel; I'm crazy tired yet again, and my whole world, my whole self, is all a little—all very—wrong. My instinct bickers with my brain for a second, then I sink down against the door. "Yeah," I tell him, "it most definitely *sucks*."

"Oh, gimme a break, would you?" he says, sitting up. "I mean, put me straight if I'm wrong here, but you're not the one at the mercy of the freakin' she-wolves."

I sort of wish I were still standing with my hand on the doorknob, so I could just say, Kate style, *okay, fine, whatever*, and make a very fast exit, and I sort of…feel vexed.

"*She-wolves?!*"

"Ah, jeez. C'mon, River! I mean I know you're supposed to be one and all, but for real?! I mean…these wimmin… I mean, c'mon, River. You know what I mean."

"I don't."

"You do! Wimmin ain't supposed to be like this! Wimmin are supposed to be all…you know…femin-ine and female-ish. You know, all *ooh* and *ahh* and—"

"Killers! You said *wimmin* were killers!"

"Yeah. I mean, you know. That too. That and the *ooh* and *ahh*."

Yet again, I have no idea what he's talking about. Only I can't be bothered to even act like I do. "What ARE you talking about?!"

146

"Sex vids!" he says, as though I should know exactly what he means.

I stare right back at him. At his alien weirdness.

"Don't say you've never seen one…" he says, a confused half smirk on his hairy zombie ghost-boy face.

"I've never seen one."

"Sure you have!"

"I haven't."

The smirk transforms itself into a frown.

"Well, that might explain a few things," he says.

"Like what?!"

"Nuthin'."

"LIKE WHAT?"

"Like you ain't like a girl's supposed to be. Like none of these wimmin are! I've seen them. I've been watching. They're not right."

"According to…"

"No. Come on! Don't give me that! If you truly ain't seen your first sex vid yet—and you shoulda done; how come you ain't?—you've seen game wimmin, right?"

I squint at him. Global Agreement No. 7 says *Everyone has the right to be listened to* and I am being tested by it right now, because I have the feeling this is not something I want to listen to.

"Wimmin in games, they're pretty much the same, 'cept some of them are kick-ass too. Cruel, kick-ass be-oo-tiful killers. They ain't *hairy* in the pits and legs. They look like wimmin, even the ones don't wear lipstick or got short hair. They're *wardrobed* like wimmin. They've got *nice* clothes. You know, that fit tight. And I'll tell you another thing, River, wimmin wear *brassieres*."

It's as much as I can do to stop myself banging my head against the door to shake the amazement from my head. *What is it—he—talking about?!* I pull myself together.

"Up until I found you, precisely how many women had you met in your life?"

"Plenty," he says, lying back down in (my) bed.

"Actually, physically met?"

"You ain't a woman, River. You just ain't."

"How many?"

"None."

It satisfies me immensely, the silence that follows.

"Wait up," he says. "Up until you happened to come across me, precisely how many *men* had you ever met, huh?"

"You're not a man."

"How many?"

"None, but at least I know some real facts about them."

"Name ONE."

"Men kill."

"Okay, name TWO."

"Oh, take your pick: rape, guns, knives, prisons, war. How about those?"

"How about them, eh?" he says, but quietly.

"It's true?" I ask. I'm actually astonished; all that stuff I'd half listened to but had somehow lodged in my brain, until this creature arrived, I never thought for one moment that people could have really behaved like that. And now this: that people—that XYs—are still behaving like that?

"Only fathers have guns. And it's hard to get a knife. You can make one though, if you have to."

"Rape?" I ask the question, almost unable to believe there could be any other answer than no.

"That happens."

I suddenly feel incredibly cold. I'd get a sweater from my—*my*—chest of drawers, but this—what this *boy* is saying—is so chillingly shocking to me, I feel I can't move. I can hardly even speak.

"Do you *know* who your father is?" I ask.

"Father is the father of the unit. The FU! The one with the gun." He sits up again, looks at me. "River, do you know who your father is?"

"No! No one does...do they?"

"No! I mean, there's guessing. It's all bullshit. Every boy wants to claim the toughest bastard is his daddy, don't they?"

"I wouldn't know."

"Yeah, course." He lies back down, stares at the night-light. "I keep forgetting you ain't a boy. I keep forgetting that. Say, has the *mumma* got a gun?"

"No! Of course she hasn't!"

"She's the boss though, ain't she? She's your FU, right?"

"She's my mumma!"

"*Big shot*—that's what I heard the old one say. The mumma's in charge of stuff."

"She's a National Representative."

149

"And that would be?"

"People voted for her to represent them—you know, at the National Council."

"I do not know, River. Indeed, I do not."

"But you must have heard of the National Council? I mean… you're old enough to vote. You are voting, aren't you?"

"Swear to God, I do not know what you're talking about."

I feel as though my world has just tilted on its axis; if I got up and looked out of the window, I wouldn't be surprised if I saw the stars of the southern hemisphere out there.

"You are joking."

He does not respond.

"People choose people to represent them. People choose people they trust to make decisions on their behalf. Decisions that will benefit everyone." In my mind's eye, I see our ha-ha-harvest field. "In the long term."

"This place is weird as hell," he whispers to himself. "You've been duped, River. No one in this world thinks about anyone but themselves."

I can't take any more. I feel as though I'm sinking where I sit—into a swamp of horribleness. I get up to leave.

"See you later," he murmurs.

I can't help myself. I want facts. "Why did you run away?"

On the basis of the horrible, horrible insights I'm getting into his horrible, horrible world, I'm expecting a Kate answer. A *DUH!* of spectacular proportions, because who would not run from the world he is describing?

"I don't wanna say about that." Then, "I thought I'd die," he says, his voice dripping swamp misery.

The swamp of horribleness, it's soaking right up to my heart. I should have gone while I had the chance. I can't move. I am trapped in it.

"I wanted to die. I thought I would. I just kept running because I wanted to see the ocean. Do you know what that is? The ocean! Goddamn endless water! Sooner or later, that's where we'll all end up. Did you even know that, River? Did you even know every bit of land we walk on came from under the water and that it's all going back to under the water? It's all crumbling…right from under our feet."

"I'm not sure that's quite right," I say, and I sigh because, you know what? At this moment, it seems as right as anything else. "The Himalayas would take a very long time to crumble."

"Whatever," he sighs back. "I'm tellin' ya: it ain't dust to dust. It's water. That's where we all came from, that's where we're all gonna go back to."

I draw a deep breath. It's as though I somehow know how this will go. I am tired—so tired—but I cannot withhold knowledge.

"Well, you made it," I tell him. "The ocean is just over there."

"Just over where?"

"You saw it, on the map. Not the ocean—the sea. Just over there." I point at the bedroom wall.

"How far?"

"It takes about ten minutes to—"

He's pulling on his cloven hooves. He's standing in front of me, in Kate's big knickers, pulling on *my* satin bathrobe.

"Show me," he says.

"I really don't think—"

"Show me or I'll just go myself. The old one said I could. The unit *mother* didn't say different. They said I could leave any time."

He takes hold of my arms and I feel a massive flinch of terror.

"Never gonna hurt you. Code of Honor. Show me the freakin' sea-ocean. River. ***Please.***"

I don't move. I can't move. In the moonlight, I watch a single tear roll from his zombie-ghost-boy eye. The possibility that *he* might be human blossoms weakly in my tired, tired mind.

Very weakly.

"No," I tell him.

CHAPTER 14
A CHAT

Nudity.

Over breakfast after not enough sleep, me and Mumma sit at the kitchen table, faces screwed up with the effort of trying to comprehend what it is that Kate is saying. The chat she wanted to have—postponed—is now happening, and it's the weirdest *chat* we've ever had.

Kate is saying that it is not okay to go around with no clothes on—not ever—if *Mason* is around. I do not understand this. Nor does Mumma.

"But *why* exactly?" she asks, frowning deeply.

Kate, who's already beginning to get a little touchy about the chat, screws her face up too, thinking hard, me and Mumma waiting with bated breath. "It's just how things were," she says.

"But...*too bad, so sad, bye-bye*?" I ask. I'm seriously NOT understanding; it doesn't make any sense at all. And if it once did, it surely shouldn't now, when nothing else that once-was is.

"No!" Kate says. "Not in this case!" Ordinarily she'd have a go at me for speaking in uptalk at home, but it doesn't even seem to have registered. "This has got to be a rule," she says to Mumma.

"But why?" says Mumma, and I am thinking the same. I mean, it's not like we all wander around naked all the time anyway, but if there's swimming or we're messing about trying old clothes on or we're allowed a winter sauna, it's not a big deal, is it, to be naked in front of people? I mean, even if you really, really, really liked someone, even if you were aching, absolutely aching, to be close to them you wouldn't—

"Is this to do with *rape*?" says Mumma, speaking the shocking thought that has presented itself in my mind too.

I know what rape is. Some years ago, Astra, a mumma in a community just north of here, was raped. The report of the case was public, as all 150 Court cases are. There was shock and there was anger and there was huge sorrow. Gifts were sent to Astra from all over the region, and as part of the restoration she decided upon, as was her right, she will now advise and support in any similar cases. That's how restoration works; the person and the community who suffered must decide how the perpetrator must address what they have done, but they will also decide what they need. Astra chose to advise and support on rape, of which there are so few cases—so few it had almost faded in my memory. Except we girls got a talking-to from the granmummas about "no means no," which didn't make a great deal of sense to us, because what else would "no" mean?

"It's just how things were!" Kate is saying.

Rape. I feel such revulsion and such alarm.

"I think we really do have to call H&R," Mumma says.

"No!" cries Kate. "You're getting this all wrong!"

"What *right* way is there to get this?" Mumma says. I've never heard her so...rattled. My calm Mumma is NOT calm.

"Seriously, don't even go there," Kate tells Mumma. "It was another world, okay?" She wipes her sweating brow. It takes a lot for Kate to sweat these days; she says age has made her bones cold. *Ready for the grave*, she mutters darkly as, even in the heat of summer, she reaches for a sweater.

Nothing makes sense and I can't seem to find a thing in my head to help with making sense of it. Clothes—or towels—wouldn't really stop anyone from doing something so incredibly dreadful, would they? They wouldn't even slow anyone down for long, would they? And slowing down isn't the same as stopping. How could anyone have so little self-control?! How could anyone... Why would anyone... WHY WOULD ANYONE, EVER, WANT TO DO THAT TO ANOTHER PERSON?

"Did men have to never be naked too?" I ask. It is, I feel, the last intelligent, logical question I can pull out of my baffled, horrified brain before it explodes.

"Yes!" shrieks Kate, like it's obvious. "No nakedness, all right?"

155

Mumma is slowly shaking her head, as confused as I am. "We don't really understand," she murmurs.

"You don't *need* to understand." Kate sighs. "Look, I'm really sorry to have to be saying this. I do know how messed up it must sound to you...but there was a time when—*argh*! Things were so messed up that a woman could get blamed for what a man did. A woman could get blamed; they'd say she was too naked, too drunk, too whatever. You ask any of the old gals, and they'll tell you the same! It wasn't right. We all kind of knew it wasn't right—"

"*Kind of?*" says Mumma.

"You had to be there," says Kate coldly. "And you weren't."

"No," says Mumma. "But if you are saying that this XY is capable of rape, then we really do need to call H&R. Now."

"I'm not saying that," says Kate.

"It sounds like it," says Mumma.

"I'm not. I'm just saying... God! It's almost impossible to speak to you!"

My mumma opens her arms, letting her palms rest on the table as if she is waiting to embrace whatever burden Kate has to pass on.

Kate dabs her sweating brow firmly, as though pressing once-was thoughts back down into her mind.

"Look, why don't you try to think about it from Mason's point of view?" she says.

"Which is?" I ask. I truly cannot imagine his point of view.

"He's never even seen women and girls before—"

"Yes, and we've never seen an XY," says Mumma.

"A *boy*," says Kate. "He's overwhelmed. He's outnumbered."

"We're being very kind."

I nod, vigorously, in agreement with Mumma. I am being especially kind, I think (e.g., *my* room).

"Look, *no one* walked around naked," Kate mumbles. I see her thinking, hard. "It was…*courtesy*," she says, beaming as she hits upon the word. Beaming because she knows that me and Mumma, that's a thing we understand. That's a thing *everyone* understands. How you're supposed to treat people: respectfully and kindly, even when you wish they hadn't come over/weren't saying what they're saying/want to scream at them. And strangers and newcomers? *Utmost* courtesy.

"But—" I get out, which is the cue for Kate to lose it completely:

"COURTESY!" she shrieks. "THE SAME AS GODDAMN PLEASE AND THANK YOU! CLOTHES ARE COURTESY! YOU NEED TO LISTEN TO ME BECAUSE YOU DON'T KNOW! THIS IS NOW A RULE IN THIS HOUSE! NO MORE WANDERING AROUND STARK NAKED, OKAY?!"

I have many thoughts all at once:

1. Kate, as she has just demonstrated, has no time for courtesy. Rare—the occasion on which she shows it.

2. I don't get how never being naked could have been courtesy.

3. I was brought up to think when we can't decide what to

do, we have to think firstly about the environment (so one towel, not two) and secondly about the survival of people. I don't understand where this naked thing fits into that or any Agreement—international, national, or local—that I know of.

4. I've seen the old magazines Kate and the rest of the granmummas have. Women wore all kinds of crazy, funny things (some even see-through!). The men in those magazines? Mainly they wore suits, and generally they wore a lot more clothes, unless everyone was on the beach, in which case the breast-less men wore shorts and the women covered their breasts. Breasts are…breasts. They're normal. They're… Why would you cover them but leave an absence of them uncovered?

C-O-N-F-U-S-I-N-G or what?

Mumma and I stare at Kate.

"Look, what I mean is that I'm fairly sure Mason might find naked women a bit of a shock," she says quietly.

This is, it seems to me, a reasonable statement. "I was quite shocked," I tell them, "when I saw *him* naked."

Mumma shrugs. "People are often shocked by what is new to them," she says. "And then…they move on. They have to move on," she says to Kate.

It's such an important comment—one that we all understand. After the sickness, the whole world had to move on, didn't it?

"I can't," Kate says. "Not on this issue. So it's me. This is about me. Forget about Mason. Who knows what he thinks, and now is not the time to go asking him. This is about what I can and cannot deal with. I can see that it's *incomprehensible* to you, and that makes me feel…very old. I was brought up in a different time. There's hardly a day goes by when I don't see that, when I don't see how…the things I thought were normal, they were just how things were. And then everything changed. But I still feel how I feel. It's how I was brought up. It's hard to undo that. It's in my head; it shouldn't be, I'm sure, and you wouldn't understand anyway. I don't expect you to get a word of this. What would you know? But I'm telling you…you can't go around naked for a while, okay? You can't because *I* can't handle it."

I've never heard Kate speak like this. The granmummas and their views are always treated with respect—if not for their wisdom, of which they often have plenty, then for their having survived a time so terrible none of us can quite imagine how they did it. But what Kate is saying now seems not to come from the granmumma spirit that is so respected. It seems to come instead from a place of quiet personal confusion and distress.

"You'd prefer us not to be naked when Mason is around?" says Mumma gently, in uptalk.

Kate has run out of puff and patience. She just nods very hard at us, eyes wild.

"Then that's what we'll do," says Mumma. "Subject to review."

Kate, her quiet self immediately shoved aside, rolls her eyes at "subject to review," which is fantastically cheeky of her considering she just got her own way without proper discussion and while demonstrating blatant disrespect for at least two Global Agreements. That's so Granmumma of her.

"River…you need to ask him if there is anything he'd like," she instructs, pulling herself together.

"Why me?"

"Because he trusts you."

"He does not!"

"Okay, so *trust* might not exactly be the right word, but there's a bond there."

"*Code of Honor*," I rasp, doing a fairly brilliant, if somewhat cruel, impersonation of the ~~creature~~ boy.

Kate ignores me: "Exactly."

"What if I don't want to?"

"Listen, sweetie pop," coos Kate, "I know you're freaked out, but this is important."

When Kate calls me *sweetie pop*, I love it. I melt.

So I ask. *On my own*. Kate whispers she and Mumma will wait outside.

I whisper, "*NO WAY*."

Kate ignores me and knocks at *my* bedroom door. There is no response. Mumma looks at Kate in alarm.

"I don't think he understands about knocking," Kate whispers. "Ask him if it's okay for you to come in."

"Is it okay to come in?" I shout.

Silence.

"Say his name," instructs Kate.

"May-son." I say it very theatrically. I know I shouldn't even before Kate bats the back of her hand at me.

"Whatever," it croaks from behind the door.

Kate turns the handle and shoves me into *my* room, where the ~~creature~~ boy lies in *my* bed, looking sick and sorry for himself and generally stinking. I leave the door wide open behind me. I might have to run.

"We were wondering if there is anything you'd like. Or anything you need."

I don't say it in a way that you'd describe as being *nice*. A part of me… So maybe I don't feel okay about being so rude, and Kate and Mumma are sure to tell me off about it, but I somehow cannot find it in myself to be more polite or sincere to this ~~thing~~ boy.

"Like what?" it croaks.

How would I know? I'm thinking, in a panic, truth be told. I just thought I'd ask the question, get the answer, and get out. I conduct a speed rummage in my brain for the things I like when I'm sick.

"Well, you know…maybe some books?"

OH NO. WHY DID I SAY THAT? I AM NOT LENDING IT MY BOOKS.

"Picture books?" he asks…with the tiniest twinkle of curiosity.

"No, books with words."

"Can't read good."

Oh how I envy Mumma and Kate, who, out of sight, will be free to faint from shock. I compose myself.

"Or…some flowers?"

He looks at me as though I am weird and crazy and even more strange than he is.

"Soup?"

I have the eeriest feeling it doesn't know what soup is.

"Or…a bath?"

At my final offering, a flicker of what could be interest crosses his hairy face.

He clears his throat. "Imma think about that," he says.

"Well…great!" I say, Kate-and-Mumma-listen-how-nice-I'm-being loudly. I make a last attempt to sound sympathetic. "So, you think, and just let us know if there's anything else you want."

Outside, one of the cows starts up bellowing—probably Dandelion, she's always got something to say—and the boy grips hold of the bedsheets, legs twitching to *go*.

"It's just a cow," I tell him.

He looks at me and—oh!—what I see on its face is littler-one fright.

"You know, *moo*."

"I been hearing a whole lot of things," he says, eyeing me.

"Like what?" I don't even mean to ask that, not really. It's just, who doesn't know how a cow sounds?

"Things."

I have to think really hard. If he doesn't know what a cow sounds like, it wouldn't know…

"So you probably heard the rooster."

He just looks at me. Does that word mean anything to him?

"*Cock-a-doodle-doo!*" I do my best littler-one-style rooster impersonation. "Or the sheep. You know, *baaa!* Or the pigs— *hrr, hrr, hrr—weeeeee.*"

It's grinning at me—full-on grinning.

"Are you laughing at me?"

"Nope…well, you know, some."

"I think the only thing that's funny is someone not knowing what a cow sounds like."

"That ain't my fault, is it? Where I come from we ain't got no cows."

"Everyone has cows."

"A unit don't. A unit's got no animals 'cept the ones running it."

"*What?*" There's the tiniest creak from outside the room, and I remember Mumma and Kate are outside. "Look, just let us know, okay? There must be something you'd like. Something that would make you feel better."

I've done my job. I've asked the question. Unable to bear the confused frown on its face, I turn to leave.

"River, wait!" it croaks.

"Yup?"

"I never saw no gym room here."

I don't know really what it means. "I don't think we've got one of those."

"Well, where'd you keep your 'quipment?"

"Equipment?"

"You know, treadmill, weights…"

What on earth is he talking about? "I'm not sure. I'll find

out," I tell him—preferable to say that than ask what he means. Kate might know.

"I need to get back in training."

"Okay. Anything else you'd like?"

"Well...d'you think they'd issue me with a game box?"

NO IDEA. WHAT ON EARTH IS IT TALKING ABOUT?

"I'll find out about that too."

I try to leave again.

"River?"

"Yup?" I say, over my shoulder.

"Thanks," he says in a small voice.

You're welcome or *my pleasure* would be a more courteous reply, but I'm so surprised to be thanked I can't get the right words out.

"That's okay," I reply, also in a small voice.

CHAPTER 15
SANITARY

For anyone who's thinking about keeping a boy, my advice would be: don't.

Having a boy in your house is no fun at all.

In fact, it's the opposite of fun.

Please note: I am saying "boy" instead of "XY" or "it" or "thing" or "creature." I am even trying to think it. I am making an effort. It is not easy.

♀ ♂

Kate could indeed understand every word Mason spoke and said that she would obtain a "game box," an item several of the granmummas are, apparently, "bound to have," which is news to me.

And I end up at Lenny's that night, asking whether she's got such a thing as:

"A treadmill."

"And what's that?"

"A running machine."

"What on earth do you want one of those for?" she asks.

"I want to get fit." That's what Kate told me to say. It sounds weird.

"What? Why don't you just do more work?" says Lenny, genuinely perplexed.

"And it'll help me study. You know…oxygen…exercise."

I'm vague on the specifics. It's biology, isn't it? Machines are my thing.

"You can always come and muck out Milpy," she says. "That should focus your mind."

Lenny takes care of Milpy and machines, animals and broken things. Every young person in this village spends time with her, learning about creatures and how to fix stuff. In the once-was, the granmummas say it was mostly *men* who did the fixing of things. That seems pretty weird to me, and not just because there were *men* involved. I mean, why would it be mainly XYs that did that? How did that ever happen? (But I don't not get it in a way that seriously troubles me; unlike Plat, I'm not interested at all in finding out. It's just how it was: *too bad, so sad,* etc.) Then, when all the men had died or gone, if a thing got broken, you'd just go and get another one. When I first heard that, I was shocked because it was so unimaginable, but the population had halved, so there was plenty to go around—and plenty for years to come as the number of people continued to decline. Lots of things that used to get made didn't get made, and more and more things got broken until Mumma's generation grew up and got us organized. *Reorganized*, Kate would say—and that's right and fair and true, because if it wasn't for the granmummas, there'd be no "us" to get organized.

Anyway, animal care aside, now no one grows up without knowing how to do stuff, and unlike the ha-ha-harvest experiment, Repair & Maintain is permanent. Cars, washing machines, turbines, solar panels—even littler ones like Sweet know how a plug should be wired. And around here, it's Lenny who teaches that, because the mummas are too busy and the granmummas… are the granmummas. There's not a thing that goes on that they're not running or at least involved in, apart from R&M.

"We did our part," Kate says every time she hands me whatever broken thing she wants fixed.

To be honest, R&M is a kind of refuge. It's the next-best thing to our free time on Tuesday nights. It's the time and place when we just get to *do* stuff. It's not like school, where no matter how keen you are, you feel the weight of pressure to do well upon you. We are told it's an honor to feel that pressure because we will take—we have to take—our world forward. We learn that before we even learn to wire a plug.

"Look, I really don't know about this," Lenny says, scooping back the wild curls of her hair as she picks her way through the vast storage barn where she keeps machines and once-was gadgets of all kinds for parts. Kate says it's like *Raiders of the Lost Ark* in there. I don't know what that is, and I've never bothered to find out, but Lenny's barn is a place of once-was mechanical and electronic wonders and curiosities. It's my idea of heaven.

"River, really, why do you want this?" says Lenny, hunting in her pockets for a hair tie.

"Because of...why...I said." Kate said to say another thing if things got tricky: "My mumma is fine about it. She Agrees."

I've never done that before, but *If Lenny gets funny about it, you'll just have to play the mumma card*, Kate said, and Mumma winced—so hard—and then nodded. Kate told me what to say but—UGH!—this is as weird and as unpleasant as lying to Plat. I feel I could faint—like a boy!—just saying it, I truly do, so I prop myself up on the nearest object.

Lenny studies me.

"Do you even know what a running machine is?" she asks me.

"Yes! Sure! That's why I want one!"

"You're leaning on one," says Lenny.

I spin around. So...that's a running machine? I must have walked past it a thousand times! Walked past because it just doesn't look like it'd be useful for anything...other than running, I suppose. And, really, why would you—

"Great!" I tell Lenny, shutting off my own "this thing is ridiculous" thoughts.

"You can't have that one. It's electrical," she says, twisting up her hair and tying it.

"Electrical?!" I am truly shocked. In what world would people use up electricity *going for a run*?

"Mmm-hmm. The plug's a bit of a giveaway, I'd have thought. Remind me, what is it you're studying again?"

I can feel myself burning up, to have been so flustered with the lying I didn't even notice what's plain to see.

"There's a mechanical one somewhere at the back there, so you're going to have to help me shift all this stuff…if you're not too unfit."

AAAAAAAAAARGH! That's what my arms and my back and my legs have got to say about carrying the stupid *weighs-a-ton* running machine through the silent village night.

My whole life, I have been surrounded by *empathy*—that's what Mumma calls it. To me, it's just…life. You never get lost in yourself or your worries (e.g., the screaming of your body in muscular pain) because you'd always tell someone—and usually, even before you find the words to tell, there's always someone around who'll see how it is—because that's how life works, isn't it?

It still is. Sort of. When Lenny feels how I'm struggling—I am too flustered by the situation to speak—she takes more than her fair share of the weight of that thing.

"Where do you want it?" Lenny pants, looking grimly at the stairs; she knows my room is up there.

"That's okay!" Kate says to her, handing her a granmumma-baked cake. "Thank you so much!"

Lenny looks at me; she *knows* something is going on.

"Yes, thank you so much!" I chirp. I feel extraordinarily bad.

"I can't do this," I tell Kate as she shuts the door.

"Your mumma will help get it upstairs."

"No, I mean I can't do *this*. Lying to everyone."

"Yes, you can," says Kate. "It's easy."

"It's awful. It's impossible."

"No, it's not." She sighs at me.

"It is!"

She points that shaking finger in my face. "It's not," she says. "I'll tell you what's awful and impossible. Awful and impossible is watching your family die around you. This boy? He's our legacy—and our hope."

You can't argue with that, can you? I mean, you wouldn't even want to…but, not for the first time in my life, it quietly crosses my mind what the world will be like when the granmummas have all gone, when the anguish and anger and sorrow of the past is no longer standing in front of you, pointing its shaking finger into your face.

The boy was astonishingly unimpressed with the treadmill. He didn't say anything—not to begin with—but even I could see the confusion and disappointment on his face.

"Is there something wrong, Mason?" Mumma asked, sweating from the effort of getting the thing upstairs.

"No, sir" was all he said.

Then, when Mumma had gone, Kate asked him again:

"What's wrong, dude?"

"It's like… Where's the screen?" he said.

"What?" I asked.

"You know, the screen—so you can see how you're doing. So you can see where you're runnin'. I run mountain routes mainly, but I do beaches too—only for the ocean views; the slope angle gets boring. You're just on a steady up when you're runnin' on sand, ain't you? Hey! How do you even adjust the angle on this machine?"

"You don't," said Kate.

"And…heart rate?" he said. "Distance? Fat burn-off?"

"If you're sweating, you're running," said Kate. "This is the best we've got."

And he looked at her, and it was such a look… I don't know what the boy version of pity looks like, but I'm guessing that was it.

"They said that," he murmured. "They said you wimmin was lost without us."

"Who said that?" asked Kate, and I felt myself tense up. I know Kate and I know her tones and I know how she fires questions when she's angry.

"The fathers," he said. "The unit fathers."

I watched Kate battle with herself and make her decision: to remain calm, to not push it.

"We are not lost," she said calmly. "We are running the world."

And then she left—before she could flip out, I suspect—and

171

I left too, because I'd practically broken my back dragging that stupid machine into this house, and I didn't want to hear another word about anything.

♀ ♂

So Kate had been right about Hormones—in her own, antagonistic way. My periods aren't regular enough yet for me to know how I am with them. Lenny most especially tells us how, yeah, they can be annoying if you get a lot of pain, but periods can also be very useful. She says you've got to learn to know them and to use them, and even in my limited, erratic experience of them, I can kind of see how that is right. Me? I've already noticed that I focus better before my period, that I design better, and that I get serious bursts of energy. Plat says she's the opposite; she just wants to snuggle up and read. Last men's week, Yukiko told us how XYs also have hormonal cycles, also governed by the moon, but that, because they didn't actually bleed, this was never really talked about in the once-was. I didn't pay much attention, as usual. But that night, changing my sanitary pad, I thought about it. I thought maybe Mason was at a particular stage in his cycle—and right on cue, he walked into the bathroom.

I was on the toilet. I'd finished peeing. I'd just put a clean pad in my knickers. I'd dumped the used one by the sink. This was the incident:

Mason, sweating from his first "best we've got" treadmill run, walked in. We have no lock on the bathroom door—why would we? If the door is closed, the bathroom is occupied (i.e., someone is having a poo). Peeing is hardly private, is it? Pooing is another matter; no one else should be subjected to your smells. So the door wasn't even closed; I was just changing my pad and having a pee.

"Shoulda knocked!" he says as I get up off the toilet, hauling up my combats. He doesn't even close the door. (I don't think doors mean much to him.)

"Yes," I mutter, as loud as *YES!* Though my brain is jumbled and jangling; only Kate knows how you're supposed to behave around XYs. Peeing probably counts as nudity.

"Gotta go," he says awkwardly, but he doesn't just go ahead and pee, so maybe Kate has talked to him as well?

And that is when the incident happens:

"Who got hurt?" he says, spotting my used sanitary pad. "They hurt you, kid? Did they?!"

"No more than usual," I tell him, picking up the used pad. A couple of years ago, we had a bit of a crisis with them; home manufacture of hemp pads broke down after the weather had an angry summer—the cotton producers, suffering because of the same meteorological anger, could not supply, even if we had a trade to offer. All we had was... For nearly sixty years, there had been a mountain of clothes for men and boys. It was, of course, plundered by necessity. Clothes adapted, fabric cut free from design and resewn, but there was still a mountain—an almost untouched, weirdly sacred mountain that had been kept but had no purpose. Until there was one, to which the granmummas

173

agreed. The pad I had worn, the pad I had bled all over, is machine washable. It is made from dead men's shredded clothes.

His face—it's all alarm.

"I'm having a period," I tell him. I expect, to him, I am probably making a face he doesn't understand either: pity. *How could it be*, I am thinking, *that you could not know what a period is?*

Kate appears at the bathroom door; her face is ALARM MAX.

"Get out!" she tells me. A reversal of her usual "Get in!"

I get out. I am not upset. I do not understand. I anticipate another chat.

As I said, having a boy in your house is no fun at all.

CHAPTER 16

THUMP
THUMP
THUMP

I wake, every morning, to *THUMP, THUMP, THUMP*.

I go to school. I get asked and asked and asked questions about the **boy**, even though he's officially dead and gone. No one is supposed to do that, to go on about what happened, but everyone except Plat does.

It's easy for Plat not to. We are painfully, expertly avoiding each other.

I come home, every evening, to *THUMP, THUMP, THUMP*.

It starts almost as soon as I enter the house. The boy has been told by Kate that he cannot run when I am not home. So I'm thinking he must be watching for me—from *my* window. No one seems to need to tell him I'm home.

It stops, always, at 11:00 p.m. It starts, always, at 7:00 a.m. There is no break on the weekend; on Tuesdays and Wednesdays, he runs the same as if they were just like any other days. The *boy* has no weekend.

The only upside is I've hooked that machine up to generate electricity. Every *THUMP* is wired into the village grid.

"He's used to a routine," Kate, who hates routine, says.

"This can't go on," Mumma says.

Joy. JOY. **JOY.**

She's home for dinner, has been quizzing Kate and hearing what I already know (i.e., THE ROUTINE). The boy gets up and does "gym." *THUMP, THUMP, THUMP.* He showers (Despite repeated offers, he has yet to take a bath. *Can't swim*, he told me.); he has breakfast (toast—he claimed he'd never eaten it before, but now he just loves toast and jam or honey); and does whatever he does with a game box on the *personal* computer Kate managed to procure. Repeat that—gym (*THUMP, THUMP, THUMP*), shower, eat (toast), computer—three times over, and then he goes to bed. There's never any hot water anymore, and even the granmummas who are keeping us supplied with jam and honey are starting to question the quantities involved. Soup has now been introduced to his diet, but it has to be puréed to oblivion; he's suspicious of any lumps.

It is ANNOYING, and it is BORING. I'd never have thought having a boy would be BORING.

"But what is he doing on the computer?" Mumma asks.

"He's gaming," Kate says.

"Gaming? What is that?" says Mumma—clueless as me, I'd say. I stare hard at my plate.

"Playing games."

"What kind of games?"

"Shooting people or aliens! Or enemies! You know! Killing stuff! Or blowing them up or, I dunno, just generally zapping them," says Kate.

Mumma's jaw is hanging open—mine is too.

"Look, there's more to it than that," says Kate. "You had to be smart about it. You have to work out all kinds of things. And it's good for hand-eye coordination."

"Hand-eye coordination," says Mumma.

"Sure." Kate laughs. "And fun! It was exciting! It was FUN."

Mumma's jaw clamps shut. Mine stays hanging. Those "games"? I really want to see them. I've slacked off on my "I am the trusted one" duty. I am ready and willing to step back up.

"And that's it?" asks Mumma. "He plays games?"

"Yup," says Kate.

"And no studying?"

"Nope."

"None at all?"

"Seeing as how your mouth's open, why don't you put some food in it?" Kate says to me.

I oblige, but it's hard to chew and swallow when this is all so mind-bogglingly interesting.

"He can't read. He told us that. I don't really think he's ever done much in the way of studying. I don't think they bothered with it much. I don't think they bothered with *anything* much."

I hear anger and sorrow in Kate's voice, there so plain Mumma hears it too.

"Oh," says Mumma.

THUMP, THUMP, THUMP is the boy's contribution to this fascinating conversation.

"Well…" says Mumma, thinking. And that's when she says it: "This can't go on."

My brain snaps into here-and-now life: as fascinating as this whole "boy" thing has become in the past few minutes, I want it done. BOY GONE. No more questions because NO MORE THUMP, THUMP, THUMP, AND NO MORE BOY. And Plat! River and Plat!

"He needs time to adjust, that's all," says Kate. *Adjust* is a very un-Kate word.

"He needs to go to school," says Mumma.

WHAT?! Wait just a second!

Kate lays down her knife and fork.

"He does. They all do," says Kate.

"I don't know about the rest of the Sanctuaries," says Mumma. "I only know about *this* boy. But even if we could somehow pass him off as…*one of us*, I don't think he's ready for that."

To my utter relief (and astonishment), Kate does not argue.

"Zoe-River," she says, "I think this boy has been living in a bad way. And I don't think it's just him. It cannot be just him. You have to find out about it, you have to tell people about it, and you have to stop it."

My mumma is staring straight at Kate. The THUMP, THUMP, THUMP stops.

We all look at the ceiling.

It's not 11:00 p.m. It's only 9:35 p.m., according to the kitchen clock. Always wrong—never *this* wrong.

My mumma looks at Kate. "I will try my best," she tells her.

There is the sound—most alarming and unexpected—of feet padding down the stairs.

"I invited Mason to join us for dinner," Kate says. "You know, so he can adjust."

"Perhaps you could have told us?" Mumma whispers.

"I didn't think he'd come."

The kitchen door creaks open. The boy creature emerges, shuffling into the kitchen in trousers and a blouse that belongs to Kate and his cloven-hoof shoes. He's all red in the face and sweating, breath rasping louder than Kate's, like he's still running.

"I'm late," he pants.

"It doesn't matter," Kate, who'd screech at me for tardiness, says as she ladles out a delicious plateful of the insect stew, with fat chunks of superfresh vegetables and brilliant dumplings, a dollop of creamy root mash, and a scoop of buttery greens spiced with crushed juniper berries.

"So...how are you feeling, Mason?" Mumma asks.

He clears his throat. "What?"

"Don't say *what*. Say *pardon*," comes out of my mouth without a thought involved (it's a standard instruction to littler ones).

"River! Courtesy!" says Mumma. "How are you, Mason?"

"Okay, I guess." He shovels up a spoonful of stew that's destined never to reach his mouth. "I ain't puked in days. Lost fitness though. Lost a lot of fitness."

"Ah…and how are you *feeling*?"

I am beginning to think that the boy creature must be quite stupid because it looks to me as though this isn't a question he understands. He shifts about in his seat, frowning.

"You know, *emotionally*," Mumma persists, floundering.

"For crying out loud, let the boy eat," says Kate. "Maybe he doesn't want to talk about how he feels right now."

I'd expect Mumma to come right back at Kate (who's a stranger to courtesy of the verbal type), but she doesn't. I've never seen Mumma look so lost and uncertain—and over this! Mumma is the smartest person in our 150, but she's never been brilliant at the feelings side of things. Nevertheless, she does try, when she remembers, and it's a kindness to be accepted, isn't it? It's a kindness to be asked, sincerely, how you are feeling. The way this boy creature is acting is just… I don't get it. He must be stupid. Look at him—now he's staring at his spoon. (As though he's never seen an insect before?)

There's this few minutes in which nobody says anything, but nobody is eating either, and it's an awkward few minutes because you just know everyone (except the boy creature?) has a lot to say. Me, I don't speak because I daren't. It's like there's a fire in my head, huge lumps of anger, curiosity, and revulsion being chucked onto it.

In the silence, the pot of stew on the stove starts to bubble.

Mumma's phone rings. It's Akesa on PicChat. We can all see that. Mumma picks the phone up.

"I've got Mason's test results!" Akesa says, not in her normal doctor's voice; she is very excited.

"What test results?" says Mason.

"Ah, he's there with you," says Akesa. "That's good. I've got questions—well, just one, really."

"I'm really not sure this is such a good idea," Kate gets in.

"What test results? What tests? I never did no tests here."

"Zoe-River…" Kate warns.

"I never did no tests here. God almighty! Did you steal my sperm already?"

I should think if any of us were eating, we'd all choke, Mason included; he looks wild with panic.

"I ain't been well," he gibbers.

"Let me speak to the patient," I can see Akesa's face asking, upside down across the table.

"No one has stolen your sperm," Kate is saying.

"What *freaking* tests?!"

"LET ME SPEAK TO THE PATIENT!"

Mason snatches the phone. "I ain't been well. I'm getting fitness back. I need T, that's all."

Mumma, flustered, gets up to put the kettle on.

"Not that kind of tea," Kate bellows at her, and she sits back down.

"You mean testosterone?" Akesa asks.

"What else would I mean? I ain't had an injection for a while. That's all it'll be. If I've flunked a sperm test, it's 'cause I need a T-jab! I ain't been well!"

It's like he's speaking to all of us now, panic and fear and misery rolling in his eyes.

"You need to calm down, Mason," Kate says softly.

He nods frantically at us all. "I'm calm. I'm calm," he mutters; he is not calm at all. "But you can't just kick me out of here because I flunked one sperm test!"

"Is that what would happen in the Sanctuary?" asks Kate, glaring at Mumma.

"No-sperms get sent to the food factory. That place is just hell with better hygiene. I ain't ending up in no she-wolf food factory!"

"That's not going to happen," says Mumma. "We don't do that kind of thing here."

"No one's taken your sperm, and no one's *going* to take your sperm," says Kate. "So let's just listen to the doctor, eh?"

He nods—less frantically but most unconvincingly.

"I've checked and rechecked to confirm: you *are* infected with the virus, but I can find no sign of any reaction to it whatsoever, as all earlier samples showed."

The sound of Akesa's voice—oh, it's lovely to hear in this room. It's her calm, sensible, factual words that we ALL need to hear—well, maybe not all of us. Mason's face is scrunched tight.

"You're going to be fine," Akesa says.

"Hear that? You're going to be fine!" Kate says to Mason, the sweetest smile on her face. "He's going to be fine," she says triumphantly to Mumma.

"Although I expect you don't *feel* fine right now," says Akesa.

"I just need a T-jab," he says to her, his voice as tense and scrunched as his face and his body.

"You weren't being injected with testosterone," Akesa says.

"Well, now, see, that's a lie," Mason says.

"The testosterone was in the implant in your arm."

"Liar. And I know so. Think I'm a fool?" says Mason, clutching his arm. "That was a transmitter tag! I cut it out myself! Right there in the jungle! That was a transmitter." He looks up at me. "So they can track you, so they can find your body if you're dumb enough to run."

"It was a testosterone implant," Akesa says. "The injections you had I think were a tranquilizer. I found traces of it in your blood."

"It could have been something we gave him," says Kate.

"No," says Akesa. "I saw what you gave him, and this is some other kind of synthetic opiate. He has extensive injection scarring." She pauses. "You were being drugged. How often were you given injections, Mason?" asks Akesa.

"Every week, same as every boy," he says, his hand clutching the phone so tight I think it might break.

"And for how long?"

"Since they put the tag in."

"And when was that?"

"U-Beta. I was twelve."

"This is a disgrace," breathes Kate at Mumma.

Akesa clears her throat. "You've got the virus, Mason. It's in every single sample, but you're not reacting."

"This is it," says Kate. "They've found a cure…"

"Not exactly," says Akesa. "He's been…modified."

"What?" says Mason.

"You don't know?"

"Don't know *what*?"

"I had to search pretty hard to find it, but I've looked at your chromosomes, Mason. You've got a splice of X in your Y chromosome."

"I do not know what you are freaking talking about." Mason speaks quietly at the phone in his fist.

"Nor do we," says Kate.

"He's been modified at a genetic level. It has to have been done at the IVF stage. It's minute, obviously, but it's there: a tiny section of X chromosome has been introduced into his Y chromosome. It's utterly brilliant. I have no idea whether he could pass it on to his offspring—and I doubt it—but it is enough to protect him and his sperm. The virus cannot attack him; it's blocked. I suppose, essentially, the virus reads him as female."

Mason turns to me. "What'd she say?" he asks.

CHAPTER 17
STEW

"That you're part girl?"

Now doesn't seem the time to give Mason a biology lesson, so I say it in uptalk as simply as I can.

"Well, I wouldn't quite put it like that," says Akesa. "Let's just say, where you'd expect to be entirely male, there is a small female element."

Mason hasn't stopped looking at me. "I'm part girl?" he asks me.

"Kind of, mm-hmm."

The neglected bubbling pot of stew on the stove sends out an angry stink of burning. Mumma—without taking her eyes off Mason, off the phone, off the whole crazy scene—gets up, shoves it off the heat, and sits back down again.

"If you have any questions, I'll try to answer them as best I can," Akesa is saying to Mason. He lays the phone down on the table, gets up, and leaves.

He doesn't screech or groan his chair. He doesn't even slam the door. He just stands, turns, and goes.

"Oh, well done, *Doc*. Really well done," Kate says, and reaches a shaking finger out to kill the call.

"Shouldn't you be happy about it?" I ask her, though she's too busy staring at Mumma to listen. "I mean, won't it mean they can leave the Sanctuaries now?"

As the *THUMP, THUMP, THUMP* starts up, the weird and dreadful prospect of hordes of Masons roaming the land again looms large and scary and a little too realistically in my mind.

"So, we're making genetically modified boys now, are we?" she says to Mumma. "*Until a solution is found*. Sixty years, no cure. Now this? How long has this been going on?"

"I did not know anything about it," says Mumma.

"You're a National Representative," says Kate.

"I did not—"

"What is it you do know about?"

"Not this," says my mumma. PicChat rings on the notebook in her study. My mumma doesn't go to answer it, and then it stops. Notification that a message has been recorded beeps; I know that sound. I've heard it so many times. So has Kate. PicChat rings again. No one moves.

"Sixty years we've been waiting for them to come home. Sixty years. If I ever find out you knew anything about *any* of… this business…" Kate says.

"Katherine-Thea," my mumma breathes. "I—"

The notebook stops ringing.

"I'm sorry," Kate manages to say. "It's stress. It's… You know. What we went through."

THUMP, THUMP, THUMP.

Mumma does know. Mumma knows especially because her own mumma witnessed the sickness. Her own mumma, Thea, was just a tiny girl who was left alone at the airport. A tiny girl whom Kate saw. Kate, who had just given up her own baby brother, whose broken teen heart still held love. Kate went and asked her, *Where's your mummy?* And the tiny girl didn't know, and there was no one to ask.

At the side of the deserted motorway, Thea watched, weeping, as Kate's howls announced her boyfriend's death.

Thirty years later, Kate watched, weeping, as Mumma, then a teen herself, announced with howls of grief Thea's death from breast cancer.

That night, Kate stopped crying. She put her might behind creating a new future, as all the granmummas were doing.

And Mumma did too.

♀ ♂

"Should someone go and talk to him?" Mumma asks Kate.

I really, really do not want to, so I am incredibly relieved when Kate says, "No, we should just leave him for a while."

"But he seemed *upset*," says Mumma.

187

"Look—everything about him, everything about the way he behaves, it's old-school, all right? How boys and men used to be."

"Maybe that's why people wanted to get rid of them."

I know I should not be saying it, not now—but I say it. It is out of my mouth and in the room. It's just a rumor that gets whispered from time to time, that the sickness was a deliberate act, the purposeful introduction of a virus to eliminate the majority of XYs. I've even heard granmummas joke about it when some terrible event from the once-was gets mentioned, and there were, as far as I can tell, so very many terrible events. But I've never heard Kate joke about it, and she is now looking at me with what you could call *disgust*.

"People do say that," I mutter.

"Not all of them behaved like this, but a lot did," Kate says to Mumma.

"The ones that did gaming?" Mumma asks, struggling to understand. "Blam, blam?"

"No," says Kate. "Some, maybe. Don't get hung up about that. That was just… Things were different. *People* were different."

"You mean men and boys?"

"No. Everyone," says Kate, frowning so hard her eyes close in concentration, in the effort of explaining the once-was that neither Mumma nor I can imagine—and I don't want to either. "Everyone and everything was different, and that boy… To me, it's like time travel or something. He seems to me like how boys were."

"But it's been *sixty* years," Mumma says.

"I know. *Go figure*," says Kate. It's one of her expressions; it means… Well, I've never understood what exactly, but from the way she uses it, it means something like *Work it out for yourself, but I think I already know the answer.*

Kate gets up and gets the apple brandy and two glasses. Two. I'm not even going to be offered some. I know I shouldn't have said what I said, but I found him. I saved him and—okay, so Mumma is lying at a national level, but I am having to lie directly and on a daily basis to our friends and neighbors. And I don't even drink apple brandy, but I—

"What about me?"

Kate sets down the bottle and the glasses.

"What about you?" she says. "You know, sometimes, you really are one prize brat."

"And you…really are one prize bitch."

It's Kate speak, that. Pure Kate speak. Pure Kate-at-her-worst speak, coming out of my mouth. The fact that she doesn't react to it is even more disturbing.

The *THUMP*, *THUMP*, *THUMP* stops. I hadn't even realized I was so aware of it.

"Eleven o'clock," I tell them. "I'm going to bed."

That's what I say—and the sound of my own voice makes me cringe because I know even this simple thing I'm saying is not coming from a good place. And the knowing of that makes me as mad as this whole *situation* makes me mad. Angry mad and crazy mad and every other kind of mad there is.

I feel bad. I know everyone is upset. I am, Mumma is, the

damn boy is…and so is Kate. I know, in my heart, that her upset is deep and old and s-e-r-i-o-u-s.

Still, I can't seem to help myself. I screech my chair and I stomp to my room.

My room?!

I insisted Mumma and I move my study desk from my bedroom down to the utility room, even though there is no space in there for it. I squeeze past it, raking clothes—for which there is no chest of drawers or wardrobe or cabinets—to the end of the smelly, old cot and clamber into it, clothes still on because I'm too mad to take them off.

I'm too mad to even shut my eyes. I'm too mad to even look and see what the sky is doing. I stare through the darkness at the beautiful Kate-made study desk I love so much—my little world within a world: a fold-down desk inside a cupboard filled with shelves and hidden drawers. *For your secret things*, Kate said when she gave it to me for my seventh birthday. My secret things were my little, fiddly electromechanical projects—things I took apart and struggled to put back together again—the bones of birds, and feathers, feathers, feathers. I imagined that if I ever got to build aircrafts, I wouldn't just make technically brilliant machines; I would remember the beauty of the birds that inspired human flight. I would make *beautiful* planes, a whole fleet of them, painted to look just like birds.

Those secret things? They weren't really secret at all. I had no secrets.

CHAPTER 18
GAMES

I hold out for two days.

I hold out, clinging to my own bad mood like it's a life raft. My own bad mood is the only thing that makes sense to me. The *feeling* of being in a bad mood, that is. The *reasons* for the bad mood make no sense to me, and that in itself makes the bad mood worse, which is fine; it helps to be clinging on to something large and solid. But I have been brought up to pay attention to thinking as well as feeling, so in spite of myself, I do think too. My conclusion is that I am in a bad mood because there is just too much going on. There is too much emotion in this house. There is too much disruption to too many lives; everyone is in their own state of turmoil: Kate, Mumma, me…and *Mason*. My bad mood dictates I must act as though I do not care or notice, and I don't quite know exactly how much I do care. Mainly, I just wish I'd never found him. But I do, most definitely, notice that he has withdrawn. He's in his—MY—room all the time. I hear Kate and Mumma talk about it, Mumma being concerned and Kate saying to leave him be. Kate pressing Mumma to investigate the Sanctuary situation. Mumma saying she is consulting. Kate telling Mumma she'd better not be snitching, that she will never speak to Mumma again if the boy gets taken. Me, clinging silently to my bad mood...and Mason clinging to his...? Less silently. All you can hear from MY room is *THUMP*, *THUMP*, *THUMP*. Either that or the gaming grunts; he's eased off on the *Noooo!*'s and *Yesss!*es.

I do, really, want to see what those games are like.

♀ ♂

While Mumma is in her study on her notebook (investigating, I suppose) and Kate has gone off in her own anxious, bad mood to the midweek Friday social night at the granmummas' house (they play cards; they claim no gambling is involved—everyone knows different), I decide to do a little bit of investigating/Friday social of my own.

I knock on the boy's door. (Knocking on my *own* bedroom door!) When there's no answer after the second knock, I open the door: Mason, slouched on *my* bed, jumps out of his skin! He chucks aside whatever piece of his computer equipment he'd got hold of and whips off the headphones he's wearing.

And all he does is glare at me.

And all I do is glare back.

My room. I take a step inside. Obviously, it's not the first time I've looked in. Plenty of times when he's been in the shower, I've poked my head around the door to mourn my bedroom, which looks so strange now: walls bare (I said I wanted my pictures), filled with machines and other "gym" stuff, but almost empty of any kind of smell apart from baking powder, cider vinegar, and soap. He is very keen on hygiene, both personal and household. It is incredibly clean. It is not like my room at all.

"You could at least say hello," I say.

He grunts.

That makes me furious.

"I've basically saved your life *twice*. This is *my* room you're living in. You didn't seem to have any problem speaking to me before, so…"

He picks up the computer equipment, some kind of control set, and clicks around with something.

"What? You won't even say hello?"

"You could too," he mutters, putting the controls back down.

"Could what?"

"At least say hello."

We glare at each other. I'm probably the glaring loser right now because he's got a point. I didn't say hello, did I?

"Hi," I manage to say.

"Hi," he says.

On the huge screen he's got sitting on *my* chest of drawers, there's an image of a cobbled city square—ancient, medieval—and in the middle of it, a man with a sword stands, looking this way and that, but not otherwise moving.

"Nice talking to you," Mason says, and picks the controls back up.

"Now who's being rude?"

"What?" he says. "Oh, wait—*don't say what. Say pardon.* Look, *River*, I've got nothing to say. What would I have to say?"

Tons of things, I'm thinking. Tons of stuff I don't know about and I don't really *want* to know about—and...HOLD ON! I've got tons of things to say—tons of things you'd think *he* might want to know about.

"I thought...maybe you'd like to ask me some things?"

"Nope."

"Maybe you'd just like it if I told you some things?"

"Nope."

He puts the controls back down and wipes his hands on the blankets; he has loads of blankets, because Kate says he's not used to the cold. What cold? Our house has never been so day-and-night warm. So he's sweating—palm sweat. I know palm sweat; I get it when I have to speak in public. Palm sweat means nerves.

"Are you nervous?" I ask him. I know I shouldn't do that; it doesn't help me at all when people notice and ask, but he's a boy, isn't he? Would it even signify the same thing?

"Nope. You got something else to say, or are you just gonna go? 'Cause I really do just want you to go."

"Yeah, and I wish *you* would."

The second I say it, I regret it. However true it is.

"And *I* wish I could. But there ain't nowhere for a freak like me *to* go, is there?"

"I'm sorry," I tell him—and I am. I am, obviously, sorry he cannot just up and leave my life and take this storm of lies and upset with him. But I am also, I realize, genuinely sorry because he cannot do that. Because he never meant for this whole thing to be happening either. And now...I suppose we just *all* have to live with it. "I want to see that," I tell him, pointing at the screen. "I want to try it."

He delivers one weary stare.

"Well, then just forget it," I tell him, reaching out for my bad mood. I need it; I can feel waves of annoyance—waves of yet more *goddamn* emotion—rising around me.

"Five minutes," he says. "Five."

I roll my eyes. That's how you speak to littler ones.

"Ten max," he says.

I take the deal. I shut the door behind me, and I walk over to the bed and reach for that piece of equipment he's got.

"Nuh-uh!" he says. "You take the old one's controller."

He points at my dressing table; there's another piece of equipment just like his.

"Kate's been playing this too?"

He nods. "She ain't bad."

I grab the equipment. Before I got to fly real planes, I tried simulators to learn the basics, and this equipment, this controller, looks pretty simple to me. I sit down on the side of my bed with it.

"Knock yourself out," says Mason, removing his headphone jack and switching to screen sound.

It is infuriatingly difficult.

After I've been sword slaughtered, horribly and effortlessly, about five or six times, I could pretty much slaughter someone myself.

I am just kidding. Of course I am. But honestly?!

"You are so dead!" Mason laughs. We're well over the ten minutes, but neither of us is bothered about that. I don't know him or XYs enough to know for sure, but his laughter...it seems...genuine. And not unkind. It reminds me of how, when I was tiny, Kate couldn't help but laugh a little at the minimachines I made; she laughed, but I didn't feel intimidated by it. It was a kind and appreciative laugh. I don't feel intimidated now. I feel totally wound up. Determined to conquer.

"Seriously," Mason says, "River, you are about the worst player I've ever seen, and I've seen plenty. In K-Beta, I taught all them kids. I taught them: this is how you fight."

"Again," I say to him. "Let me try again."

I get slaughtered.

"Again."

I get slaughtered.

"Again."

I get slaughtered—but I wounded him first.

"Again!"

I get slaughtered. Mason says I need to slow down just a little bit, watch where the sword swings are coming from. Jump clear.

Not really listening now.

"Again!"

I hack one assailant to death only to get felled by another.

"Again!"

Mumma comes in, Kate, wheezing, shooting inhaler, right behind her just as I do it: I plunge my sword into my medieval opponent's heart.

"I just killed him!" I shout—my whole body feels like it's jumping with excitement, my hands twitch with a strange, new tension.

In the kitchen, in front of Mumma, Kate says there is a new house rule:

I am not to go into Mason's room.

"But…it's *my* room," I say.

"I agree," Mumma says. "With Kate," she adds—in case there could be any doubt.

"We were just playing!" I protest.

"And I don't want those *games* in this house," Mumma tells Kate.

"It *is* just a game," says Kate.

"Where's the fun in that?" Mumma says. "Where's the fun in death?"

It was fun—I mean, not *fun* fun, when you laugh so hard your cheeks ache, but it was fun! It was the most *fun* I've had in weeks. I'm not even looking forward to tonight's harvest supper, which is usually the *wildest* fun, because of this situation.

And I think about that. And I try to imagine: What if I were Mason? What if that gaming thing truly was all the fun I could ever expect to have? I think about that all night as another angry storm rages; the weather, this autumn, it is *furious*.

I creep upstairs. I don't knock.

"Yo," he says through the darkness. He is sitting on the window seat.

I close the door and sit down opposite him.

"Venice was all I had," he says, and I look where he is looking. Even in the darkness, I can see the screen is gone, the PC too. "I didn't even play it much no more. I just liked…so when you're not fighting, you can explore. I liked climbing around that city. I knew every stone in it. I knew every person. I knew Leonardo. I saw his drawings. I saw it all."

"You should have told Mumma that," I say. It's all I can think to say. And it's true.

"I…I wanna see the ocean," he says. "I just want to see the ocean. I want to see one real thing."

"Everything is real."

"Not to me it ain't. That there," he says, pointing at the empty space the PC occupied, "that was the best real I had."

CHAPTER 19
SWAMP

The estuary looks really beautiful. It has a thousand moods, and now, with the first soft glow of the coming dawn gently kissing the stars goodbye, it looks...*serene*. That would be the word for it. The world is still and cool and fresh after the storm, and even the water, resting between tides, lies gray and smooth and calm.

"Well, this is shit, ain't it?" he says.

It is, absolutely, the last thing I would ever have expected anyone to say in the face of such gorgeousness.

"I mean—WAIT! Is this actually shit?" he says, extracting his feet with loud sucks from the softly sheening ripples of estuary mud.

"Of course it's not! It's just...mud."

"It stinks!"

Does it? I wouldn't even notice that. Mud just smells like mud to me. If I smell it at all, it smells like…home. It smells like *life*.

"And you've been lied to big-time," he says. "This ain't the ocean."

"It is. That is to say, it's the sea. That is to say, it's an estuary, isn't it?"

"You said ocean."

"I said sea. You saw the map. You saw the globe. What were you expecting? A view of the American coastline?"

"Can you see that from here? Can you see America?"

A slight wind—tiny but full of spiky chill—ghosts up off the water as more and more light floods the sky.

"It's all lies. Everything's lies. We been lied to, River. You and me both. I'm part girl, so say you. Ain't no goddamn ocean."

He turns to me, and all is hopelessness on his face. Hopelessness and bitterness, crushing disappointment.

I lead him out onto the spit. I have to tell him, *Follow where I tread.* I have to be that specific about it because there's a way you have to go, and he (obviously!) doesn't know and keeps wandering off and hitting yet more mud sinks, where streams finally carve their way to the sea. I lead him out until we hit the beach—that's the stony place we swim from, on an incoming tide. Even if you go out a little too far, all that will happen is you'll get swept home fast. Unless you go too far and know what you're doing. This is the place me and Plat rafted from.

"So, this is the beach—"

"This ain't no beach," he mutters. "Beaches got sand. Beaches got bikini babes. Beaches are hot."

"And that's Wales," I tell him, pointing at the land across the estuary. "Those islands? That's Little Holm, that's Steep Holm. Out that way, there's Lundy. Gull cities! Over there, Exmoor—seriously tall cliffs, brilliant prehistoric stone… arrangements." I remember, just in time, what Tamara said they should be called: *arrangements*, not circles, because they're not circular, and they're small—tiny!—but they must have taken discussion and agreement to build. (Tamara even adores ancient evidence of organization.) "And that," I tell him, "is the ocean."

I point my finger at where there is no land in sight.

It's like he hadn't seen it. How could he not have seen the space?

"America?" he asks, staring in wonder at the horizon.

"It's there."

"Can't see it."

"It's thousands of miles away."

"How many? How far?"

"Depends which part. Five thousand. At least."

This fact seems to do something to his legs. He sits. He sits on the beach and holds his head in his hands. If my whole life hadn't gone a little overly dramatic, I'd think he was being overly dramatic. Right now, it's just perfect. Got an XY *wigging out*, as Kate would say, with dawn now seriously blasting us.

"We really do need to go home now," I tell him, picking up a

201

pebble. It's what I do when I get stuck on math problems; I come here and skim stones.

"*Home?* River, I'm so lost right now I don't even know which way is up."

I know I should probably say something or do something—but what? Give him a hug? I know that's what I would do if another person spoke so upsetting a thought…but I don't. I feel…exhausted. Exhausted because I haven't had enough sleep for ages, not just this last night. And exhausted because this is EXHAUSTING. How on earth do you even begin to explain the world to someone who seems to have so little clue about it? So all I find I can do is look back at him and shrug. I can't even manage a reassuring smile… That would be the right thing to do now, wouldn't it? To at least smile. I CAN'T.

I feel my hand close around the pebble: smooth and cold and true.

"The whole world's a lie," he moans. "And I'm a lie too, ain't I? I'm a goddamn girl."

"Part girl—no, it's not even that! It's tiny. It's just a tiny, tiny sliver of girl. And in any case, what could possibly be so bad about that?"

He huffs out air and rolls his eyes like it's obvious.

"I don't really understand. I don't understand at all."

The pebble is warming in my hand. My heart, it's fluttering, flitting. It doesn't know where to land: compassion or contempt?

"Know what I think? I think you could have gone through your whole life without even knowing about that. Why should

202

it make any difference to you? Honestly, trust me, Mason, you were you before you knew this, and you're still you. You're *always* going to be you."

I hurl the pebble.

I am very, very good at skimming stones. Plat thinks she's better. She isn't!

The pebble bounces—one, two, three, four, five times. Not bad, considering. Nine's my record. I turn to him; he's staring, open jawed, at the place where the pebble sank, ripples spreading on the flat, quiet sea.

"Stones bounce on water," he says. "Stones freaking bounce."

And I try very hard to remember when I saw that for the first time, because I must have been amazed too…but I can't. I don't know what to say to him, and besides, we really do need to go.

That's the thing about a dawn, isn't it? When you've been up all night, even the smallest glimmer of it seems so incredibly bright. Apart from the disconcerting possibility that others have dawn lessons on the weekend (I've been so distracted I don't know anyone's timetables), the village won't be up for a while yet to start on the preparations for the harvest supper, but still—daylight. I don't want to be out here in my pj's with a shivering boy in a too-short, pink bathrobe when my friends and neighbors open their curtains.

"Come on," I say to him. "We'd better get you out of here before the she-wolves wake up." And he looks up at me, and it's like all the fight and fire have gone out of him and he's just plain wide-eyed scared. "I'm joking!" I tell him. "But we really should go, okay?"

"'Kay, River," he says in that small voice I heard once before, and he gets to his feet, but in a stiff, shaky way, like one of the oldest of the granmummas.

I don't take the chance of going back through the village. I cut right around it, keeping well clear of the school, looping, zig-zagging on the maze of footpaths, made narrow by the summer's lush growth, dying off now, but still—

"JESUS!" he cries out, and I turn to see him scratching frantically at his nettle-stung legs, bare from the knees down under MY bathrobe. "Goddamn she-wolf plant attacked me!"

I pick a dock leaf and offer it to him.

"You need to rub it on your skin. Trust me. Do it."

My heart flutters again. Compassion? Contempt? Confusion? No! Never mind what! If we don't get a move on, we'll get spotted, and I do NOT want to have to deal with any kind of escalation of this situation.

"Like this," I say and bend to rub his legs.

He jumps back away from me, then forward again because— "Jesus!"—he hits more nettles.

For crying out loud. "Do you want me to help you or not?"

He doesn't answer; he's just standing there…all done in. So I reach deep. I reach deep to find how I'd speak to a littler one or the oldest and the frailest of the granmummas: kindly and in their own language. I'd find a way to connect.

"Code of Honor, this will help" is what I say.

He snorts, scoffing, like I'm making some kind of joke—but he doesn't move, so I rub those super-furry legs with the leaf. I can't even tell whether he's so scared and tense his legs would always feel like that, or whether that's what stupid amounts of running do, but his muscles—they're rigid, rocklike, and the whole of his legs feel unnaturally lean. They feel *wrong*. Maybe it's because he's not eating properly, or maybe this is the way XYs are. Only Kate would know.

"Better?" I ask him when I'm done rubbing.

"Little bit," he says in a strained, anxious, weird voice.

It really is like dealing with a littler one.

"Don't focus on it," I advise, wondering if there's calamine lotion at the granmummas, because those reaction bumps on his skin really do look pretty terrible, the worst I've ever seen. "And avoid these plants," I instruct, pointing at a nettle.

We have just got to get home. I speed up; he yelps at fresh nettle stings, and I ignore it and try to distract him, the same way I would do with a littler one who was bothered by something that will be okay and can't be helped:

"That's Lenny's farm," I tell him.

"A farm!"

"And this is where we grow vegetables and other things." I really don't want to talk about the polytunnel full of marijuana and chilies right now.

He peers over the hedge at the wrecked field. Pretty much anything edible H&R and their helicopter didn't mash has been plundered for the harvest supper. "You eat that stuff?"

"Yes—I mean, no. That's just what's left. It's the end of the season, isn't it?"

He shrugs.

"Over there's the school," I tell him as we zigzag, him jumping over nettles behind me like, like…a deer leaping, springy and scared.

"That's the church." I point at the tower.

He stops leaping for a moment.

"A house of God," he says.

I forgot about him being religious.

"Yeah, sure. We try to take care of it. I mean, a little. The roof's falling in. Lenny still uses it for storage and stuff, but there's a terrible damp problem, and we…just haven't got the resources. People come first, don't they?"

He nods. I am not convinced he's being anything other than polite, but he doesn't even know what "polite" means, does he?

I've got no time to dwell on it. In my mind, I've calculated and made a decision. We'll cut back into the village past the granmummas' house—quicker that way, and even if any of them are up (they might be—even apple brandy doesn't always knock them out), they're not going to say a word to anyone but Kate, are they, about me and the XY sneaking home?

"This is where most of the granmummas live," I tell him as we hurry past.

"The old ones?"

"Mmm-hmm. They…prefer their own company. We sort

206

of speak a different language, I guess. They grew up in the once-was."

"The once-was…"

Never really thought about how to define it. It's just the past, isn't it?

"The time when men and boys were around."

"We're still around."

"You know what I mean. *Around* around. Living outside the Sanctuaries. What do you call that time?"

"I don't."

"No, come on. You must call it something."

"I don't. *We* don't."

"But…who do you think… I mean, how do you think… So you're in your Sanctuary—"

"Unit."

"What did you think was happening in the rest of the world?"

"I don't know. I didn't 'think.' It's…whatever, isn't it? No one thinks about that kind of stuff."

"But, seriously, what did you think was happening…out here?"

"I dunno. She-wolves…plotting."

"Plotting to what?"

"Rape us. Kill us."

I turn, I stare him straight in his furry face, and I tell him: "Maybe you need to rethink that. On the basis of the evidence. Maybe you also need to think about how come the Sanctuaries even exist. Where do your supplies come from? Your food? Your electricity? Your clothes? Ev-er-y-thing?"

"We got food factories. My clothes is just from the warehouse. We got supplies. We got everything! And when I run, I make electricity. I make power."

"Power? I've hooked you up; your running machine is hooked up. Wanna know how much power you're making?"

He shakes his head, and I tell him anyway.

"Not even enough to run a light bulb."

"I've been lied to about stuff," he says. "Seems I have."

I feel bad immediately. I check my feelings—I'm not scared of him, at least not quite like I was. The little parts I get to know and see, it gets harder and harder to be scared. He is *clueless* and afraid. All he has over me now is, I suppose, physical strength and speed—and I'm not even sure of that. For all his weird muscles, he's skinny, he's been sick, and he hasn't been eating right. It's another thing I'll have to ask Kate about. It's so hazy in my mind, the community studies lessons I dozed through, dreaming instead about what me and Plat were going to do. How—exactly—did XYs dominate the once-was? Were they all super-fit and scary?

"This is the Memory Garden," I tell him.

It is a mini-arboretum of trees, beautiful, now-dying flowers planted all around. Some trees old, some newer, all hung with cards and messages and bows and yet more flowers (dead and living; real and fake) and chimes and the things the granmummas leave. They hang books—once-was stories about boys stranded on islands, boys who were wizards, magical creatures on great quests. They hang objects: there's a little, black, flame-painted bike; a skateboard; tiny tennis shoes; bigger tennis shoes; hoodies; T-shirts; jeans; DVDs; and *condoms*. Oh, and they hang home-grown marijuana joints there too, alongside ancient cans of beer—or sometimes just the plastic that held the cans, the plastic that will take a thousand years to die. And I know now what that black, dangling lump is—a *game box*.

He's looking at it all. He's not speaking.

"People plant a tree here when they've given birth to a son."

He just stares.

"And then they decorate the trees," I say to fill the silence of his staring. I am suddenly uneasy. I feel as though I might have made a very terrible mistake, because what would that feel like? To never know who your mumma was? "And, on the boy's birthday, we bring cake and have a little party."

"On January the first…"

"That's your birthday, isn't it?"

"It's everyone's birthday," he says.

"It's not mine. Mine's November the second."

"I was born on January first, same as every boy."

"*Mason*…I don't think that's true. I mean, maybe you were born on the first of January, but… Look. That's Aidan's tree. He was born in November—a hornbeam for the berries. Nathan, born in December, so…holly. That's Luke's—September, evergreen oak. Then there's Finlay, July—so the horse chestnut, for luxuriant shade. Stanley-Tiger, August—*Davidia involucrata*, ghost tree."

The ghost tree has already lost its leaves, as though it had anticipated this wild-weather autumn. It is pure shape. It is a beautiful shape. And behind it, the tree Kate planted for Jaylen: a silver birch. The first one died, but you can still see the stump; the next one to be planted is very old now too but hanging on.

"Does my…*mumma*—would *my* mumma have a tree like this for me?"

It was mainly the granmummas who planted trees. The mummas' generation, they tend not to.

"She might do, yes. I mean…even if there wasn't a tree, I know for sure your mumma would remember you."

I meant to make things better. I feel as though I have made things worse.

He is rooted to the spot, staring at those trees.

"Let's go home," I whisper, and he nods, but he doesn't move, so I take him by the arm and I turn him around. I steer him down the lane and—

I STOP BEFORE HE DOES. NO. NO. NO.

It's like he's in some kind of dream state, so I actually have to pull him to get him to stop. And he looks around at me like he's just remembered I'm there, and he looks at where I am looking—and I feel fright surge through him, so I take his hand to hold him still, and I hiss, "*RELAX!*"

An apparition is skipping toward us, puddle jumping. Not jumping over puddles, but—SPLASH! SPLASH! SPLASH!— into them. It's Sweet. It would be Sweet! Of course, my heart groans, *It's Sweet…* In self-constructed, garishly painted papier-mâché butterfly wings; her face adorned with autumn leaves

210

stuck on with smears of mud; ancient, way-too-big, red rubber boots on her feet, and she is clutching an enormous bright-yellow chicken-of-the-woods fungus.

There is no place to run. No place to hide. And no time to speak before—

"I've got a chicken!" she announces, splashing up to us. "You're hairy. Who are you?"

"Courtesy!" I try—desperately. "This is…my cousin…the cousin of my cousin. I don't even know what you're doing up at this time, but—"

"It's not my fault! It's the storm's fault! It woke me up!"

Concern of a new kind rips through my existing troubles like a…like a bolt of lightning. "Sweet! You didn't go out in the storm, did you? You know you shouldn't do that! It's dangerous!"

She studies me for a second. "That's why I went into the woods," she says. "It's safer! Don't you know anything about lightning?! When the kz-kz-kz-kaboom happens, it'll just get the trees because they're taller. I wasn't scared! You *are* very hairy. You're the hairiest person I ever met."

"You're the weirdest thing I ever met," the boy growls before I can stop him.

"Have you got a sore throat?" Sweet asks. "I had a sore throat once. You have to tell the granmummas."

"We will. We've got to go now," I hear myself saying. I squeeze the boy's hand and I feel him squeeze back—not hard, like I did, but a frightened pulse of acknowledgment. And I draw him on, down the lane, Sweet dancing around us, puddle splashing.

"My throat was SO sore I couldn't even speak, and when I did it came out *ruh-ruh-ruh* just like you!"

"You shouldn't go out in storms…and you should take the chicken to Willow," I say over my shoulder, casually and with grimly retrieved normality. "She's the best at cooking them."

"Yes," says Sweet, puddle splashing past us, "but I want to see the hairy girl."

"Well, you can't," I snap, "because…*she*…is poorly. Go. Go on—go."

Sweet assesses the situation. She assesses the fierceness in my eyes.

"You know I said I liked you a little?" she tells me. "It's not that much."

"Go!"

She shrugs, puddle splashes back down the lane.

"I'm not allowed outside in my bathrobe!" she cries. "And how come *she* gets to wear the dead-boy shoes?!"

I do what I suppose people did for centuries. I cast my eyes up to the sky. It is so much bigger than us and so very amazing. It is no wonder people thought there had to be a God. And it is no wonder people thought God would live right there, in the sky. I look up and I see…

THE DREAMBIRD.

CHAPTER 20
DREAMBIRD

Stress makes you deaf. That's my conclusion.

It makes you deaf temporarily, but it does not make you blind. The second I clap eyes on that beautiful aircraft sailing in, I hear it too. EASING POWER! DESCENDING! DESCENDING!

"River?" I vaguely hear Mason say.

DESCENDING! DREAMBIRD DESCENDING!

Designed in India. Chinese aluminum. Japanese tech. Revolutionary fuel-economic engines. Lower-speed maneuverability. The first supersonic plane to be built in...OVER A HUNDRED YEARS?!

I sky-gawp.

DREAMBIRD. DESCENDING. DESCENDING. DESCENDING.

Only one place it could be going.

I sigh at the sky, my heart soaring high as that plane.

"I don't like planes," Mason mutters.

I tune back in. "What would you know?" I snap. Gotta ditch him. Gotta go.

I drag him by the hand the rest of the way up the lane. Mumma and Kate, all snaggle-sleepy haired and frantic looking are coming out of our door. Who cares?

"Sweet saw us," I say, releasing the boy's hand, releasing him into their care. "She'll say something; she's bound to. Told her *she's* my cousin's cousin, and *she's* poorly—sore throat. I've got to go—"

Kate opens her mouth to say whatever. I can't do this right now.

"It's the Dreambird! Did you see it?!"

My mumma opens her mouth too.

"Just tell them everything," I urge Mason. "*Tell* them. About Sweet, about the lies. Tell them!"

His face twists in fear and confusion, and I do not have time to make it right.

I do not. I'm gone. I race back up the lane.

"Back A-S-A-P!" I shout, already wondering if there's enough fuel in my bike to get us to the training airport.

"**Pj's!**" Mumma shouts.

True. Drat. True. Drat. I'm tempted to ignore it, but…

I race back down the lane, straight into the house and up to MY room. I'm midchange—i.e., naked—when Kate, Mumma and the boy come in.

"Put some goddamn clothes on!" Kate shrieks, pulling the gawping boy out of the room.

"I am!"

I am too. I'm dressed in seconds, ignoring Kate telling me we need to talk and Mumma telling me to just hold on a moment.

"It's the *Dreambird*." I speak into their faces as I come out of the room. I know Mumma will know how important this is, and not just because I've gone on about it in the past, but because it's such an international BIG DEAL. Kate? She'll have heard, but it will have bored her. She won't have cared enough to register: DREAMBIRD. Both cases: whatever they've got to say, I don't want to hear it. And as for the harvest-supper preparation? It's too bad. There is always a terrible mess afterward anyway, so I'll work extra hard on the cleanup.

"Later," I hear the boy say as I clatter down the stairs to grab my backpack.

Five minutes later, I crash into Lenny's barn and grab my scrambler.

"Given up on the running then?" Lenny shouts with a huge grin on her face as I fire my bike up. Lenny is the one person in my life who will absolutely understand this. We both *adore* machines.

"Dreambird!" I shout, and speed on out of there, scattering chickens.

♀ ♂

It is so good to be on my bike. I'd forgotten how good it was. You get a certain amount of freedom to ride when you've first built your machine. Then, after that, you're fuel rationed, unless it's a journey you need to make. And I need to make this journey; Yaz and Yukiko will back me up if it comes to it. This is for my education, and my education is for the good of everyone—a fact I try to not let add to the pressure to do well that already haunts me.

I take the main road. Through the woods would be quicker, but that route is hardly repaired at all—there's not enough justification for it. And although it'd probably be fine, and fun, on a normal day, to be dodging road ripples and potholes at speed, I cannot risk a *prang*. That's a Kate word that, as far as I can tell, covers anything from a bit of a dent to a total write-off (if she's driving). So I'm main road all the way. A scrambler's not built for pure speed, but my bike is loving the road, and so am I. For the first time since the boy arrived, I feel FREE.

♀ ♂

"No admittance."

I almost can't believe I'm hearing the words. Not just because I need to see this aircraft so badly my whole body is burning—flaming!—with feverish, *passionate* desire, but because, well, I mean, *who says that to anyone about anything?*

"No admittance," says the H&R person inside the gate. We couldn't shake hands and kiss cheeks as courtesy demands because there is a massive fence between us, so we just touched palms through the chain link as we greeted each other, me saying, in huge excitement, "Hi! I've come to see the Dreambird!"

She saying what she said: "No admittance."

Stunned and hurting and longing, I try EVERY plea I can think of:

"But that's the Dreambird!"

"I'm studying aeronautical engineering!"

"But this is the training airport!"

"I've been here lots of times before!"

"I'm going to work here!"

"I just rode 120 miles to get here!"

"I'm out of fuel! I had to push my bike the last several miles!"

"But...*please*, that's the **Dreambird**!"

Each results in the same answer—"No admittance"—until I hit on:

"My mumma said it would be okay."

"No admittance."

"My mumma is the southwest rep on the National Council."

The H&R person walks away from the fence. I feel wrong in myself for having "played the mumma card" as Kate would say, but my yearning to get close to that incredible machine is too great. I can see it less than a couple of miles away, parked outside a hangar, and already, with every plea, I have looked and seen how that hangar is fenced off from every side. I WILL find a way in...though perhaps I won't have to. The H&R person makes one radio call after another, with people calling her back.

The H&R person walks back to the fence.

My heart is singing!

"No admittance," she says.

My jaw drops.

"That's the final word on it," she says. "It has been Agreed."

The plane of my dreams, the plane I really, really need to see, is just sitting right there on the asphalt.

"No admittance."

I wheel my bike around the perimeter fence. I know where to go and ask for fuel. There's a depot. Mariam's cousin Laila-Jewel works there—we know each other. We know each other enough for her to immediately see how upset I am.

"What are you doing here?" she asks as we shake hands and kiss. "Ah! I don't even have to ask that, do I?"

"How's Jewel?"

"She's great! Running rings around the granmummas and doing so well at school—*better than Mariam*," she whispers, then laughs, "Better than me, at any rate!"

From out of the back of the depot, I can see the object of my desire, and in my bones, still rattling from the ride and aching from the push, I can feel my wasted journey hurting.

"What is this no-admittance thing?" I ask.

"I do not know," she says. "NO ADMITTANCE! Infuriating, isn't it? The Dreambird's in, and no one's allowed to go and see except…"

I tear my eyes off the plane to look at her.

"I've got to refuel it. 8:00 p.m."

That's so late. That so doesn't matter. I'd wait for a week to see this. A week? I'd wait for *months*.

"I expect you need to go to the workshops," she says, "before you come back and assist."

My smile is a thousand miles wide.

My smile is so wide I daren't even visit the workshops. All everyone will want to talk about is the Dreambird anyway, and all I'll do is end up telling everyone I'm going to get to see it up close, because to do otherwise would be not just withholding knowledge, but a further lie on top of a mountain of lies I'm sick of telling.

So I go to the museum hangars instead. They're open 24/7 and the granmumma pilot and the engineer who are on hand to explain anything you might need to know have seen me so many times before they leave me be—though from their smiles alone I know they know exactly why I'm here, and I know they're as desperate as me to see the Dreambird.

"No admittance, eh?" is all the engineer says as she and the pilot offer me cup after cup after cup of tea, which I sip, stern faced, over my notebook as I examine plane after plane after plane, the specs of which I already know by heart. And when they have gone, I climb into the cockpit of the Fairey Delta. It's my favorite. It always has been, and I think it always will be. I knew about it long before I knew anything about the Dreambird. It was flown by the granmummas' daddies' daddies' daddies. Just being inside that ancient, little, blue beast of a dream of a bird makes me happy. Makes me feel connected to generations of people like me who just wanted to know: What can we do?

I sit in the cockpit, in the dark, and I beam. In my imagination, I am not just flying that Fairey, I am at the controls of its daughter's daughter's daughter's daughter: the Dreambird. And I will see her.

At 7:30 p.m., still beaming with joy, I go to find Laila-Jewel.

♀ ♂

I remember very clearly the first time I saw a BIG plane up close. Not the Concorde in the museum, which littler-one me found cozy as a playhouse inside—and packed with too many kilos of seriously once-was electronics—but an Airbus. Inside, that was an incredible sight: nearly a whole plane full of seats from the time when people thought nothing of burning millions of gallons of irreplaceable fossil fuels, going to places they had no need to go to. Though if you ask Kate, she'll tell you she really did need to go to Ibiza with her cousins Cheyenne and Bianca.

And on the outside? I just remember how tiny I felt, how amazed I was that this enormous beast of a bird could ever even leave the ground.

I feel tiny again now. I am in awe. Laila-Jewel knows it—she understands just what this means to me.

"It's quite something, isn't it?" she whispers to me as I stand there, in a borrowed blue fueling jumpsuit, dumbstruck because, even in the darkness lit by floodlights, I can see how truly extraordinary the Dreambird is.

I am now, I know, going to study extra, extra hard. I am going to **ACE** every single subject I have to ace—because I want to be part of the team that builds aircraft like this. And if we can do this, surely it is possible that, in my lifetime, we could go back into space.

It's genius. Weight challenges maneuverability at lower speeds. Deltas demand long runways. This one won't.

The wing is *exquisite*. It curves divinely! A curve more complex than a Concorde's twisting ogee. Seamless riveting, but I can see there're hydraulics. It must have lift—superlift!—smooth, smooth cruise (I'm visualizing this subtly complex wing being tested in a smoke tunnel, how it'd just grab any speed of headwind you could throw at it and glide on through), AND deceleration capacity. Hydraulic maneuverability.

It's got it all.

Delta paradise.

I study online with students in India. I can't wait to see them again. I can't wait to tell them, *Congratulations! You did it.*

This *bird* is amazing, and it is beautiful. And I would love, love, love to see inside. I want to know about the engines. I want to see inside the flight deck—and there are lights on in there. I can see the pilots doing preflight checks, and I know, in my bones, that no amount of "no admittance" is going to stop me.

"Amazing, eh? Amazing," Laila-Jewel says, winding the fuel hose back in.

It's Laila-Jewel who will stop me. She helped me. I cannot abuse her kindness. I've been useless to her. I try to help wind in.

"I've got it," she says.

"Why would they do this?" I ask her, my heart torn apart because I am seeing my own true love right in front of me, and yet, it's forbidden. "Why would they fly this in and then not let anyone see it?"

"Not let *you* see it, you mean," she says, climbing into the cab of the fuel tanker.

I run around to the other side and get up into the cab.

"They've been showing it off all day, but only to the invited," she says, swinging the truck around to avoid numerous containers as we circle the plane to put fuel into the tank on the other wing. "So we've just had to invite ourselves, haven't we?"

We pull up and get out.

"And how am I supposed to work in this light?" Laila-Jewel says.

It's not that bad. Once you've got your dark-adapted eye in, you can see the Dreambird fairly well. I could just climb up to the flight deck, and even if they threw me out immediately, I'd get to have at least one glance at the panels. The trim controls must be utterly brilliant. The calibration on the hydraulics… I want to see the *precision*. I want to see. Laila-Jewel *would* understand if I just climbed those steps and dared to say hi. And, really, how much trouble could there be? Maybe they wouldn't tell me to go away. Every pilot I have ever met—and most especially Mariam—would never tell a keen person to go away. Mariam

222

has shown me every last feature of the Explorer, even though helicopters aren't really my thing.

But…my life is complicated right now, and that complication complicatedly involves other people. Kate, Mumma. The granmummas. And the boy. The *damn* boy. This mess at home—I feel snarled up in its many tentacles. I want to be bold, but I do not feel free to be bold. This *boy* mess is holding me back.

I back off into the darkness, and I calm myself. I check my feelings. I've seen the Dreambird. I don't want to get Laila-Jewel into any kind of trouble. I am just grateful I got to see this amazingness.

I need to record it. That's what I need to do.

I pull my notebook out of my backpack. I set it to camera/night. I click, click, click on those incredible wings. I back off to get a long shot. I look at the shot—No! I want the WHOLE THING. I back off farther. I take more shots. I look at them.

They're the best that I can do in *crummy* light—Kate word—with a crummy notebook camera.

It's the Dreambird. When—how—will I get to see it again? I switch on the flash. One shot with flash.

I take it.

No one, not even Laila-Jewel, seems to have noticed.

I look at the shot. Got it! I study the shot. This is it—you can even see the awesome complex wing curve, and… What is that?

On the picture, my eye is drawn to a small, white thing. A small, white thing sticking out from one of the containers. A small, white thing almost like a little flag…or a hand?

223

I stare at the containers. No flag. No hand. I look back at my pic. It does look like a hand. I enlarge the pic. It's blurry, but it looks like a hand...

I approach the containers. A row of them, ready to be loaded onto the plane. They're not regular containers, the kind we get coming in on ships at Plymouth and Avonmouth. They're smaller, perhaps about the size of my new utility-room bedroom, a few cubic yards only. Vents in them. Barred vents.

I walk up to the last one in the row. I breathe, sucking came-from-nowhere bad feelings in and out of my lungs. I speak.

"Hello?" I say.

"Hello and goodbye," a slurry voice says back.

I lean in closer. I put my hand up to the barred vent and—SNATCH! A hand grabs mine.

"Get me out of here," the voice slurs.

A face appears, presses sideways against the bars as the body it belongs to, gripping my hand, hauls itself up.

It is a face I am now almost immediately certain is an XY's face, but older than Mason. It's harder looking, leaner and much, much hairier...and odd. This face seems odd. For a moment, I think I am looking at a huge grin, but as he turns his head, I see the smile is not a smile at all. It exists on only one side of his face. A bald, pink-fleshed scar cuts through his beard from his mouth to his cheekbone. His eyes are rolling like he's about to faint or fall asleep.

"Oh shit. You're one of them, ain't you?"

He laughs, hard and bitter.

"I caught myself a woman. Take it that is what you're supposed to be?"

"No. Name's Mason," I tell him. He tightens its grip; I think my wrist might be about to break. "Code of Honor."

"Code of Honor my ass! You ain't Mason," he slurs.

I don't say anything. My mind is in free fall. A jolt of bone-breaking pain in my wrist reminds my body I am on Earth.

"Let me out."

There's just one bolt, way down low on the door to the container. Down too low for any hand from inside the container to reach.

"*In God's name, please!*" he hisses, and my wrist truly does feel as though it's about to snap. "*All I want is to die free!*"

I have, instantly, in my head: Mason. How desperate he was when I found him. How he thought he would die. How he behaved. His tears. How it seemed as though he was nothing but a scary creature, how I now understand—I think—that he was just *scared*. How fear makes people behave. How fear made *me* behave.

I unbolt the container, my wrist immediately released as he shoves the door open. His eyes roll in his head as he breathes in deeply—so deep it's as though he were sucking in the whole of the night sky—the stars, the moon, all of it.

"Death, I am so in love with you," he says.

Someone did this for Mason, I'm thinking. *This is where he ran from. This is where he ran from not even knowing that—*

"Hey!" a voice is calling. "Hey!"

It's H&R.

"HEY!"

I am the kind of person who needs time and space to work things out—quietly, on my own, with no interruptions. I have seconds.

"I can get you out of here," I tell him. "I've got a motorbike." I point. From under the wings of the Dreambird, my bike is plain to see: outside the fuel hangar, parked by the pumps. I do not know whether Laila-Jewel will have fueled her already, but I don't even know what I'm doing right now.

"Hey!"

We run. That is to say, I do. The XY I've liberated struggles to get to the hangar. I have to turn around and grab him by the hand to pull him to my bike. I leap on her. No time for helmet, boots, gloves, to change clothes. I fire her up, and she does fire up. Laila-Jewel has fueled her. I kick back that stand.

"**HEY! HEY! HEY! STOP!**" shouts the H&R person coming after us.

"**RIVER!**" Laila-Jewel is shouting, running for the hangar too.

The XY seems to have lost whatever fierceness he had. He's staggering all over the place from the run. I grab him—"Get on!"—then grab his arms and wrap them around me—"Hold on!"—and I fire on out of there.

CHAPTER 21
HARVEST

I rev my bike harder than I've ever revved any machine before, while my collapsed brain tries to quietly examine the wreckage of the situation. What have I done?!

It gets harder and harder to think straight as my whole body freezes. My hands are ice numb with cold almost immediately; my feet soon join them. My brain, with no helmet to shield my skull, feels at one with my face: stiff with cold. Even my eyeballs feel frozen. The XY is slumped against my back—slumped but somehow managing to cling on. Every time I feel those arms slip, I catch myself wondering, *Should I just let him fall? What if I just let him fall?*

He'd be hurt. I could go to get help, and someone else would have to make the decisions.

But every time those arms slip, before I can even make that dreadful choice, those arms wake up. Those arms grip like a vise.

They grip tighter when it becomes apparent that someone is coming after us. That's what it feels like—like those arms know what I don't even know myself…not at first, not for sure. I just catch weird, subtle shifts of light in the darkness. It comes and goes. Comes and goes. No side mirrors on a scrambler, so I have to glance back—there is nothing, and nothing, and nothing. Until we hit a run of straight road. I glance back—we are being followed. Headlights blast across the dark land. A car, far behind us, but coming for us.

When it comes to a choice between the main road and the sorry wreck of road where I first found Mason, I buzz past, then screech to a halt.

His arms grip tighter than ever as I reverse.

I'm going with option B: shortcut through the woods.

We hit the first stretch of rotten road, bike bouncing as I weave to avoid the places where the trees have bucked up the asphalt.

I can do this. I know this road.

Twenty miles on, I'm regretting it. My brain has completely stopped thinking. That doesn't matter too much right now, but my body is so freezing cold I can hardly control the bike. I cannot feel my own hands. Twice, I can't brake hard enough and quick enough to control the bike. Twice, I somehow get away with it— her suspension is superb; she hits the branches of storm-fallen trees, leaps, and bounces on.

Third time…not so lucky.

Luck. What is that? A thing Kate believes in.

I hit not a branch, but a whole tree, fallen. Hands too numb to brake in time. I hit it, and my bike stops where she is; we flip.

I lie on the once-was road dazed, confused, and feeling *lucky*—I can move every part of me. I pick myself up.

The XY man-boy is also lying on the road.

My bike is lying on her side, still growling power.

Can't waste a second of fuel.

I clamber over the tree, and I switch her off.

I clamber back over the tree to see the man-boy.

I think he might be dead…but he opens his eyes.

"You fucking idiot," he says.

I catch my breath. *I've just got to get home*—that's the only thought I have. Mumma will know what to do. And that's when I hear it: the low rumble of yet another autumn storm coming, and another rumble—higher, more variable, and yet more constant. The car.

It's got to be a four-wheel drive, the speed it's doing, the way the beams of its headlights are bumping around like that. Bam! Bam! Bam! Its headlights come flashing through the woods.

Bam. Its beams blast us.

I clamber back over the tree, and I fire up my bike. There's only one way past the obstruction: down, into the woods, then back up again.

And as I come back up onto the once-was road, my frozen brain grabs on to the thought: *Perhaps I should ditch him…*

I hesitate when I should not have hesitated; he pounces onto the back of the bike and the grip clamps.

I outrun the car for a good ten miles more. It had to back off and consider how to get around that tree, but get around the tree it did. I don't even have to look back to know it's there, bouncing and revving behind me. When the road through the woods forks, I choose my direction: I am not going home.

I do not want to lead this trouble to my home—that's what I think.

But this trouble? It takes fuel.

I push my scrambler hard up the other side of the valley. I'm critically low on fuel. The shortcut, even with this detour, *is* a shortcut, mile-wise, but it has guzzled what was in the tank. I'm ahead of that car, but it is still coming. My frozen brain manages one thought: *We're going to have to run for it*. I kiss my frozen hand, and I pat my bike goodbye. Then I spot my opportunity, grab it, and veer off the road.

"What the hell are you doing?!" the XY behind me shouts as we bump up into the woods.

My opportunity was not such a great one. I thought it might be a path, but it's a dead end—an end that dies just yards from the road. I brake before the woods brake for me, as they are suddenly impenetrable. I switch off and kill my lights.

"We're going to run out of fuel," I tell him, getting off the bike. "We'll go on foot."

"Go on foot to where?!"

230

"The village. It's just over the hill." Ah, I hear that car engine! "We need to hide the bike! Help me! Hurry!"

I have ahold of the handlebars. He's still on the bike. Headlight beams blast through the trees.

"Hurry!" I urge him. "Quick! *Get off!*"

He swings himself off, and I shove my bike to the ground, grabbing up anything and everything to cover her—fallen leaves, branches, bracken fronds. My frightened hands even grab and dump the mossy rocks from a once-was wall, and he helps. He helps, and I pull him away, deep into the dying bracken, just before the car bounces into sight, its beams blasting us but not seeing us.

It passes.

I ease my breath. His breath, hard in my ear, does not ease.

"Mason's alive," I tell him to calm his panic.

"That so?" he says.

"Yes!" I whisper, smiling in the darkness, waiting for amazement, for demands for explanations that I will struggle to give; waiting, above all, for joy.

"Lying bitch."

That is his reply.

His head mashes down on mine. For a half of a moment of what was left of who I used to be, I think there's something wrong with him. It. Not him. **It.** What else do you call someone who does this to a person?

There *is* something wrong with it. ***It*** is wrong.

Its lips crash against mine, poisonous and ugly. Its body presses.

I push it away. I push so hard—but it grabs back harder. So hard my shoulders feel the physics of escape. Tilt angle. Weight mass. We're on a slope. I roll.

It tips off me, rolls, its hands gripping my overalls so I am dragged, tipped, onto it. Physics. I flip and I roll, the slope in my favor, so steep its hands are wrenched free as I tumble, crashing down.

I am lying in the woods on the once-was road. Branches like bones above me.

I hear it swearing and snarling, trying to pull itself out of the tangle of brambles.

I get up and I RUN.

I race up through the woodland. This isn't my side of the valley, but I know it well enough as I get into it, and I know woods. The thing behind me doesn't know them at all—and it *is* behind me. I hear it as it comes after me. My sense, in as much as I have any sense right now, is that this *creature* is as clueless about the woods as Mason was when I found him. It crashes and blunders.

I'm fast but—"HEY!"—every time there's a flash of lightning, it spots me.

FLASH—"HEY!" *FLASH*—"HEY!"

And like Mason claimed he was fast, this blunderer…really is. I thought Mason was a man. He's a boy. This *it* is full grown. Whatever made it slurry and slow has worn off. It blunders—but it's fast.

When I get to the top of the ridge, I pause, panting, hugging

232

an ancient, wind-bent ash tree. All I have to do is get across the open land. That's all I have to do. Get across the place the trees have yet to claim for their own, the place with the rocks where Plat and I lie. Then I can get down into the woods I know so well. I can lose it for sure there. I can get home.

Its hand grabs my shoulder—

"No use runnin'," it tells me, shoving me down to the ground.

My hand grabs out into the woodland that I love, reaching for help, finding moss, leaves, and…from the feel of the bark alone—so smooth—I know it is ash. From the weight of it in my hand, I know it is healthy. A branch struck down by the storm, by the weather that can never forget.

I whack it. I whack it right around the head.

It is not enough.

"Angry now," it says, clutching its bleeding face.

So am I.

I'M NOT GOING TO MAKE IT, a voice inside my head says. WE'LL SEE ABOUT THAT, another voice says. A voice I never knew I had inside me.

I am running, and I race across the open ground—the moor—branch in my hand, running for safety.

The place Plat and I call our own. The rocks.

It is right behind me. I cannot outrun it. I make the same choice as I did on my bike. I brake. I turn. I am choosing a different route. I whack it.

It falls—oddly. It falls like a person who did not expect to fall.

233

CRACK.

It is not the impact of branch on face. It is not lightning.

It's his head. On the rocks.

Blood floods dark.

The storm flashes.

It's red. That blood. It's red. It's bright *goddamn* red.

I try to revive him.

I crash down through the woods.

Not on my path. Not on anyone's path.

I can't hear them.

I can see them. The whole village is assembled for the ha-ha-harvest do. This is what I should have been doing all day, preparing for the harvest supper. It is such a fun night.

The community studies room is hung with flags and festooned with hops, and trestle tables groan under piles of goodies: cakes and a cider barrel and pumpkins and vegetables to be shared out and apples. Apples. Everywhere, apples.

I can see the swan that's been caught and killed and roasted. Our tradition. All swans in the once-was were untouchable, belonging only to the royal family. The carcass is eaten down to its bones already. I can see Sweet clutching its enormous wings, uncooked, the feathers so beautiful. I can see the plan in her mind to wire them so she can wear them. I can see Granmumma

234

Rosie's arthritic hands collapsed on the piano she'd have been forced to play all night; Granmumma Dora's and Heloise's mouths closed on the song they were belting out with Tamara and Jade; Silver-Moon holding the drumstick she just crashed a cymbal with; Lenny releasing her loving hold on her beautiful, soulful electric guitar; Kate, on bass guitar as reluctantly as ever, grimly yanking out the power jack.

I can see them. I can see hands wipe swan grease and cake crumbs from mouths that have stopped chewing. I can see Plat, ready to run to me. I can see Mumma. I can see Mumma's love for me colliding with things I cannot imagine. And I can see you, Kate.

It's your face I see hardest. Your eyes. Your eyes that somehow know what has happened.

I can see all of this.

I can see them.

I can't hear them.

All I can hear is my own breath—in-out-in-out-in-out-in-out-in-out-in-out-in-out-in-out-in-out-in-out-in-out-in-out. All I can hear is the terrified *whoosh* of blood in my ears.

There is blood on my hands. The blood of another. On my hands, on my face, on my lips. I grabbed his head. I grabbed it, fastened my mouth onto his, and tried to breathe life into his body. I pumped hard on his chest.

I am covered—*covered*—in his blood.

And I am still carrying the branch. Even when I knew for sure it was dead, I somehow couldn't leave without that branch. Its bark is so smooth in my bloody hand. Ash, healthy ash. *Fraxinus.* Meaning spear. It's a hard wood to work, I know from Kate. She also said that in the most ancient once-was, long before she was born, ash was thought to connect the entire world—roots in hell, branches in heaven. Stem of a trunk on Earth. People thought of that tree as a goddess.

I do not believe in any such thing.

It is a branch in my hand.

Sound bursts in. There's so much sound now. There's so much activity. There's so much rushing to help me. I hear cries of fright. I hear cries of "River?!"

Oh, Plat, I even hear you.

And my own voice, speaking to Kate.

"You said they weren't dangerous."

A DECISION

CHAPTER 22
TRADE

I am vibrating with the deed.

I have done it. I have done the thing they said men did. I have killed.

I told them where the body was. I know Plat is up there now, in the rain, with the others, picking that dead *man* off the rocks. Carrying *him* down through the woods.

I have refused to wash. I am not ready to wash. As I sit at our kitchen table, I can feel the dead man's blood drying on my skin, tightening it. My hands—my killer hands—rest either side of a cup of tea, but they cannot be warmed. There is a chill inside them so deep I expect they will be forever cold. I wish I could say they feel disconnected from my body. I wish I could say something like that. But my whole body, my whole mind—all of me—feels very, very connected. Very connected and very cold. I have killed.

There is only Mumma, Kate, and me.

And Mason, our secret.

Only Mumma, Kate, Mason, me, and the deed.

I have told them everything. I have told it very clearly, from the airport to the impact, and without even a tremor in my voice. Only a warm person would falter, and I am a frozen person. I am a frozen person encased in a tightening skin of XY blood.

"Is that where you ran from, the airport?" Kate, grim faced, asks Mason.

He hasn't said a word. His head is slumped forward.

"Yes," he says, looking up. "If you're going to hell, you're gonna die anyway, so I ran."

"What on earth are you talking about?" says Mumma.

"Hell. That's where they were sending me. The place where they dump the baddest of the bad. Unit Zero. Supposed to be some kind of prison, but there ain't no rules at all there. You go, you die."

"There's no such place," says Mumma.

"There'd better not be," says Kate.

"Stones bounce, huh?" Mason says. "You tellin' me I've been lied to about hell too? What would you know?"

"I think it's really highly unlikely that such a place exists," says Mumma—more to Kate than Mason.

"It does, and that's where I was going."

"No, you weren't," says Mumma, staring at the table.

"Zoe-River," Kate says, "I asked you before. I asked you what you know about this."

"I didn't know—before. I didn't know."

"I raised your mumma and I raised you. I've pretty much raised your daughter. I did not bring *any* of you up to sit at this table and lie to me."

"I didn't know. And then I found out. About two weeks ago."

"Found. Out. What?"

"It's confidential information."

"Not at this table, it's not."

My mumma looks up at Kate. "He was being sent to China."

"*Excuse me?*" whispers Kate.

"There's a trade deal in progress," says Mumma.

"We're *exporting* boys…" Kate speaks into the silence.

"Yes," says Mumma. "There was an outbreak of the virus in the Chinese Sanctuaries. They're in desperate need of XYs. Desperate need."

Mason laughs, hard and angry. "Have to be totally desperate if they'd take a boy like me… Wait! I get it! I'll bet you're telling them Chinese wimmin they're getting prime stock, ain't you?"

Mumma looks sick. "It doesn't matter what they're getting," she says. "We're trading sperm, not personalities."

Kate—she laughs. She actually laughs. It's not like Mason's angry bark. It's bitter mirth. "**Trading them for what?!** Oh! No! Don't tell me! What? Let me guess. Boys for…for *what*?! *Insects?!*"

We have had a lot more imported insects over the past year.

I've grown up eating them, but Kate, and even Mumma, took time to get used to the idea that they are an excellent, plentiful source of cheap protein. Cheap and plentiful in theory. Though our techniques have improved, it's so hard outside tropical zones to produce enough insects of a kind and a quality that people will eat. Insects need heat.

I need heat. I need…to find a way to not be frozen.

"The insects were a sweetener," Mumma says. "Negotiation gift."

"For **what**?"

"It's confidential information." I know my mumma well enough to know she means it this time—and Kate does too.

Kate points at me, in my too-tight skin of blood. "This is your trade," she tells Mumma.

"I never ever thought that River would be…in any way involved."

"Too late now," says Kate.

"We are world leaders in IVF," says Mumma. "We have *the* most advanced IVF program. We have nothing that the world needs except a reliable, virus-proof supply of sperm."

"No, you ain't," says Mason. "You *ain't* got sperm. That's all I'm good for to you, isn't it? That's all I'm good for."

There is a silence of a whole new kind. You could call it an imported silence, because it comes from so many different places. No one owns this silence. It doesn't even belong to us: to Mumma, to Kate, to Mason, to me. It is bigger than all of us.

"I am so tired," my mumma says. She works day and

night—long days and long nights—but I've never heard her say that before, not in the way she is saying it right now. "We have to make some decisions. There is no way this will not be investigated," she mumbles.

"We could bury the body," Kate says in a low, cold voice. A low, cold, desperate voice. "We could just bury it. Deny all knowledge."

"I want to wash now," I say out loud, scratching at my own skin. Flecks of dried blood peel off—ping off—in every direction. "I WANT TO WASH! **I'VE GOT TO WASH!**"

I sit in the bath. Yes, I am having a bath because this is—is it not?—a *special* occasion. I feel like the water should be red, but it's not—it's just mud grubby, with a terrible tinge of pink. My mumma is washing me. My mumma hasn't washed me since I was a baby.

"This is not your fault," my mumma is saying over and over. "None of this is your fault."

CHAPTER 23
IT IS AGREED

I don't remember falling asleep.

I don't even remember going to bed. My mind and my body finally disconnected.

I do remember waking up. I remember waking up and creeping, not to my mumma or to Kate or to go outside and breathe in the cold night and the moon and the stars, but to Mason's room. It feels as though it will never truly be my room again.

I didn't knock. I just went in. He was not in the bed that I could see—I could see enough in the dark to know that the hunched shape on my window seat was him. My window seat, where I have liked to sit and watch the sky.

I join him. I sit at the opposite end of the window seat. I do not pull my legs up onto it as I have always liked to because there is not room for both of us. If I pulled my legs up, we would have to touch. I do not want to be touched by an XY. Not ever again.

We are silent, just looking out at the sky, though there is no sky to see. It is clouded. Hard to tell in such dark, but the clouds seem low and heavy.

I don't quite know why I have even come here. I think there are questions I want to ask. That's true, but more than that… It's the strangest feeling. It's the violence. He has come from it. He has come from a place no one else around me knows or could even begin to understand. Only Kate seems capable of imagining it, but as far as I know she has not, for *instance*, ever actually killed someone. I have.

I am in an opposite world now. That's how I feel. My world was love and duty and courtesy. My world was kindness and help, and I didn't even realize it, how kind and helpful it was. Why would I? It was my *whole* world. Now it has been split, and here I am, seeking out the company of one who has lived on the other half of a divide I never even knew existed.

Words will not come.

"Can't see no stars tonight," he says after a time. "I like 'em. I had a window, back in U-Beta. Couldn't see anything much out of it. We got walls—big walls—all around the place. But the sky? That I could see. I can tell you most every star in it. There's shapes! There'd be the panther," he says, pointing at nothing but dark cloud. "That's got a claw to it. And the lizard—that crawls almost flat on its belly. 'Cept if you look hard enough, that lizard's got legs. And the snake got its head rearing up like it's about to attack."

I am quiet. A strange, strange thought is happening in my head about how the stars got named and by whom. I think I know what he is talking about: how the constellations we should be able to see would look if those clouds weren't in our way.

"You thought you were going to prison. To hell? What for?"

That's what I say; I'm not even sure if I mean to say it. It's just that I feel so bad right now, so deeply troubled, that I somehow need to know how a person could feel worse. I need to know what terribleness would take a person to a place where they would choose death over life.

"I stabbed someone."

"Did you kill him?"

"No. I ain't a killer."

At those words, I slump.

"Christ! Sorry, River—"

"Did you *want* to kill him?"

"Did you?"

"I...wanted to stop him. I just wanted it to stop."

"That's how it was for me too. I wanted to stop Lion, and it didn't seem like there was any other way. Lion! Never met a boy that chose himself a more stupid name. You ain't got no name otherwise 'cept 'boy,' but *Lion*?! Who'd choose that? That's a name says 'pick on me.' Only no one did because—hey. Guess what? In Z-Beta the FU is called *Killer*. That'd be another stupid choice of name, but Killer he was. Father of the unit?! He was the meanest of the mean, but, oh, Killer loved his li'l pet Lion."

"Why did you do that?" I ask quietly. "Why did you stab that boy?"

"'Cause he was gonna stab Jed. Jed was my friend. Where I come from, you can't have friends. You'd better not get to caring about a person. You'd better not let that kind of stuff show. All you've got is Code of Honor. And the code…it ties you to whomever."

"Like you and me?"

"S'pose. I don't even know about that anymore. I don't know anything, do I?"

He shifts about on the window seat. "Reckon after Jed, you are the closest thing to a friend I've got."

"What happened to them? What happened to these people?"

"Well…I stabbed Lion, I did. Mess of blood like you've never seen…"

He trails off. I have seen a mess of blood. I have been covered in it.

"Lion got right up off his sickbed and did for Jed. End of. Jed…he's killed. Dead and gone. Me? I got a one-way trip to hell."

If he'd told me any of this sooner, I wouldn't have believed such a nightmare of a world could be possible. Now I know… and I feel I am now part of this nightmare. And if he had told me, would it have stopped me from letting *that man* out of the container? Perhaps. Perhaps not.

"You shouldn't feel bad for what you did," he says. "I met

plenty in them units I'd have killed if I could. Not just stopped: killed. Plenty *any* boy would have killed. He even tell you his name, this one you did for?"

"No."

I've killed a man with no name.

We sit in silence for a moment, both staring at our invisible, imaginary beasts in the sky.

"He…had a beard, like you, only more of it," I say. That alone—the memory of that alone—makes me WAKE UP. Makes me feel SICK. I get up from *my* window seat. "And he was older and…"

On my own face, in the darkness, I draw it—the slash of the scar from his lip to his cheekbone.

Mason draws in a massive gulp of breath. "River!" he breathes out, his voice too loud in the silence of the night.

"Be quiet!" I tell him. I cannot stand this. I cannot stand to think about that *man*. I truly can stand no more. Of any of this. I walk out.

I leave the door open behind me. It's his business to close it.

I have no interest in closing doors or opening them. I have no interest.

With this whole situation, I am done.

♀ ♂

I suppose I do manage to sleep again. It doesn't feel like it, but when my eyes were last open, it was still night, and now…it is

248

day. Plat is sitting on my creaky cot, the house and the whole village quiet around us. The silence blasts. And me not even noticing it at first. Just like I don't even really notice how strange the light is.

"Oh, Plat!"

We hug for a very long time.

"I didn't mean to do it, Plat. I didn't mean to. I mean, I meant to. I meant to hit him. I meant to stop him. I didn't mean to—"

"Shh! I know. Everyone knows. It wasn't your fault. It was *self-defense*."

"Self-defense... Plat, what is that? Is that a legal thing?"

"You had no choice, did you? It's not like you meant to kill him. You just wanted to stop him."

My hands—so cold still—feel the memory of the deed. "Plat...when I hit him, I think I wanted to stop him so much—"

"You could not possibly have known what would happen."

"No..."

My voice, my whole being, is quaking. I feel faint. "I can't breathe. Open the window!"

Plat jumps up, opens the window, and helps me over to it. I suck in lungfuls of autumn chill—such a chill. This is why the light is strange: in the night, snow has come. Snow in October, falling on a world that just won't be ready for it, so many plants and animals not prepared. But that's how it is now. That's how the once-was still is; they'd hoped the Earth would bounce back in no time, but it has been injured. Injuries take time to heal.

A pink scar under a dark beard.

"Shh!" soothes Plat, stroking my back, the silence outside so deep I swear I can hear the *swish* of her hand on me so loud it's deafening.

The silence outside. It's not just the first fall of snow.

S-I-L-E-N-C-E.

"Where is everyone?" I ask.

Plat—she just carries on stroking.

"I asked you a question," I say as calmly as I can. "Where is everyone?"

My words puff whiteness into the cool air. They are there, my words, and then gone. *Too bad, so sad*—

"What's going on, Plat?"

I'm facing her now. Feels like I'm facing some part of myself I don't really want to look at. A part of myself I am not ready to see.

"Where's Mumma? Where's Kate?"

"They said you should stay here."

"Where are they?" I'm pulling on clothes. My heart, pounding, already knows the answer. My brain wants to hear it spoken. "TELL ME."

"There's a 150."

"What for?"

"It's a court."

"About what?" I ask. My heart knows. My breath? It's short and sharp and hurting, like the outside is *in* here. Is *in* me.

A court? It can't be about me. It can't be anything to do with me, or else I'd have to be there. That's what my brain argues.

"*About what?*" I ask Plat again.

She won't even look at me. This question will not be answered.

"Oh, River, no. River, please," she says, following me as I crash down the stairs, as I shove sockless feet into my boots. No time to lace them. No time for a coat. "Don't go!"

I'm gone.

♀ ♂

Court normally happens in the community studies room at school. I run there, stumbling through the snow, Plat—I think—trying to plead with me...or was she just stumbling along with me? I'd stopped listening.

The community studies room is empty except for the littler ones, messing around when they should be studying. Messing around when at least some of them would normally be in court too—too young to vote, but not too young to learn. I suppose it has been Agreed that whatever is going on in court is not something they need to know. And as I am not there either, I suppose it has been Agreed that it is not something I need to know. But Plat? One look at her face tells me she knew the court wasn't here. She has let me run here. *Playing for time*, Kate would say.

"So where are they? The granmummas' house?" That's next most likely, though we've had courts and other community meetings in Lenny's barn before—and even in the church.

"I don't want you to go there."

That's all the answer I need. But Plat—Plat wouldn't miss a court.

"Why aren't you there?" I ask her.

"I've abstained," she says.

On what should have been my first 150 Court, I had to abstain because it was *me* facing restorative justice for punching Jade, which I did when she said the only reason I was so quickly accepted into the 150 was because of my mumma. I wouldn't have punched her for that; I punched her because of the nasty and very untrue things she said about Mumma. She said we were privileged, that Mumma abused her privilege, that we got new tech before anyone else did (we don't), and that the only reason Kate—"that old witch," Jade called her—was still alive was because my mumma had a guaranteed supply of inhalers. None of it was true. I felt Kate rage possess me. I punched. Jade punched back. I punched again.

Her nose bled. I came back to myself, and I sat and comforted her. Her arm reached up around my shoulder, and she comforted me back. But I was a 150 member, so it didn't—it couldn't—end there. Not for me. I had taken my first step into mummahood. I was becoming an adult, so I had to face justice as an adult.

The restoration decided upon was that Jade should apologize to me and that I should help her in whatever way she chose for six months or until she decided otherwise. I thought she never would decide otherwise. For a week, Jade reveled in the arrangement, even though the court was clear that I should be thanked by her for every deed done. It was a harsh Agreement; it tested us both. At the end of the second week, Jade had had enough. *Justice has been done*, she told the 150. I wasn't even that grateful to her for losing patience with the process. We both knew she shouldn't have said what she said and I shouldn't have done what I did.

Justice truly had been done.

Since then, I abstain a lot. A lot more than I should do. Abstentions are rare. So rare that if it occurs, it usually means a 150 member can't separate her feelings from the facts. Most of us, most of the time, are more than capable of making decisions. It's how we are raised, what we are raised to do, and it started right back in the granmummas' time, when life was one agonizing decision after another. Me, I love facts. I *know* facts. You give me a mathematical problem, and I will show you the answer, even if I have to skip a thousand stones to work it out. You give me Casey needs a hip operation versus Silver-Moon's mumma has leukemia, and I abstain.

Plat, she *never* abstains.

"Please, River, let's just go home. Yours, mine—I don't care! Let's just go home. We'll talk about it at home," Plat is saying.

I run, stumbling, for the granmummas' house.

"Don't do this," Plat says, putting herself between me and the granmummas' door. "Please don't do this."

I can hardly hear her. What I hear is the pounding of blood in my own ears from the running and—

Didn't it feel like this last night, when I killed a man? The crashing pounding of blood? The *whoosh* of life when a life has been taken.

"Give me one good reason," my brain forces me to say to Plat.

"Because I love you," she says.

Oh, Plat. P-L-A-T-I-N-U-M! I love you too. But Plat…she also loves the law and politics and justice and *reason*. "Because I love you" is hardly Plat's style. "Because I love you" makes no sense to me right now.

"It has been Agreed, River."

"What has?"

"The verdict."

My brain sputters.

I feel… I think I must feel as baffled and angry as Mason ever has. But I am not Mason. I have a right. I take hold of Plat's hand. I squeeze it. Then she stands aside.

I push open the door.

I scan the room, and the room scans me.

It looks so normal—and so *not normal*. Every sofa, every table, every chair, every everything in the granmummas' enormous kitchen, has been pulled to the sides so the 150 can cram in; even the doors to the never-used dining room have been flung open to accommodate the crowd.

They sit or stand, higgledy-piggledy, but roughly in a circle. That's what a court always looks like—no one separate, all in a circle.

I am in the middle of it. No one goes into the middle. I am in the middle.

In that circle, part of that circle, sits Mason.

He stares back at me…with just the slightest shake of his head. A quiet *no*, but around it, there's a ripple; evidently, the community has been introduced to Mason, and evidently many of those who are not granmummas are still struggling with the fact of his existence, just as I did.

I was right: none of the littler ones are in the court to observe. Only 150 voters: teens like me, the granmummas, the mummas—but not my mumma?! I scan the room again: no Mumma—only Kate, who gets up from her place next to Mason and comes to me and says, "You shouldn't be here," even as other neighbors get up—to comfort, to chide, to… I do not know what this is.

"Well, I am here," I tell her very quietly.

I'm not *biologically* related to Kate, but sometimes I feel more like her daughter than Mumma's. I *sound* like her sometimes. I do know that. *Sounds like* is not the same as *thinks like*. I do remind myself of that. I remind myself of that now.

"Everyone should sit down," says Yaz. "That includes you, River."

Yaz was deputized to be facilitator of the 150 when Mumma isn't around, but it turns out Mumma *is* around. Yukiko is holding an open notebook, filming the proceedings. An open notebook on which PicChat is up and Mumma's face is scanning the room—and sees me.

I see her register that. Register me. Register me and ignore me.

Granmumma Rosie gets up from her chair and goes and perches on the arm of a sofa. I am being given a seat. This is not the usual way of things; if you're fit to stand, you stand. Plat pushes through the circle to stand behind the chair. I go, and I sit, and I am grateful to sit. My knees are shaking. Plat's loving hands rest gently on my shoulders.

"Yaz, what was the result of your investigation?" my mumma asks.

I look at Mason.

"That I'm guilty as hell," he says, looking straight back at me.

"Yaz?" my mumma says.

"Manslaughter," says Yaz.

"That's right!" says Mason. "I slaughtered him!"

Yaz wheels over to him. "This is being recorded now," she advises. "We're going for the lesser charge. On the basis of the evidence."

"Basis of—lesser'n what? What are you saying?"

"Lesser than murder. It was not deliberate. It was accidental. It was self-defense."

Mason squints at her.

"And it was not, in any way, premeditated."

"Pre-what?"

"You didn't think about killing that asshole prior to… *accidentally* killing him," Kate tries to help out.

"Oh NO! NO, NO, NO, NO!" cries Mason. "WAIT THE HELL UP HERE! I thought about killing that bastard about ten thousand times a day!"

256

"That's not the point," Kate murmurs. "Trust me: you didn't mean to kill him."

My heart—my deafening, pounding heart—feels like it could burst straight out of my chest and lie there beating, bloodily, in front of everyone.

"But *I* did it," I tell them all. I do that; I speak.

"Got witnesses says I did," Mason blusters on. "Whole village of she-wolf witnesses. And I did." He seeks out the camera. "I did it, and I meant to."

Sweet has a toy, a kaleidoscope. She loves it. I don't love it. It makes me dizzy, makes the world split and twirl. I feel like I'm looking through it right now. I feel like I'm *feeling* through it.

"*Accidental?!*" he says to Yaz. "This ain't no accident. I *meant* to kill him."

"But it's in your best interests to—" Yaz tries.

"My best interests?" Mason rages. "*My* best interests? Put it down as I meant to kill him or the deal's off."

"What deal?" I ask out loud, but to no one in particular. My heart lies like a stone at the bottom of the kaleidoscope world.

"I've got a reputation," Mason says to Kate. "And maybe that's all I've got, but I'm telling you—"

"Stop filming," Kate says to Yukiko, and Yukiko does. "Scroll back. Wipe the conclusion. Recap. Charge is murder. Plea is guilty."

The court ripples with consternation, and I see Kate stare Mumma down.

Plat gently hugs my shoulders.

257

"But *I* did it," I tell them all, my heart pounding with fright.

"This is a done deal, sweetie pop." Kate speaks across the room to me. "Don't mess this up."

"But I did it…"

"Do not mess this up or we're all in trouble. All of us."

Every head in the room nods. My community is unanimous. Our 150 is united in Agreement…and Mason is too. As he nods, he fixes me with a stare and a long, purposeful grin. A long, purposeful grin I don't even have a name for—sad? Glad? Angry? Wistful? A kaleidoscope grin.

I sit back down, feel Plat's sweet hands curve around my shoulders, offering a comfort I can't even feel.

"Are we ready to record this?" asks Yukiko.

Granmummas, mummas, and the oldest teens nod. Mason nods.

Yukiko hands the community notebook to Casey.

"I don't think I can," she whispers. "I mean, I just don't think—"

"I'll do it," says Plat, stepping forward.

"Your career!" exclaims Zara, her mumma.

Plat, she just takes hold of that notebook. "Recording," she says.

She points the camera at Yaz.

"A *man* was killed—"

"Murdered," Mason chips in—is waved down to silence by Kate.

"A man was murdered. Method and location information online with this report. Pictures same. Witness reports same.

258

Postmortem report"—it's only now, when I see Yaz look to her, that I even realize Akesa is in the room too—"available shortly. Cause of death: blow to head—"

"De-liberate," Mason blurts.

"—resulting in catastrophic brain hemorrhage," Akesa says.

"We have the perpetrator," Yaz says.

Plat turns the notebook camera to Mason.

He runs a hand through his hair. That's what he does, I know, when he is anxious. Is it only me who sees that hand is shaking?

"Yo, hey," he speaks to the camera. "It was me. I did it. I meant to. No one asked me to 'fess to nothing. I hid out in the woods for weeks after I run from here. No one"—he shoots a look at Yukiko, who mouths words—"aided or a-betted," he says slowly. "I didn't get no help from no one, and I did do it, and I did mean to."

Plat shifts the notebook away. There's a ripple in the room as Mason reaches and grabs it back. "Code of Honor," he speaks into the camera.

Yaz takes the notebook off Plat, speaks directly into the camera.

"We have an admittance of responsibility," she says. "Assessments confirm that although the perpetrator is suffering from depression and anxiety—"

"What? Who's saying that? Did you say that?" Mason demands of Akesa.

"—his mental health is otherwise sound, although he appears to have a variety of delusions of a...*culturally transmitted* nature."

259

"Now what is that supposed to mean, she-wolf?!" Mason snarls.

"We don't know how to restore," Yaz says to my mumma.

"Understood," my mumma says. "As the case involves a *boy*, it'll be decided by the National Council. Thank you to the 150 for their deliberations and for Agreeing not to discuss this case outside the court…and to the accused, for being so helpful. The court can go home."

There's a murmur of—relief? Is it that? It's so hard to tell which way is up, which way is down, which image is true.

I look at the window because I cannot look at anyone else. It's snowing again. I hear a single flake falling. Falling. It screams, sounds like a jet crashing.

♀ ♂

"Come home now," Kate says.

The room…it's empty. I don't know how it got to be empty.

Only Plat and Kate and Mason remain.

"Come on," Plat echoes, helping me to my feet.

My legs are numb. I can hardly walk. I walk.

In the lane, stumbling home through fast-falling snow, I say again, "But I did it."

"He's taking the rap," Kate says, breathing so deep on the night air a fear about her lungs manages to burst into my stunned brain. "D'you understand?"

"They talked to him," Plat is saying. "He Agreed."

"He Agreed," Kate echoes.

"Code of Honor," Mason whispers to the sky, astonished by the falling of snow.

CHAPTER 24
RIGHT AND WRONG

"It's not right."

That's all I keep saying. To myself—and to Kate, and to Plat, and to Mason. And what gets said in between chills me colder than I have ever been.

"You're worth ten of him," Kate says, sitting me down at the kitchen table. "Sorry, Mason, but that's how it is."

It's shocking—so shocking—to hear these shocking things coming out of Kate's mouth, but what is apparent to me is that this isn't some kind of hate or anger speaking; it's logic drenched in sorrow. Muffled by snow.

"Guess so," says Mason.

"But…he's a *boy*," I say. I'm not even sure what I mean by that—not anymore. I was brought up to believe they were precious. Dangerous but precious?

"And he'll still be a boy, wherever he ends up," Kate says. "D'you understand? It's his job to *produce sperm*, and it always will be. Maybe in another sixty years, it'll be different. Maybe it'll take another hundred years. It's harsh, but that's how it is. You though… River, I don't know what restoration would get decided on if you took the blame for this, but I'm pretty sure it'd be bad news—for your future. For *our* future."

"*Took the blame?* I DID it. The whole village knows I did it! This is not right."

"You're the only one thinks that," says Mason. "I mean, ain't that how it works around here? If the most people think it's right, it is right."

"We'd just say that it had been Agreed," Plat says quietly. "But Kate *is* right: you've got to think about your future."

"What about *his* future?"

"What about it?" Mason snorts.

"His future is set," says Kate, grimly.

"The way you're talking…you're making it sound like he's a different species or something."

"Ain't me that's different," he mumbles.

"He might as well be a different species," says Kate. "Didn't what that man did to you prove that?"

I feel sick at the memory of it, sick and angry. And I wonder what it's going to take, and how long it's going to take, to find a place to put that memory—far, far away from everything that is good in my world.

"That wasn't Mason."

"No. But Mason wasn't *raised* like you."

"He's still a person though, isn't he?"

"Technically, yes."

"I've read about this," Plat says, "about the way some men used to talk about women—now listen to how you're talking about *him*."

I've never seen this, Plat challenging Kate. Makes my numbed brain—heating with anger—wonder again why Plat abstained.

"It's *not* the same."

"How is it not the same?"

"Because in between then and now, we nearly got wiped out. Them and us. All of us. The whole of the human race. This isn't *prejudice*. This isn't *sexism*. This isn't anything other than practicality. Wake up, girl! It is **not** the same!"

"Then how come it *sounds* the same?" says Plat.

Kate sighs, gets up, and shoves the kettle on the stove.

"You weren't there. You don't know how it was," she says. "You, River, the mummas, all of you: you're clueless."

Kate says that to me a lot. Usually it's about whatever I'm wearing. She says it wasn't just men who died; it was fashion.

"No voting, no education, no legal rights, no decent jobs, no decent pay, no control over *fertility*. Wasn't that how it was?" says Plat.

"Not in my time. You're muddled on your facts. Things had changed."

"Not for all women."

"No." Kate turns around. "For sure. And for the rest of us, in the countries where everything was supposed to be just peachy… it wasn't at all. It was a different kind of bad. It was a sneaky, poisonous kind of bad. So sneaky I hardly even knew it at the time. Equal but not equal. Different *standards*. And it was normal."

The kettle screams, so quick to boil in our superheated house. Kate shoves it off the heat.

"It was so normal we never really questioned half the things that went on," she says. "I never questioned it. I never even thought about it until River came along."

She sits back down at the table. She grabs my dread-frozen hands, clutches them within her age-frozen hands—her hands that are tool-cut scarred from years of hard work.

"You have freedom," she says to me. "I didn't even know what it meant until I saw you. Sweetie pop, if my mother could see you, she'd be so amazed and so proud and"—Kate wells up; she doesn't really do positive expressed emotion—"she'd also tell you to shave your legs and use mascara."

Kate's mumma sold cosmetics to her neighbors. That's how she made *money* Kate's daddy couldn't touch. Her money.

Kate shrieks with crazy laughter. Emotion overload.

"Ah! I'm just kidding! Well, I'm not, because you really would look a whole lot better if you'd—oh, don't listen to me. My mother, she would have been blown away by you," Kate says, wiping away those rare tears before they can fall.

Mason, he shifts back his chair slowly—a quiet grumble.

"And I think your mother would be proud of you," Kate tells him.

"I don't know what she-wolf dropped me," Mason says.

It's a savage comment. If one of the littler ones said anything like it, we'd…just ignore it. You've got to circle back around to such obvious expressions of anger. Kate performs a handbrake turn:

"And your father would be proud too," Kate says.

"I doubt it," Mason says. "And he ain't here to ask, is he? She just killed him."

"For which I do most sincerely thank you," Mason says into the silence that follows.

The silence continues.

"Your father…?" Kate says.

"I tried to tell you last night, but you up and left," Mason says to me.

"He was your *father*?"

"Unit father! I don't know who my *father* is any more than anyone does—any more than you know who your she-wolf mother is!"

"My mumma…she's my mother."

Mason, he stares at me. "She's your *real* mother?"

"Yes."

All this time, it never occurred to me that he would think otherwise. The resemblance alone, surely? My heart fills with pity for him.

"What will happen to Mason?" I ask Plat.

"Whatever the National Council decides," she says.

"He'll probably end up in goddamn China," says Kate. "I am sorry, you know," she says to Mason, "but we can't challenge this whole trade thing right now…even if we wanted to. There's just too much at stake." She looks at me.

My head is full of thoughts. Thoughts I don't want to be there. Thoughts that feel as alien in my head as Mason being here in the first place. I am used to thinking hard, but it's math I know. Correct and incorrect. Things you can work out, even if it takes a long time. Seems to me people have been puzzling over this whole girl-boy thing for hundreds—maybe even thousands—of years, so how would someone like me, who never really listened in community studies *and* only met a boy for the first time in her life a few weeks ago *and* pretty much hates any kind of slippery debate—how would someone like me know what's right and wrong here?

"If Mason were a girl," I say to Plat, "what would the restoration be?"

"The Agreement is clear," she says. "Usually the victim's family would have the first say on what the restoration would be. Although there isn't really any 'usually,' there are so few cases."

"What if the victim had no family?"

"I don't think that has ever happened."

"But what if?"

"The communities involved would be asked. They'd be consulted anyway, as part of the process. As would the perpetrator's family."

"What if the perpetrator had no family?"

Plat shrugs.

"But he has," says Kate. "He has! Mason has a mumma! Everyone has a mumma!"

Kate places the ring on the table in front of me. It is her *engagement* ring. Silver, with a diamond. A once-was ring, a gift from her boyfriend. It's not that people don't wear such things anymore. They do; people exchange and wear all kinds of rings. Mumma wears one for the National Council and another she won't talk about. I grew up thinking it was for me until the day I told Kate I thought that, and Kate laughed, so I asked Mumma, and Mumma said it was *also* for me. But *this* ring? It is so precious to Kate, yet never ever worn. I have only been allowed to see it a few times in my life. I have never been allowed to touch it, and now she is giving it to me.

"We should never have asked the National Council to decide restoration," Kate says. "Plat is right: his *mumma* must decide."

Mason, Plat, and I are silent—as we have been for the past ten minutes as Kate shouted on the phone to Akesa, to the granmummas, to persons unknown, as she rummaged in her bedroom.

"We can find out who she is. All those tests Akesa did? Let's just say his DNA info is not secure. It could be hacked—very easily. It could be matched—very easily. Uh! Do I have to spell it out for you?" she says as we all stare blankly at her.

"Clueless," she mutters. "You're going to go to some people who can locate his mumma. Now you take this," Kate says to me, sliding the ring across the table with one work-scarred finger, "and you go to this address."

I see her finger hesitate for a second before it leaves that ring. The first time it has been out of her possession in sixty years. She lays a crumpled scrap of paper on the table: *BABYLAND, BULLRING*, it says, block capitals in her atrocious handwriting.

I look up at her, still not quite understanding—or perhaps not quite *willing* to understand.

"You're saying this isn't right, aren't you? You're saying it's not right Mason should take the blame," she says to me.

I nod, uneasy.

"If you've seen a problem, you have to come up with a solution, don't you? Well, lucky you, I've thought of it for you. You take this ring to this place and you trade it for his mother's identity."

"And then what?" Mason jumps in.

"And then you'll be safe," says Kate. "Trust me: she'll keep you safe."

"I don't trust no—"

"Oh, put a sock in it, would you? You'll be fine. And if you're not fine, you can come right on back here and have a good old whine at me."

"No, I—"

"What? You'd rather be shipped to China? How gutless are you? This is a chance, and you need to take it."

Mason falls silent again.

I pick up the piece of paper as though holding it would make any of this—or her handwriting—any clearer. "I don't even know where this is," I tell her.

"The Bullring—it's in Birmingham?" Plat says.

"Correct," says Kate. "There's a train at 5:00 a.m., gets into Birmingham at seven. If you leave at four, you should be okay."

"The snow?" says Plat.

"Three then," says Kate. "Two thirty just to be on the safe side."

"By horse?" says Plat.

Kate frowns—so do I. But I'm thinking, *This is crazy and scary and typical Kate, but this* is *a thing I can do*.

"My bike can handle snow," I say, meaning I can handle snow. And then I remember: my bike is dumped in the woods, miles away, tank empty. There is the Bonneville in the workshop, but even if it could handle off road—and it can't—it is almost as precious to Kate as her ring; the only use it ever gets is a once-a-month trip up and down the lane—*So I know it's still alive*, Kate says.

"Can I take your bike?" I ask Plat.

"You can't take a bike. It won't matter if you even manage to wheel it a mile away before you start it up: everyone will hear."

"I'll wheel it two miles!"

"Better to take the little pony," Kate nods, in agreement with Plat.

I glance at the kitchen clock; just gone midnight now, though it could be somewhat wrong. I grab the phone Kate's been ranting on: 12:10 a.m. I recalculate based on ONE horsepower:

270

Milpy plodding in snow, in a bad mood—she's bound to be. She won't like this.

"I should go now."

"I'll get you some warmer clothes," she says to Mason. "Well, obviously you're going to have to take him with you," she says to the look of horror on my face.

"No. I don't want to."

"You *have* to take him."

"Oh. Wait, what?" says Mason. "No. I can't do that. No way. Did you see the way them she-wolves was around me back there?! All staring at me like I'm some kind of freak!"

"That's because you are a freak," says Kate. "To them, I mean. Because they know what you are. I mean—look: most of them have never seen a boy, or ever expected to—"

"They. Stared. It was…not *courteous*."

"Ha." Kate smiles. "So you're speaking the language now, are you? Your mumma's going to love that. Trust me, if we put the right sort of clothes on you, no one's going to bat an eyelid."

Mason tugs at his fuzzy beard.

"Facial hair is hardly unusual," says Plat.

"I never saw no one in that room with this much."

"That's because Hope's mumma wasn't there," mutters Kate.

"She abstained too?" I ask.

"No," says Plat. "She Agreed by proxy. She was too…*upset* to attend. The point is, *Mason*, facial hair is not an issue. Especially not in Birmingham."

"I wouldn't know anything about that," he says. "All I know is how a female is supposed to look."

Plat and I shrug helplessly at Kate, who rolls her eyes. "All right. I'll shave your face if it's going to make you feel better," she says.

"It will not make me feel better," he says.

"Oh, get over yourself," says Kate.

"Fuck you," Mason mutters, then glances up at us. Only Kate seems to be not remotely shocked by his words. He lowers his gaze.

Oh, but in that glance, I see it: his fear and his helplessness.

"River, I don't think you should go," Plat says. "Look, I wasn't thinking straight just now. I'm not disagreeing with the principle. I see the argument that *Mason* should be treated fairly, and I understand why Kate—and the rest of the granmummas—would want this."

"You understand *nothing*," says Kate.

"But I don't think you should go—with him—because we cannot be certain that he won't attack you, as that other *XY* did."

The memory, loose in me, chills my blood. Even Kate is quiet for a moment.

"Code of Honor," Mason says.

"What is that?" says Plat. "That means nothing. That's just words."

"That's all I've got," Mason says. "I wouldn't do that thing you're saying. I wouldn't hurt River. I owe her my life."

I don't feel relieved at hearing this. I feel again a burden I do not want to carry: his gratitude for having been treated like a human being. I want to be free of it. I want him gone. The kaleidoscope is back, being twisted this way and that. I did a thing I could never have imagined doing. I didn't mean to do it, but I did do it. And he is prepared to take the blame for it. Any which way it all twists, I see Mason—and I do not want to see him. I wish I had never seen him, but…

"I trust him," I tell them. And it astonishes me that this is so. "We need to hurry."

Kate nods, but still she turns to Mason.

"You listen to me," she says to him, pointing her scarred, shaking finger in his face, "if anything happens to my great-granddaughter, you will die. Slowly and painfully. We will hunt you down."

This is not so very far away from the kind of casual threat Kate would make to me in jest. She was particularly fierce with me when Plat and I pulled off the raft trip to Gloucester. But I have been hunted down; I know what it feels like to be running for your life—and so does Mason.

"I know it," he says.

"That's it?" says Kate. "That's all you've got to say?"

"What else am I supposed to say? You're issuing a threat. I'm telling you I've heard it."

"You could reassure me that nothing will happen to my granddaughter."

"I already did. Sayin' a thing twice ain't gonna make it any truer."

Kate scowls at him.

"Please, shut up now," I tell her, and we go to my poky room, Plat and I.

I am so grateful that she stays, hunched on my creaky cot, as I shove items into my backpack—no more than I'd take to my cousins' for a weekend stay, which seems too much. I won't be gone for more than a day, will I?

"How long do you think this'll take?" I ask her.

"It doesn't have to take any time at all," Plat says.

"Plat."

"River," she says, standing and putting her loving arms around me, "don't go."

"I have missed you so much," I tell her.

I have, I have, I have.

"But I'm going."

CHAPTER 25
THE CHILL

And so I go. I leave the village—my village. My everything.

Milpy doesn't like this, not one bit. Nor do I.

What I used to know is that there is nothing in this world that can hurt us. I knew there was no such thing as all the things people and horses used to be scared about.

Now I know some of those things exist.

One of them is right behind me.

We are not speaking. What is there to say?

He is shivering, shaking almost uncontrollably. The heat in the house was cranked up for him, but you'd think he'd be okay with his layers, even on this snowy night.

Finally, I can stand it no more.

"Here," I tell him, pulling off my riding cape, a huge water-proof tent of a thing. "Put this on."

"What about you?"

What about me? I've got my coat on underneath. I've got layers underneath that, but I'm facing the wind, and the wind is immediately poking its chilly fingers wherever it can. I'd rather deal with its ice than deal with—

"Just put it on, would you? And don't flap it around. Milpy doesn't like it."

Mason puts the cape on and scoots forward and wraps the cape around himself *and* me.

I feel myself tense, but it is very sensible. There is room for two. And if it were Plat—I wish or, in this situation, ANYONE else from the village, anyone else in the world—I wouldn't hesitate. And almost as soon as I think that, I do not hesitate. I button the cape up. I shove my hands through the armholes and gather up the reins.

His body is so cold inside this cape it feels like the wind is now at my back.

When Milpy stumbles, his arms grab around me. Through layers, I feel the grip of fingers, icier than the wind clutching, and I shudder.

"Sorry," he mumbles, withdrawing his hands.

"This is like in olden times," he says after a while. "You know, when there was knights and stuff, saving chicks."

I shift and turn my head to look at him. I mean, really, in *what* world…

"'Cept the horses was smaller then, I reckon," he says.

"She's a Shire horse," I tell him.

"Hobbit thing?!" he says.

"No, I mean she's meant to be big. It's her breed."

"That so?"

"Yup."

"You know about Hobbits and stuff, then?" he says after another long pause.

"Yeah, I…can't remember it that well, but everyone reads those kinds of books at some point, don't they?"

"Not me. K-Beta Unit Father used to shove on story discs when he was supposed to be doing whatever FUs are supposed to do. Y'know: fitness talks, lectures about antisocial behavior. He was all right in some ways. Sometimes."

"Z-Beta. That's what you said. You're from Z-Beta Unit."

"That was way down the line. I'm talking about K-Beta. I was…seven? Think I must have been. Started off in A-Beta. New unit every year."

I can't help myself. I calculate immediately. "That'd put you in G at seven," I say out loud.

"Not if you're bad. If you're bad, you skip units. You sink so fast it's like there's rocks tied to you. I saw that on a game. Had a choice to shoot a man or just tie him up, weigh him down, and then shove him into the river. So you think, save a bullet, tie him, shove his pockets full of rocks, and push, 'cept you do that and you can't be sure, can you? You can't be sure what's gonna happen. If you ain't tied him up tight enough or stuffed enough rocks into his pockets, any man'd find a way to get loose and rise again."

I hear the sound of skull on rock. In a flash of lightning, the sight of a flood of hot blood on cold, wet rock. I shut my eyes, squeeze them tight, to shut it out, as though shutting my eyes can make it not so.

"Maybe this is me rising," he says. "Or maybe I'm just sinking farther. It's kind of hard to tell. I am just glad you ain't got tangled in this too, River. Any more than you are, I mean. It's good that you're cutting yourself free."

Cutting myself free? That he sees it like that shocks and *annoys* me, but what is even more disturbing is my feeling of knowing with absolute certainty: I am never going to be free of this.

CHAPTER 26
BRITISH RAIL

"That's where we're going?" Mason asks, looking over my shoulder at the flood of lights on snow.

You can smell the smoke of the station guard's fire even from up here. We have stopped—that is to say, Milpy has stopped—at the top of the steep, twisting path that leads down to the station. A shortcut down from the road. A path I have decided we need to take. Time is not on our side.

"Yes."

"There wimmin there?"

"Yes." (*Who else would there be?*) "Come on," I tell him, unbuttoning the riding cape. "We need to get down."

As the cape falls away from me, it releases a fug of human and horse sweat so warm a little cloud of vapor puffs into the chill of the night—a night that's starry now: clouds gone, moon blasting, snow crisping with frost. I jump down…and he hesitates.

"Come on," I tell him.

"I can't."

"It's easy! Just swing your leg around and slide down."

"No. I mean…I can't. I don't want to go down there."

I look at his face in the moonlight. What I see on it is fear.

"You can and you will," I tell him. I'm telling it to myself really; I do know that. And I think, perhaps, he might almost know that too.

He shifts his leg around, manages to hang there for a moment, as I've seen the littlest of the littler ones do, climbing, when they are convinced the drop below them might require a parachute when really they are inches from the ground. He is inches from the ground. I tug the cape, and he falls, knees buckling, into the snow.

He gets up, dusting frost-powdery snow from his legs, shivering. Shaking.

"There's nothing to be afraid of," I tell him. That's what I say with my heart full of fear. "We're going to be fine."

I look down at the station. It looks warm and welcoming—like home.

I think about going home.

"You sure I look okay?" he's saying.

I look at him. He hands me the riding cape.

It's hard for me to say; he is so transformed. Under a garish, woolly hat, his shaved face looks thin and frightened—on top of a body that is bulky with layers. At Mason's own insistence, the layers include a dress of Kate's and breasts made of socks, which are visible beneath the shapeless, baggy sweater that was added on top, because the coat Kate also donated will not close up over the bulk. His sock-breasts have become dislodged. They look wrong. Wonky is normal, everyone's breasts are wonky, but one has migrated to shoulder height and both have become strangely lumpy. I lay my hands on his chest, and I wiggle and squish those socks into a decent shape and configuration.

Milpy stamps. *What is going on here?* she demands to know.

"There," I tell him.

"I look normal?"

Now really isn't the time to try to explain to him that people come in all shapes and sizes, dress in all kinds of ways. That's true for the village, and that's even more the case in Birmingham, from what I can remember. It's got to be five years since our last school trip, but I still recall being amazed at how many different kinds of people there were. However, he is also wearing socks over his rubber-hooved feet in snow. We didn't have any kind of footwear large enough, no boots that would fit him.

"Do I, River? You gotta tell me, because I got freakin' fear of them she-wolves."

And then there's his voice. That it's deep isn't a problem—plenty of people have deep voices. It's what that voice says that's NOT NORMAL.

His appearance is the least of our problems.

"Yes! But...look, you need to keep quiet, okay? Let me do all the talking."

"We gonna have to talk?! To she-wolves?!"

"*I'll* do the talking."

"Okay, River, okay," he says, shaking with cold…and fear?

"You put this on," I tell him, handing him back the riding cape. "We need to walk the rest of the way."

"Then you take it."

I'd love to. Any more of this chat and I'll die of cold (and nerves?) right here. "You put it on. I've got my coat."

He hesitates.

"Put it on!" I call over my shoulder as I grab up Milpy's reins and lead her on and down.

The moonlight is so bright, but this path, deep in snow, is treacherous—bad enough for humans, for Milpy, it's an outrage. I sense it's going to take a whole ha-ha-harvest's worth of carrots to make up for this.

"I'm sorry you ever even found me," he says. "I'm sorry about it all, River."

Yes, so am I, I'm thinking. But what has been found cannot be un-found. What has been done…cannot be undone.

I wish, with all my heart, that these things weren't so. But they are.

"Hush," I tell him.

I stop just before we reach the station. I choose a level patch on the snowy path where there's a collapsed and rotted once-was bench, a brass plaque (IN MEMORY OF EDWARD) hanging on by a single nail. I stop and I watch. An angry horse and a shaking boy wait with me. I've got no way of telling what the time is, and I do not want to miss the train. All I can do is watch as more and more cars and motorbikes and horses and vans and lorries and carts arrive.

Milpy, furious, is stamping her feet; Mason is stamping too—the cold must be eating into him from the feet up.

"Okay, let's go," I tell them as soon as the flow of arrivals slows. The train must be coming very soon.

The angry horse? She's eager to continue. The boy? He just comes trudging after us.

When we reach the station, I drape Milpy's reins loosely around the fence, so she'll think she's tied but won't hurt herself if she has a random panic, which is what Mason is having.

"I ain't never been on a train," he mutters, teeth chattering.

I've made him stand in his rubber hooves in the snow. Scared? Yes, he probably is. Freezing from the feet up? Definitely.

"Shh!" I tell him, heading for the waiting room. I stamp the snow off my feet before we go in, and Mason does the same, and I wish he hadn't because the socks he's wearing have frayed on the rocky path and his hooves are showing. I'm tempted to leave him outside, and I almost do. The waiting room is deliciously warm, so I go to shut the door behind me quick as I can, only to realize that my cape-and-hoof companion has failed to follow me, so I grab his hand and pull him in before anyone can complain about the heat from the blazing wood burner escaping.

The hard metal seats that used to be in the waiting room are dumped outside, rusting, and the room is filled with armchairs and sofas, on which people—mainly granmummas and littler ones—lounge, sipping tea or snoozing and now stirring at the blast of cold. The only positive thing to be said is that the room is dark apart from the glow of the fire and the notebook and lamp on the station manager's desk...but not dark enough: "Big sister! Where are your boots?!" a littler one pipes up as the room looks at us with weary half interest.

"She lost them," I tell the littler one as I smile and whisper *good morning* at the waiting passengers. I'm so glad it's so early—at any other time, courtesy would mean I'd need to formally introduce us; right now, everyone is too sleepy to care.

"Who are you?" the station manager asks—almost rudely. The train must be about to come in because she's tapping away on her notebook like mad, hurrying us on, glancing at a railway control console I don't understand on which lights are blinking. "Need names," she says. "And reason for journey."

I didn't even know we'd have to do this, sign in for this journey. On the school trip, someone must have done that for us. The station manager has her hand hovering above the keyboard.

"So...we're *May* and River."

She types superfast into her notebook.

"Going to the National Council."

She looks up at me. "Are you River of Zoe-River? From the tech village?"

"Yes," I whisper.

"Your mumma's our National Rep, isn't she?" she whispers back.

Whispering is no good in this place. Granmummas in that waiting room nudge each other as they sip final slurps of tea, pulling on boots and coats that are warming by the fire.

I nod. "Could you please take care of the horse? I've got horseradish vodka," I tell her.

The manager peers out through the window. In the darkness, Milpy is just an angry hulk of a shadow, but somehow, as though she knows we are speaking about her, she tilts her head. Moonlight glints off her eye. Yup, she is furious.

"I don't drink," she says.

"And honey! I've got honey!" And I do. Or rather, Mason does. I elbow him and he jumps to it, wrestling the backpack out from under the riding cape. He hands it to me, and I rummage and set TWO jars of honey down on the manager's desk. The crazy seasons make hard work for the bees, so honey is still a precious, precious sweet. Two jars is A LOT.

The station manager eyes them—as other eyes in the room are doing—then gently slides them back at me. "I don't need honey," she says. "Just tell your mumma we need another points guard at the interchange."

"Oh, I really can't…" That's what I start to say, whole roomful of people listening now. In my village, everyone knows me, knows I can't—and won't and wouldn't—make any kind of special plea.

"I've told my 150 that Ella needs assistance," the manager says.

"Assistance?!" a mumma in the room chips in, confirming my fear that everyone IS listening. "Her eyesight is going! She needs to stand down! She's dangerous!"

"She's a granmumma," another granmumma says. "Don't you forget that."

"I am not forgetting that," says the mumma. "How could you even think I would? How could any of us ever? She is still dangerous!"

"Train!" cries the granmumma, shaking the sleeping girl at her side because—THANK THE EARTH!—the train is rolling in.

"Tell your mumma," the manager says to me, bustling out of the door. "Tell her we need assistance at the interchange."

"I really can't," I say—too late. She's gone. Everyone else is bustling out too, though I notice the looks in my direction. At least they're not at Mason.

I leave the honey.

We follow the bustle out onto the platform. Goods are being loaded at a frantic pace: I see winter cabbages, parsnips, potatoes, other root veg, and apples, apples, apples (where we live is good for them, and you can store them until spring if you know how). I take a look back at Milpy.

"Horse is mad as hell," says Mason.

"Thought I told you not to speak," I whisper back, looking at Milpy. I'm glad I left that honey, because I'm fairly sure she's not going to be a gracious guest. I grab Mason's hand and bundle him onto the train and we find ourselves some seats. Though this train is mainly goods with only a couple of passenger cars, there is plenty of room for everyone…but everyone seems to want to sit by me.

Which means sitting near Mason.

He's got the window seat. I've got the aisle…and the crowd.

So your mumma's a Rep, is she?

*National! Her mumma's a **National** Rep!*

Does she know what's happening about Cornwall?

Oh please, what about Cornwall?!

No fish! That's what you do, isn't it? It's not even been that stormy—

We risk our lives! What would you know about the sea?!

I know when people aren't pulling their weight!

***Fish!** My Crystal-Rose needs cancer meds. Will you tell your mumma that? Crystal-Rose in Taunton East.*

Yes, but what about our comms?

What about comms?!

The satellite's going to go down. Think about that!

Yes! What's your mumma doing about comms?

What's your mumma doing about fishing?

*What's your mumma doing about **health care**?*

Crystal-Rose. Health care. Comms. Fish. *I don't know* is all I can keep saying—because I don't. *I'm so sorry. I can't help you. I don't know.* And all the while, Mason, next to me—he's freaking out. I can feel the tension in his whole body and most particularly in his hand. It's still clutching mine, and it's covered in sweat.

"What's the matter?" I whisper to him out of the corner of my mouth, because although no one seems remotely interested in him, my knowing he's a *him* is making me so anxious. If these people saw what I can still see plain as day—IT'S A BOY!—there'd be questions so much more tricky than fishing—or even cancer.

"It's so fast," he whispers back, voice all shaky. He glances at me; the lights in the car are low, but his eyes glint in them like those of a small creature: bright and round and crackling with terror.

I don't travel much, except on the motorbike or on Milpy, so I understand a tiny bit, but still! "You've been on a plane," I whisper through gritted teeth. He has been on a plane, and I never have. "This is at least a thousand miles an hour slower."

"I couldn't see outside!"

"Then don't look. Shut your eyes."

"Is she travel sick?" a granmumma asks. "I've got ginger," she says.

"Granmumma stash," Crystal-Rose's mumma mutters.

"It's old," says the granmumma, ignoring her and shaking out the bag, "but it's still good."

Crystallized ginger—it's a lovely, precious thing. I can't say no to this kindness, so I pick up a lump with a *thank you so much* and hand it to Mason, who takes it in his hand without looking. He's too busy staring out in terror at the snowy, moonlit land whizzing past.

"We had a long journey," I tell the crowd. "We've really got to sleep right now."

"Put that in your mouth and suck on it," I whisper at Mason, tapping the hand that's clutching the ginger. "Close your eyes.

Lean against this." I pull off my outer fleece (I'll be warm enough without it, just) and stuff it behind the other side of Mason's head. "And try, please just try, to at least pretend to sleep."

I squash against him, squeezing his hand HARD and hoping he understands: YOU MUST DO THIS! He puts the ginger in his mouth. Lays his head against the fleece.

"Ut's hot," he mumbles, rolling the ginger around his mouth.

I "snuggle" closer for the purpose of whispering, "Do not spit that out."

"I dun't like it."

"Shuddup. Close your eyes."

Around me, I listen to the discussion rumble on, and *discussion* is the right word, because that's what it becomes. Although these people are all from different 150s, they are so used to talking things through, the element of bicker disperses as soon as there is no longer the possibility of bumping an issue straight up to National Council level. The Train Council forms; advice and information are exchanged; suggestions and solutions are offered. Even the Cornish fishing situation is clarified: only granmummas will go out when winter storms threaten. When *every child is our child*, who would allow a person to risk death for cod?

The discussion eases into Agreement: *We have to have comms or we have nothing*, Crystal-Rose's Mumma says to murmurs of Agreement as Mason and I "snuggle" in a rigid sort of way— Mason because of the terror of the whizzing-too-fast world (and possibly the ginger), and me from the terror that someone might realize (How can they not?! Isn't it obvious?!) that my traveling companion is *as rare as a rhino*, as Kate would say—rarer, in fact, because the last I heard, rhinos and most other once-was endangered species are really doing okay now.

XY numbers, they have become controlled. Unlike in the early days, when supplies of frozen sperm ran low and the human reproduction rate plummeted, the IVF program has offered choice. Granmummas like Casey were brave and tough enough to step up and give away sons because it seemed to be the only way the human race would survive. Now, it is considered that we are safe. Human beings are no longer in danger. There aren't yet enough of us for the world to be as it once was, but who would want that anyway? Most things I have ever read or heard about the once-was seem either unbelievable or undesirable (with some exceptions, such as an abundance of chocolate, chicken tikka masala, and Ibiza, because when Kate told me about that holiday she took with her cousins, it did sound like a whole lot of crazy fun).

You can choose. I will be able to choose: whether to have a child and whether to have a boy. They can be selected for. These days, the choice to have a boy that will have to be given away is made before conception.

Mason…when was he born? Did his mumma choose?

My eyes are tight shut, but I cannot sleep.

CHAPTER 27

PINK AND BLUE

"River, I think we're here," Mason says.

As if I didn't know it. As if I have been sleeping. I turn my head a little, and I look up into his face, and my heart lurches—most unexpectedly—with feeling. Pity, I suppose. His eyes—they're weasel small and bright still. Such fear. Like me, I don't think Mason has slept at all.

Our traveling companions have gone already—I was waiting for them to leave—and they are out on the platform, unloading a chaos of goods, so I take us through to the end compartment, where we exit without any further tricky questions being asked. As we walk up the steps into the station, it feels like any confidence I had is still sitting there on the train, waving me goodbye.

It's not just that the reality of what I have come to do is

closer now; it's Birmingham. IT FREAKS ME OUT, as Kate would say.

It isn't even light yet, but the place is buzzing. The vast station concourse is packed with movement; every kind of person seems to be there, lugging goods, chatting, shouting! BUSY, BUSY, BUSY, and not a single face I know—not that I would want to see a face I know. I clutch Mason's hand tight and pull him out of the station into the cold, cold air, and I breathe in deeply and nearly choke because the air itself, though cold with snow, is *wrong* to me. It's full of strange scents and full of strange sounds, and there are people, hundreds of people, absolutely everywhere—walking, talking, SHOUTING! People on foot, people in bicycle-drawn rickshaws, people pulling carts, people on horses, people leading horses pulling carts, electric cars, motorbikes. The swirl of it all around us, elevated roads swishing up and down to the station, a crisscross of routes where packed streets meet.

And I look up, and I see Mason grinning—*grinning!*—at me. Grin so huge it's like a shout. His hand is no longer in mine.

"This is where my mumma lives?!"

"No! I mean…I don't know. Maybe?"

"I *hope* so! This place is amazing!" he says, turning this way and that. "Skyscrapers! Freeways! It's *Grand Theft Auto* AND *Assassin's Creed*! They got cars AND carts and horses! It's the business! This place is THE business! Look," he says, pointing, "they got KFC! They got McDonald's! I *know* them signs!"

Those signs are so once-was they're filthy and broken and there's moss growing on them.

"Can we get a burger?!"

He looks at me, as excited as a littler one on her birthday.

"Those places don't exist anymore."

"But there's signs!"

I shake my head.

"Toast?" he says. "If they're just selling toast, we could get that, couldn't we? We could get some toast? And soup! I don't even care if there's vegetables in it! I don't even care if there's insects!"

There is nothing I'd like better than a pile of toast right now, and a big fat cup of sage tea. And to be back home, in the kitchen, and not in this scary city, and for none of this to ever have happened. But it has happened, and here we stand: the killer no one knows is a killer and the boy no one knows is a boy, and I am so very tired and hungry—and cold. It's already eating through my coat. Even the cold is hungry.

My confidence is heading home on the train. My stomach agrees with Mason. My heart is already at home, happy in my own once-was (and eating toast).

"River…this place is amazing, ain't it? River…River, you okay?" he says, hopping from one cold foot to another, grinning.

"Yeah. Sure. Come on."

He grabs my hand as I take off down the street. I hardly even notice it; I need to do what I need to do, and what I need to do is ditch him. I will not mess this up.

It's barely light. My anxiety is so strong it propels me at speed through the crowds, slipping and sliding, dragging gawping

Mason, slipping and sliding behind me. I just need to do this thing. Get it done. Do it. Deal with it.

We slip and slide, searching, until I realize I am actually going to have to ask someone where the address I've memorized actually is. This is me—a person who is too scared to ask a stranger where the place I'm looking for is…until I spot a mumma who looks to be in a terrible hurry. It's her I ask because I know she won't have time to ask a single question back.

I clutch Mason's hand, willing him to stay silent, as I ask her: *Please, where is the Bullring?* I do not ask her about the rest of the address: Babyland. Her answer depresses me deeply; I should have asked someone sooner. We need to go back to the indoor market next to the station.

♀ ♂

In the countryside, I have a great, easy sense of direction. In this city, I struggle. It takes longer than it should—and another, excruciating question asked to another hurrying mumma—before we get back there.

Stalls in once-was shops surround us. Stalls selling *food*. Food is not at the top of my plan. But the smell of it? I try to resist. I have to resist! And…I've got nothing left to trade except a bottle of horseradish vodka, which would be too much payment for some food, plus better to hold on to it in case of emergency. My stomach is telling me this is an emergency, but not one that should require the trade of my last asset. I know, if I asked, any one of the stallholders would feed us. Courtesy would demand it. I just find that I don't want to ask. It's not just that I'm too shy and I've never had to do that before, to ask strangers. I'm scared that to ask would be to invite questions I don't want to answer but courtesy would insist I reply to. I don't want to lie, and I definitely don't want anyone to realize Mason is a boy, so we walk on—until I see a littler one about to scrape leftover porridge into a pig-swill bin. Our stomachs are growling so loud I can't even tell whether it's his or mine.

"Could we please have that?" I ask.

"But it's not nice now!"

"We don't mind, really."

"You've got nothing to trade? Or chip coin?" she asks, a little surprised.

"No." I didn't have a chance—and wouldn't have dared—to take chip coin from the community allowance for this trip that is in opposition to my community.

"Granmumma!" she calls. "These people are hungry!"

She calls so loudly everyone left inside the food place hears. And every granmumma in the food place—we're in the one called *McDonald's*—brings food. A serious amount of food. Kate says that in the once-was many people actually could not *afford* to eat; now no one would ever go hungry, but the granmummas remember the Time of Crisis, the time that came in the years after the sickness, when there was not enough food to go around. The time when the granmummas learned to hunt, as well as to grow and to farm—all of which, for reasons I don't understand, had been mainly XY things. You only have to say to a granmumma, "I'm hungry," and you will be fed until your stomach is fit to burst.

Within minutes, we are having plates and bowls of food offered. There's all the usual stuff you'd expect—insect stews and baked potatoes and baked apples stuffed with sugared damsons—plus foods I've never even seen or tasted before. There's something that looks like a meatloaf, which surprises me because it's unusual to see much meat for sale or trade. It's very tasty though.

"You like it?" the granmumma stallholder who must have made it asks us.

Mason nods enthusiastically, reaches for a second slice.

"See?!" she calls out to everyone. "They like it!"

"That's because they don't know what it is!" the porridge girl's granmumma says, and everyone laughs. Someone starts with an old, old song Kate likes—something about swinging from a chandelier—and everyone joins in. Not in some grand, organized way like it's the choir, but just people singing, how it happens when you don't mean it to: a patchwork of a song. Everyone adding parts—pretty parts and not-so-pretty parts, but somehow they all get to the chorus.

"So, what is it?" I ask the granmumma stallholder.

"Vole!"

I stop eating. We eat a lot of things Kate considers should not be eaten. The insects are so delicious even she's okay with them, but there are plenty of foods she refuses to eat, such as *rodents*. She says she ate them once, because she had to, but now there's no need she won't touch them. I'm a little queasy about rodents myself, particularly ones that look as dear as water voles.

"We had an infestation of them on the crops! Difficult to prepare, but waste not, want not, eh?"

Mason reaches for a third slice of vole meatloaf. I'm thinking he does not know what a vole is.

"Thank you so much," I tell her, kissing her cheeks.

"This is really, really good," he mumbles through his stuffed mouth as I drag him away, my stomach churning.

Signs above once-was shops blast my searching eyes as though they were still lit, and none are what I'm looking for. There used to be so many shops! Clothes and shoes, more clothes and shoes, pharmacies, mobile phone shops, and a place that sold only perfume. Then, up on the floor above us, I see the one I am looking for.

I drag Mason up the stopped escalator.

Babyland.

It looks closed. It's dark inside.

I press my desperate hand against one of the glass doors—a gap between and underneath them so huge heat must have just poured out in the once-was—and the door, it opens.

It looks as though it has been empty for years. *Sixty* years. It's full of shelves and rails and hangers thick with dust and empty of clothes. High on the walls are tiny speakers from which music softly crackles down, another tune Kate would probably know. But it's the walls that draw my attention. The weirdness of the walls.

297

On one side: PINK. Pictures of babies and littler ones wearing PINK. PINK. PINK. Bows in hair, flowers on dresses. One even holds a pony dolly, a PINK, impractically long-maned, *blue*-eyed pony that could not look less like the only little pony I know if it tried.

Massive pictures. Massive PINK pictures. And one word: GIRLS.

Other side: BLUE…and one word: BOYS. Are these…supposed to be XY babies?! XY littler ones?! The blue-picture littler ones hold toy boats and trains and rockets. One or two look grubby; they have been messing about in mud.

PINK.

AND.

BLUE.

AND.

WEIRD.

"What in the hell is this place, River?" murmurs Mason.

"I don't know…but it must be the wrong place."

I look at him and he's just staring into the gloom…and I have a jolt of almost feeling what this moment might mean to him: no mumma.

"I'm sorry," I whisper.

Still, he stares. The music in the shop stops.

"We have to go now. This can't be the right place."

We'll walk around, just check there isn't another Babyland— could there be?!—and if there isn't, which my sinking heart tells me there probably won't be, then what?

"There's no one here!" I tell him, so loud in this dead place.

"There is," he says, still staring.

A shiver runs down my spine; it's almost as though I can hear those PINKS and BLUES chuckling. He points through the gloom, where there's a small, black, glassy dome on the ceiling, and as I look, a red light on it blips.

"That's just something someone left on," I tell him. "That happens. I've seen it."

I have. Plat, Tamara, and I once found an abandoned house way out in the countryside, a house that was still connected to the grid and was filled with machines that were still gobbling up power after all those years. In Kate's day, when the grief had melted enough to allow thought to begin, they realized this was going to be a problem. Brigades of people—mainly teens like Kate, there being hardly any littler ones then—were organized to go into empty homes and SWITCH OFF. The mummas praise this event; the granmummas do not like to speak of it. I think they found a lot of dead XYs.

"That's a security camera," says Mason.

I don't know what a security camera is, but I do know, "We need to go."

"They're watching."

"No one is watching."

"They are. I seen it move. You watch. You can see it inside that glass. It's moving. They've seen us."

The children on the walls grin and chuckle. I do NOT believe in ghosts. As a door at the back of the shop cracks open,

I jump, sending a rail of hangers clattering to the floor. Light floods in as fast as adrenaline floods my body.

"How can I help you?"

I'd be guessing that the person asking the question is having a bit of a wild, dress-up day. Maybe it's her ha-ha-harvest festival? She is wearing red, shiny shorts and a matching corset, a black leather carrying belt and black fishnet tights (I've worn tights like that which belonged to Kate), and boots—boots that are also bright red and are stacked so high you'd think she could fall at any moment.

I'm speechless—from the fright, from the shock of this amazing costume, from the whirl in my head that is managing to spit out the thought that *We've got the wrong place.*

"I wanna find my mumma," Mason says.

I told him not to speak. I told him. The way he speaks is SO *wrong*.

Her huge, black eyelashes (False! We mess around with those too, making them out of feathers) flicker for just one second, taking Mason in.

"What's the trade?" she asks him.

Mason looks at me. I pull myself together and step forward.

"This," I tell her, pulling Kate's ring from the little finger of my left hand, the only one of my fingers on which it would fit.

I drop the ring into the palm of an outstretched hand with what Kate would call "killer" nails; they are red and long, and the hand weighs the ring, then closes on it, and slides it into the most minute pocket on those shiny red shorts.

300

"So, I guess you can call me Diamond," she says, breaking into a grin. "And, no, I do not want to know your names. Right then," she says. Out of her carrying belt, she produces the kind of disposable gloves I've seen Akesa use. I think her nails must surely puncture them, but she pulls them on with practiced ease, then produces a sample tube. "Open wide," she says to Mason as she unscrews it.

Mason, unsure, looks at me.

"Open your mouth," I tell him.

He does, and she swabs the inside of his cheek, puts the swab back into the tube, and screws the lid on, tucks it into her belt.

"Come back Sunday evening," she says, pulling off the gloves.

I feel the breath go out of me. "We haven't got that long."

She eyes us both, lashes steady.

"Maternal identity only?"

"Yes."

"It's usually daddies we get asked for."

"You can find out who someone's father was? You can find out his name?" I can't help myself. I feel the weirdest shiver of astonishment. I've never heard of that. I've never really thought about my *father*. I've never thought... Does my *daddy* have a name?!

"They don't have names," she says. "They have numbers."

I cannot look at Mason.

"But, hey," she says, eyes twinkling, "what's in a name?"

"It's just maternal identity we want," I tell her, pulling myself together.

"Uh-huh," she says, still eyeing us, lashes steady. "The test takes twenty-four hours."

"I've got vodka too," I tell her. I am so far, so very far out of my depth now. It scares me so much it hurts—a little like the terror I first felt with Plat when we deliberately rowed out too far on the estuary, knowing—but not really knowing—that the tide would catch us. "It's horseradish…"

"Twenty-four hours. You can't hurry science. Come back in the morning."

I can barely nod; I hadn't anticipated this, that we would have to wait around all day and all night. I offer my freezing hand, shake hers and kiss her warm, perfumed cheek.

I elbow Mason to do the same—and he does.

"Come on," I tell gawping Mason, grabbing him by the arm.

Ghost babies laugh down at us as we walk out of the shop.

"Wait!" she calls after us. "Are you the prearrangement?"

I turn around.

"My granmumma said—"

"You?" she says, looking at Mason.

He nods uncertainly.

"Well, I'll be," she says. "Well, I will be."

302

CHAPTER 28 / ASCENT

"Come with me," Diamond says.

We follow her back through the door she came in, then up some stairs, into a tiny, windowless room with a table—perhaps where the people who sold the pink and blue clothes once sat? Then we go out past two doors, each labeled TOILET, abstract stick figures on them: one figure tiny-waisted, sprouting a triangle from its middle and both with dislocated dots for heads. There's a blast of freezing air as we go out through a door that says FIRE EXIT on to a wide sidewalk swept clear of snow.

Ugh! You're such a hick from the sticks! Kate says to me sometimes. It really annoys me. I know what she means when she says it because I asked her. It means I'm IGNORANT about the world, which I am NOT. I'm in lessons *globally* and *I know things*.

When Kate was my age—she said so herself!—they were doing things like home economics (i.e., cooking—who doesn't cook?!) and sports (who's got time for that on a curriculum?!) and post-war modern history (A subject that is now entirely redundant, in my view. Sorry, Plat). Mainly though, Kate says she was "doing": boys, makeup, clothes, and bitching—online and off-line.

Who is the hick?

I am.

Our guide turns suddenly, taking us through a glass door. A big glass door with a second set of thick wooden doors behind, insulation in a street with buildings so high it can have zero solar gain. And behind that…

For a moment, I do not even know what this place is. The huge hall is filled with all kinds of ordinary- and extraordinary-looking people. Some of the extraordinary ones make the person who has led us here look ordinary. I realize I recognize faces from the National Council, and I definitely recognize the Norfolk Rep; she came to our house once on a tour of wind-power projects. This is a *hotel*. Mumma stays in a hotel when she's in Birmingham. Mumma could be in this building. My chilled body manages to break into a sweat. I'm so anxious all I can feel is my hand. And I can only just feel that—my hand, holding Mason's. I turn and I look at him and I see… If I'm not in the village anymore, he's got to be light-years—*light-years*—away from the world he knows. Or not. He catches me looking at him and raises his eyebrows at me, eyes crackling with excitement.

"I'll show you to your room," Diamond is saying, nodding

at another mumma behind the *reception* desk, a mumma who is wearing a once-was XY-type suit, very fancy: black trousers, black jacket, black vest (Plat wore one once and looked amazing in it!) with a green bow tie and a very frilly orange shirt.

I didn't think we'd actually have to be staying here, and in any case, we most certainly can't afford a room.

"We've got nothing else to trade except the vodka," I tell Diamond.

"Do keep quiet," she says, ushering us toward a door.

I follow, dragging Mason by the hand. I just want to get out of this public space. I'm so *freaked out* right now I've even forgotten how cold I am, and one look at Mason gawping tells me he has also forgotten. It is against courtesy to stare, and he's staring. In my mind, this is just like the train, and I have to remember: no one would think in a million years that Mason could be a boy. The same way I would not have thought in a million years that a quiet-ish person called River could end up killing a man.

Diamond presses a button at the side of a shiny silver door, and the door slides open, and inside…

It's not a bedroom, as my hick self had thought it somehow perhaps could be. This is an elevator. I've never been in one.

"After you," she says.

We go in. She follows.

"I shouldn't be doing this. Waste of resources etcetera, etcetera, but honestly, my feet are killing me!" she says, pressing another button inside the elevator.

The doors slide shut and the elevator moves—UP—leaving

my stomach down. I've flown in planes and Mariam's Explorer, but I am not accustomed to this pure sensation of vertical acceleration with no view to help my brain understand the movement. My stomach surges up faster than the elevator. I shut my eyes.

"You're from the country, aren't you?" I can hear Diamond saying.

DING!

I open my eyes at the sound, see the door slide open, and I'm the first out, bursting out of that elevator. Mason, shrugging his shoulders at me, follows. Diamond strolls out after us, leads us up a flight of stairs.

Stairs are good. Stairs are solid. The elevator, apparently, only goes up so far, as does the heating, which is a thing Diamond mutters about as we climb and climb and climb, the chill in the air coming back with a vengeance, so fierce not even the work of muscles can truly warm against it.

The higher we go, the more deserted the place seems until we're passing hallways so packed with stored junk the rooms cannot possibly be used for guests.

And still we go higher, until we run out of stairs.

We stop in a hallway that is different to the others. It is smaller and free of junk. The carpet, though ancient, is plush and soft underfoot.

"River! Come and look at this!" says Mason.

From the tall window at the end of the hall, there is the most stunning view of Birmingham: the snowy city laid before us.

Diamond leans against the glass, her back to the view, studying Mason.

"I don't know what you are," she says.

Mason looks at me.

"He's a boy," I tell her. It feels like the most gigantic, dangerous confession.

She gives me the most withering look. "I'm a geneticist."

"You've been modified, haven't you?" she says to Mason. "You've been created."

Mason shrugs, uncomfortable, angry.

"We just need to find his mumma," I tell her, gripped by a sudden fear that she might be about to call H&R...but she wouldn't, would she? Why would she bring us all the way up here just to do that?

"I had to see you with my own eyes. So, now I've seen you," she says. "You never came here. You need to get out as quickly as possible, and you don't ever come back. Never speak of this. I've destroyed all records. There is no trail. There is no trace. There never would be anyway, but in this case double, triple, quadruple NOTHING. *You were never here*. Are we clear?"

I nod. I feel frightened.

"So you can keep this pretty little diamond," she says, holding out Kate's ring. "Payment is refused."

I hold out my shaking hand because I don't know what else to do. She drops the ring into my palm. My palm closes on it. It was—always—a heartbreak of a trade. Too precious.

"What about his mumma?" I ask her.

"Every child is our child," she says. "Even this one."

She points at the only door in the hallway.

"She's in there?" Mason asks.

Diamond nods, takes one last look at Mason, turns, and trudges back down the stairs.

I cannot be more shocked than Mason, but I do feel very shocked. I don't know what I had thought would happen, but somehow it feels as though this moment has come way too fast… for me, because this is goodbye. Suddenly, I feel I want to do that, to say a proper goodbye to him, but there is no time for that now. No time and no emotional space; he is shaking again, but not from the cold.

"Go ahead," I murmur.

"What if she doesn't want me?"

My heart floods with pity. I take him by the hands. "She came here for you."

He stares back at me from a place I cannot imagine. His hands slip from mine and he approaches the door. He hesitates.

He knocks.

"Yes?" calls a voice from inside. An anxious voice.

Mason opens the door.

There is a person standing there, in the middle of the room.

And I look at her, and in her face…I see Mason's.

"*My son!*" she whispers.

In her arms, the boy who doesn't cry cries.

It is too private a moment. It feels so wrong that I am there. So there will be no goodbye at all. I turn away.

The journey seems even longer on the way down. The stairs seem to go on forever. I am crying. I am crying for Mason and all the lost boys. And in my tears, I taste the bitterness of the granmummas.

CHAPTER 29
DESCENT

There is nowhere to hide from Mumma.

She is there in the lobby of the hotel. She has seen me; I have seen her. There is nowhere to hide, and I wouldn't want to anyway—all I want is the hug her open arms offer.

"River!" she says softly, cradling me as I sob. "What are you doing here? What's wrong? Darling! What on earth is wrong?"

Over her shoulder, I see them: Mason and his mumma, hurrying into the lobby. They have rushed after me, Mason scanning this way and that, seeking me out until he sees me—and sees Mumma. He looks at me; I look at him…and I shake my head. It is the tiniest movement. It is enough. He gives a nod.

He and his mumma leave.

So there was a goodbye of sorts. There was a goodbye after all.

"What are you doing here?" Mumma says again, less softly now, easing me away so I face her.

"I don't know," I say, which feels very true somehow. "I just want to go home."

She eyes me with concern. And puzzlement. And suspicion.

"Really, Mumma, I just want to go home. There'll be a train and—"

"Is Kate with you?" she asks.

She might as well be, I'm thinking. She's the past, and the past is always with us.

"No. I'm here alone."

Now I am. Now I am here alone.

"Has she… Did *Kate* send you here?"

"Mumma, I want to go home."

My mumma hugs me. "Then you go home," she says. She releases me from her embrace. "I can't come with you, I have to be at the Council. I'll be home tomorrow, then we can talk. Will you be okay?"

"Yes."

I will be okay. When I am home, I will be okay.

"River, you have done the right thing," Mumma says after a pause.

I stare at her. How could she know about Mason and his Mumma? Kate would never have told her. No granmumma would have told her.

"Your silence has protected everyone," she says.

"I don't understand…"

"If you had spoken on record at the court, it wouldn't only have been *your* future at stake; it would be everyone's future. River, the XYs are being traded for a new satellite. Without communication, we are nothing."

"The deal. That's the trade deal with China?"

"And the rest of the world."

My brain feels as though it is landing hard, back into a reality it can just about make sense of. A reality that is meaningful to me: "The Dreambird…"

We will all help one another. A demonstration of engineering excellence from India. The next time the plane comes here, the visit won't be such a secret. At the moment, we're all just working out who plays what part in this.

"That means you too, River," she says, as I stand there, brain crackling. "So go home, do—and take care."

I nod. *Who plays what part?* I am River, and I am going to build *satellites*.

"Yes, Mumma," I tell her. "Yes."

And I hug her and I kiss her.

"River, what *are* you doing here?" she says.

It feels like my mind just hit the bottom of the stairs and bounced. It went down. It bounced. It went up. It lands in a smush.

"It's confidential," I tell her.

♀ ♂

I walk to the station. Birmingham is a blur around me. Inside my head, my mind is also a blur.

I wait for my train.

My train arrives.

My train leaves.

I am not on it.

I go back up to the concourse. I stand in line for a turn at a computer. *Without communication, we are nothing.* There is only one person I want to communicate with right now. I just need her voice to quiet the clamor in my head.

Plat cannot hide her astonishment as my face pops up on PicChat in the middle of a national discussion she's attending about…*Tess*? That book Plat told me about ages ago—they're *still* discussing it?

"Apologies," Plat announces to the group. "I have to go."

She clicks off every face on the screen until we are alone. For a moment, we just look at each other, love in every pixel.

"Why did you abstain from the court?" I ask her.

She leans in to the screen. There won't be anyone else in the study room with her, of that I'm sure; no one else has the time or the brain space to worry about once-was literature. She leans in, I know, because she wants us to be close.

"I abstained because I'm just not sure—not sure enough— what the right thing to do is. I'm still not sure. I think, perhaps, that wouldn't stop me from speaking. The whole GM XY trade situation—"

"You know about that?!"

"The court was told: we're trading XYs."

"*They were told?!*" I whisper.

"They were told. Of course they were told. People needed to understand how Mason was even here alive in the first place. And then there was the question of how...that *other* XY came to be here. The 150 knows everything—and the 150 decided."

"149. You didn't vote."

"148. Nor did you."

"I couldn't, could I? I was asleep."

"And now you've woken up."

"Plat, please—tell me what to do."

"Come home."

"Tell me!"

"I'm not your mumma or your granmumma."

"I know that!"

"River, some people might be willing to take this issue further, no matter how much trouble it might cause...but not like this," she says. "No one wants this trouble. Not when it involves one of us." When I have nothing to say, she adds, "And I feel the same way. I Agree."

"I don't," I tell her.

We stare at each other.

"Then you'd have to speak to the National Council."

She knows as well as I do that I could not possibly stand in front of the National Council, in front of the world, because all proceedings are streamed and accessible, and—

"Plat—"

"No. I know what you're going to ask me, and no. I won't speak for you. Not even an *email*. Not even an *anonymous* email. If this were just—hah! 'just'!—a question of starting up a discussion about the XYs, I might be prepared to speak, but it isn't, is it? It's about you, River. If you want to put a noose around your neck you're going to have to do it yourself."

"And if I did?" I ask her. "If I did speak?"

"One question first?"

"Anything."

"Is this about love?"

"What?"

"Do you love him?"

"Plat!"

"Anything. You said anything."

"No! I don't love him!"

"Liar."

"No!"

"Liar."

"Why are you even asking me this?!"

"Because it's the first thing the council will think."

"I don't see why!"

"Because it's traditional! It's once-was! It's girl loves boy! Half the council are granmummas—this is what they'll think! They'll think the only reason you're doing this is because you are in love with him."

"Well, they can think what they like—"

"Plus, it's written in the case report."

"Someone said that?! Someone said—"

"That it is possible you are in love with him."

"Who said it? Who said that? Plat—tell me, or I'll go and look for myself."

"You can't. The case report is locked."

"No case is ever locked!"

"No case ever involved a situation like this."

Those words hit me like the smack of an ash branch in the face.

"River, do you want my advice or not?"

"I want your advice."

"Are you sure? Are you listening to me?"

"I am sure." I breathe. I try to be calm. "I'm listening."

"I think you should drop this," she says. "I Agree that this discussion—about the XYs, about everything—needs to happen. It must happen, and I'm fairly sure it will happen soon…but this is not the time or the place. If you speak about what has happened, if you speak about killing that man, there will be many, many more consequences than you can possibly imagine. This is about your life and your future, River. Don't turn it into a cause—a cause that isn't even yours. Come home, my love."

I bow my head.

"But I think it *is* my cause," I tell her. "I think…perhaps… it's everyone's cause."

She is silent; I look up at the screen. There is Plat, staring back at me.

"Then good luck," she whispers, and cuts the call.

We don't do that. We don't wish each other luck. It's a gran-mumma thing.

CHAPTER 30

WORDS

I remember this place so well from when we came here as a school: Plat so excited and me too, briefly, because I'd never been in a building like it. The National Council is an old place that was not left to crumble—like the Houses of Parliament in London—but adapted to be energy efficient. I was less excited about the politics. I mean, I knew it was important…but you vote for people you trust, don't you? And you know what decisions they're going to make because we, the 150 voters, know exactly what is going on…or we could do, if we wanted to. Plat likes to; I've never taken that much interest. Everything is online if you care to look, and everything is discussed if you care to listen. My brain has been so full of my own future I haven't wanted to listen and think about issues that don't concern me. Why would I? That's what representation is for, isn't it? Same as how I wouldn't expect anyone who climbed on board a plane I'd built to be worrying about how I'd built it. People are *trusted* to do their jobs.

In the once-was, Kate says, no one trusted the people who were supposed to represent them.

There is an elevator, I see, to enable access. I take the stairs. I push open the first door off those stairs. The first balcony is crowded—and feels way too close to the auditorium. I can see the National Council. The 150 of all our 150s: our National Representatives. I can see the bank of screens on which mummas who are too busy to be here in person can join the debate—and so many granmummas too, the ones who are just too old or too sick to come here. Though I remember the spectacle from years ago, I am still dazzled by it—though not so dazzled my eyes don't immediately see her: my mumma.

She's here, sitting, deep in thought, on a raised platform among the representatives who have been able to attend in person. Their chairs form a semicircle, the idea being—Yaz told us on the school visit—that *we*, the people in the auditorium, are the other half of that circle.

I go up higher. I walk up and up and up until, the last door I shove open…it's a fire escape, I suppose. This last door leads onto nothing but slopes of snow, a crazy roof landscape of angles and icicles, turbines still in the low gray of this winter day, cowls of heat-return funnels stand before me: faceless, howl-mouthed giants with dripping icicle hoods.

And I stand there for a moment, just breathing.

For the first time in my life, I feel truly alone.

♀ ♂

I go back down to the seats at the end of the highest balcony. There is no one much else around up here, and no chance that I will be spotted, lurking in the darkness.

The council is in discussion: how to manage the crash-risk from dying satellites.

I should be interested. I am interested. It would be a very good thing to lose myself in this discussion. This *important* discussion. It is important; so many things are—Crystal-Rose. Health care. Fish. **Comms.**

No one except Plat knows I am here. No one but me has put me here. No one—but me?—is thinking I should speak, so I don't have to.

And I know I don't want to.

Up here, I am so removed from everything…except the Global Agreements.

They are written in extravagant gold lettering above the bank of screens. They are written so high above the proceedings below it is as though they are speaking directly to me.

I close my eyes to them. It is no use. I know them by heart, the Agreements that, after grief and decades of struggle, the *world* decided upon:

The Earth comes first.
Every child is our child.
We reject all forms of violence.
We will all help one another.
Knowledge must be shared.
We Agree that we need to Agree.
Everyone has the right to be listened to.

I have grown up with them. We teens, we quote them—even the littler ones do—but usually only when we do not like what is happening to us. It's so useful to have them to point to when you want to object to something. These Agreements…they are *so* deeply a part of my life I have never had to truly think about them, any more than I ever had to think about what a "girl" is supposed to be like—or a *boy*.

It does seem to me that every single one of the Agreements was broken after Mason arrived. Even *The Earth comes first* went down the drain with gallons of hot water and endlessly stoked fires. He had never heard of these Agreements. He had never heard of them because he and his kind played no part in deciding them. And a thought more terrible than all those: they do not apply to him.

In my mind's eye, he is here with me now.

Wow, I imagine him saying. *Those are the rules?*

"They're not rules," I say out loud, opening my eyes to the empty seats around me, realizing I have, in fact, always thought of them that way. "They're Agreements…they're more like… things to aim for."

We are brought up to think we are part of everything. That power—decisions—belong to everyone.

Everyone has the right to be listened to.

I've never thought about what that means. I'd thought it meant people should feel free to say what they think—yes—but that others must *listen* to them.

What about the voices that are not heard? How can people listen to them?

I stand up on my feet.

My heart is in my mouth.

"My name is River," I shout.

The National Council—the faces on the screens, the representatives—the mummas and the granmummas and the teens who have come to witness our democracy in action…all of them look to see who has disrupted the proceedings.

I am a tiny dot. I am smaller than the smallest, most insignificant star, one of a countless multitude.

I am almost invisible.

I see Mumma. I see the shock on her face. I am so scared. I am so scared to speak. I look, and I see my mumma smile. I see that my mumma is scared too…but also, that she is proud of me. I have found my voice.

"I am River. Daughter of Zoe-River, granddaughter of Thea-Zoe, great-granddaughter of Katherine-Thea. And I have killed a man."

She is riding through the woods on what was once a road. The dotted, white line that used to separate the comings from the goings is crumbling. The asphalt is slowly being destroyed by tree roots, and small plants—so strong—sprout up all over, wherever they can. In another few years, there won't be any road left at all.

The horse, who is grumpy, pulls a cartload of cider apples: small, hard, bitter things that will be fermented into some fun. The girl has a backpack stuffed with harvest produce on her back; it is easier to carry it than have to clamber off and on Milpy just for a drink of water.

Her name is River, and she is an apprentice at the airport.

She is also an advisor to the National Council on the future of the Sanctuaries. This was the restoration that was decided upon. It is in keeping with the way of things: if you see that there is a problem, then you must try to put it right.

On her little finger, she wears a diamond ring. An engagement ring, once-was, given by her granmumma in recognition of her bravery.

It is an autumn evening.

Dark is coming soon.

She is miles from home.

She feels a little afraid.

That's when she sees it: the person standing in the middle of the road.

Not a Guy. Him. He. His. Male. Son. Dude.

Just a person. Called Mason. Waving hello.

A NOTE FROM THE AUTHOR

Dear Reader,

I thought I couldn't write this book.

The idea came about when a teen friend told me she was studying *Tess of the d'Urbervilles* in school. ("I hate Tess," she said. "She's such a sap.") I studied the same book—more than *thirty years ago*. It made my heart sink to think of generations of young people reading a story in which women are oppressed victims and men are the oppressors, no matter how much they might be encouraged to analyze it. I wondered whether it would be possible to tell a completely different kind of story.

And that's when I got stuck.

Although I might have had a lot of fun writing it—and

exorcised a few of my own demons along the way—I decided I did not want to create a simple "reversal" of the way so much of the world is in terms of relations between the sexes. It felt, paradoxically, reactionary. It felt counterproductive. It felt like such a story would only serve to reinforce binary notions of gender—notions that cause so much difficulty, and pain, for so many of us. Notions that, in my opinion, hold us all back. And I realized that I had no idea what a world run by women would be like...*because I do not know what a woman is.*

That was my shock. Biology is biology—nuts and bolts, bits and pieces—but *gender*? What is it? What does it mean?

The more I thought about what gender is and the ways in which our ideas about it are created and transmitted—through family and intergenerational influence, through education and other forms of social and cultural transmission—the more I saw gender as an entirely arbitrary construct. I support anyone who challenges that construct in any way...and I also wondered what the world would be like without it.

So this story is told to you by River, a teenage girl who lives in a world of women but who has never really had to think about gender until the arrival of a boy changes everything.

I had no idea how River's story would take shape—and I found the journey of writing it deeply challenging and surprising. Her story made me think about family and society, democracy and power, expectation and prejudice, and it became, for me, a tale about identifying oppression and finding the courage to speak up.

And it left me with a question: *Who runs the world?*
I wonder what your answer would be...

Virginia Bergin
March 2017

A CONVERSATION
WITH THE AUTHOR

This excerpted interview was conducted by Caroline Horn with ReadingZone, originally posted June 2017 at readingzone.com.

Why did you want to write about a society/global order run by women? How did you decide what that world would look like, and what was your key focus and ambition?

The answer to this question is too big for one interview! I had lots of reasons for wanting to explore this idea; some political and intellectual, some very personal…but in a creative sense, it was the biggest challenge of a *what if?* I could imagine—in fact, it was almost too much of a challenge.

I felt a huge amount of pressure to get the world "right" because I felt I wanted to represent women positively...until I realized that, in terms of gender, I don't even know what a "woman" is (so how could I possibly know what a world run by women would look like?).

I decided I was free to imagine the world however I chose, so what you have is a mishmash of ideas that interest me and that I felt could have feasibly emerged out of the dying of males.

To me, the details of how the world run by women works are not so important in the story—what is very important is that it is a world that is free of any of the pressures associated with being "female."

In terms of its timing, why did you decide that it would be set two generations down the line?

I wanted the main character, River, and her peers to be almost free of the prejudices, pressures, assumptions, and stereotypes that affect girls today. Almost—but not quite. As one aspect of considering how our ideas about gender are created and transmitted, I wanted to include the family influence of her granmumma (actually her great-grandmother) and education—although River has barely paid attention to what is said about men as it is history to her, and not relevant to her world.

Was there also some wish fulfillment in terms of the kind of society that a female-dominated world would create?

What for you would be the main positives in this world? And the negatives?

I anticipate being asked this a lot! The broad answer is NO.

The world described in the book has had to endure a terrible tragedy. I wouldn't want to see a world run by women any more than I enjoy living in a world that is currently, for the most part, run by men.

What I wanted to get at was that if we—all of us, male as well as female—could start over, what kind of a world would we want to live in?

In this story, it's women who are able to start over, and I used this to sneak in some values I hoped people might decide upon (the Global Agreements). They are very idealistic. That, for me, is a positive; people agreeing on the basics from which all other decisions flow...and it was also very important that there was a different kind of democracy, in which everyone was actively engaged.

The negatives? I think those are revealed during the story; ideals are hollow unless inclusive and acted upon—and it might take great courage to do that if everyone around you has a vested interest in not doing so.

That's my broad answer. Another answer would be that I would be very, very curious indeed to see how women would run the world. I don't think it would be perfect—and the world in *The XY* is no utopia—but right now, at our point in human history, I think we need to do things in a different way. I think people have become very disengaged and cynical about mainstream politics, but what are we going to do about it?

Why did you decide to make this female-dominated world still imperfect with questions over democracy, power, and second-class citizens?

See above. And though a huge part of me wanted this world to be perfect, I felt I would be doing a great disservice to us all if I made it so. I felt that:

1. I would be saying that women are better than men. I've lived my whole life hearing the message that men are better than women. I had no wish to invert and repeat a lie.

2. I would be saying that women are not human. It is very, very hard for people—female or male—to be perfect. Impossible? I suspect that, even in the very best—most fair/democratic/harmonious—societies that have ever existed, people were still people, and so all kinds of human "weaknesses" would have been present. Perfection is not truthful.

3. In this story, there is a big question mark over the apparent "second-class citizen" status of men. It arose in a time when the whole human race was under threat, when the simple preservation of a male was more important than the quality of life that male had...and it continued in a way that the main female characters have been largely unaware of. Unlike the situation we have today, when a

man could easily at least begin to see what women endure, the women in the story have had no access to male reality. Perhaps they should have made more effort? And is it easier not to?

4. An imperfect world is essential for a story! No conflict = no plot!

For River, the lead character, her world is "gender neutral"; she has never seen a boy, an XY, and the boy, Mason, has never seen a girl. What was it like imagining what their meeting would be like?

Nearly impossible. (It took a lot of drafts, and an earlier version of the story was written in two parts; River told one chapter, Mason the next. From that, I'd had to understand the meeting from both their points of view.)

We meet two male characters in the narrative—one boy, one man—and the man is immediately very aggressive. Is this portrayal overly negative about men?

Again, this is a question I anticipate being asked a lot! I think a story like this could be told so many different ways—and I hope people do!—but I wanted to confront the nastiest male stereotypes head-on.

In the first instance, there's Mason. Immediately aggressive—the story should explain why—and River immediately associating this aggression with a whole load of ideas about males she has never really paid that much attention to (because she has never had to).

I wanted to show how even the tiniest scraps of half-remembered "information" can become FACTS when you're threatened. It's the start of prejudice, perhaps, this generalizing—which is not to say that River isn't absolutely right to feel horrified by Mason's behavior.

Then there is Killer, the man. Unlike Mason, who has sunk, Killer has managed to rise to the top of a brutal system. He inhales freedom—and exhales violence and death. It is all he knows. Would he be like this if he had been raised differently? I wanted to think about the cultural transmission of expected behavior... (Though I should also point out that Mason and Killer are "Beta." The implication is that there could be an "Alpha" stream, where, perhaps, life might be different.)

My intention was to invoke the very worst image of masculinity...and, sadly, I don't think it's an unrealistic or unfamiliar image. I think many—too many!—boys struggle with notions of what a "man" should be like, and the story presents an extreme experience of this. What I hope is that readers—particularly boys—will use this story as a way to think and talk about the pressures they are under.

Yes, I chose the two escapees to be who they are. Yes, their portrayal of "male" is negative.

Is it overly negative? Mason, to me, is a character full of hope.

ACKNOWLEDGMENTS

This has been a long journey. I am so grateful I had company. I would very much like to thank:

My family. Most especially my sisters and my brother: Sue, Karen, and John.

My agent, Louise Lamont at LBA Books, without whom this book would never have happened.

Steve Geck; my editor, Elizabeth Boyer; and all the lovely team at Sourcebooks.

In the UK: Rachel Petty and the team at

Macmillan Children's Books, who believed in this story before I even knew how to write it.

Jacqui Pridham: you are a shining star.

Karen Legate, Jen Houghton, Jill Bird, and Ann Cahill: thank you so much for your excellent thoughts.

My friends and neighbors in Hotwells, Bristol. I have had so much support from the whole of my community, for which I am very grateful. Particular thanks to Tony Howells for giving endless encouragement, and to Hilary Hunt and Peter Ryalls for tea and sympathy.

Thanks also to my 2015 neighbors in Somerset for making me feel so welcome, particularly Richard and Carol, Tilly & Co., Alison and Keith—and Ben.

Yvonne: thank you for being there.

Dan Blore: thank you for reading and for seeing and for kindly listening to me go on a bit. A lot.

Dr. Matthew Avison (University of Bristol): thank you for your generous support and advice. I do apologize for having completely made up the science in this story.

Dear Lemn Sissay: thank you so much for *Every child is our child* (Global Agreement No. 2), a thought spoken in "A Child of the State," a TED talk. A thought I heard and felt.

Hilary Beard: you are forever fabulous—
and forever in my heart.

Tessa G: I admire you so much.

Hearts and thumbs-up to my online friends and email buddies, to the readers, bloggers, librarians, teachers, writers, and booksellers who have been so supportive over the past few years.

And finally,

Thanks to Team Granmumma:

Martha Evans, Alison Jenkins, Heather Meyer, and Allison Sylvester.

Special thanks to Ruby Sylvester-Jeyes and Aidan Beard for making me think; to Stan Sylvester-Jeyes and Luke Pridham for gaming inspiration; and to all the young people: the students I have met in schools and the kids and teens in my life.

ABOUT THE AUTHOR

Virginia Bergin learned to roller skate with the children of eminent physicists. She grew up in Abingdon, Oxfordshire, and went on to study psychology but ruined her own career when, dabbling in fine art at Central Saint Martins, she rediscovered creative writing. Since then, she has written poetry, short stories, film, and TV scripts. Virginia has written two novels for teens, H_2O and *The Storm*. She lives in Bristol, England. Visit her online at virginiabergin.com.

DON'T MISS VIRGINIA BERGIN'S THRILLING DUOLOGY

IT'S IN THE RAIN...AND JUST ONE DROP WILL KILL YOU.

...

FIREreads

#getbooklit

our hub for the hottest in young adult books!

Visit us online and sign up for our
newsletter at FIREreads.com

 @sourcebooksfire

 sourcebooksfire

 firereads.tumblr.com